Secret Wife
to the Special Forces

A Military
Reverse Harem Romance

Krista Wolf

KRISTA'S VIP EMAIL LIST:

Join to get free book offers, and learn release dates for
the hottest new titles!

Tap here to sign up: http://eepurl.com/dkWHab

~ Other Books by Krista Wolf ~

Chronicles of the Hallowed Order

One

DAKOTA

Brian dropped into his chair, but not before swiping something on his phone and sliding it deep into his front pocket. His smile was perfunctory. His expression, as always, read like his mind was somewhere else.

"Sorry I'm late," he non-apologized for the twenty-minute delay. "Damn. You ordered a whole bottle, huh?"

I grinned sweetly, pouring him a generous portion of deep red merlot. He was paying for it, after all. And once he saw the price of the bottle I'd picked out, he'd want to drink every last drop.

"Thanks babe."

"You're very welcome," I grinned, raising my glass. He toasted me awkwardly. "Can't have my man thirsty. Besides, you'll need it for all the double-talking."

"Double what?"

I'd muttered the last part into my glass, while tipping it back. It was a miracle he'd heard me. "Oh, nothing."

He wore his grey shirt, the one that shimmered to black in an almost ombré way. It clashed violently with his purple tie, but at this point who was really keeping score? As we picked up our giant menus, it seemed suddenly odd how attracted I'd once been to the man sitting across from me. It was hard to believe I'd ever considered a future with him, even briefly, during the past year we'd been together.

"What's that?"

Brian's gaze was fixed on the empty glass off to one side, in front of an empty chair. He chuckled. "You planning on doing some double-fisting?"

"I probably should be, but no," I told him. "That's for our guest."

He laughed again. "We're having a guest?"

"Oh yeah."

He shook his head dismissively, as his attention dropped to the menu. If he cared, he might've noticed the small red dot at the bottom of that glass. Or the merlot residue still clinging to the side of it, had he really looked.

But Brian didn't really *look* at anything. He wore the blinders of someone so selfish and truly self-centered, nothing else really mattered unless it pertained to him.

God, he's so oblivious.

I took an emboldening sip of wine. Not that I needed emboldening, really. I made a hand signal, and my accomplice approached the table. She slid into the empty chair while Brian was busy behind the wall of his menu, and I poured her a new glass of wine.

The payoff came when my boyfriend finally dropped his menu. The look on his face was so priceless, so abruptly panicked, I wished I could've bottled that look and kept it forever.

"Hello, baby."

In the span of less than three seconds, Brian had gone as white as a ghost. Every ounce of color was now drained from his face.

"What's the matter?" Naomi chuckled musically. "Nothing on the menu you like?"

My soon-to-be ex-boyfriend's mouth opened, closed, then opened again. He almost actually said something, but whatever it was got stuck in his throat.

"This isn't quite the threeway he wanted, is it?" I laughed, and Naomi laughed with me.

"No," she agreed. "It *definitely* isn't."

Brian finally dropped his head into his hands. The comically oversized menu flopped to the table.

"That's too bad, too," I shrugged, turning to Naomi. "If he'd been the right kind of boyfriend I might've gone for it. I'm actually pretty adventurous."

"Oh totally!" she agreed. My newfound friend jerked a thumb in our victim's direction. "But with *him?*"

We both broke into hysterical laughter, and the laughter felt cathartically good. It was such a relief to finally be through. To be putting an end to all the lies, all the scheming, all the deception.

"T—The two of you planned this?" Brian finally

spoke. "You set me up?"

"I know, pretty crazy right?"

"Like something out of a movie, really," Naomi agreed.

"It wasn't hard though," I added, "finally figuring it out. All those times you abruptly canceled plans, then turned off your phone. All the holidays you couldn't be with me, because you were spending them with her."

"Ditto," my accomplice nodded. "Dakota and I went over our dates together, and in retrospect it seems so obvious now. Still, it must've been logistically hard, seeing us both." She eyed him skeptically. "Or you know what? Scratch that. For someone like you, it was probably all too easy."

Brian sat there silently, taking it all in. He looked half dejected, half pissed off at all the laughing we were doing. I realized his anger was probably my favorite part.

"So yeah, we're both obviously through with you," I told him, matter-of-factly. "We're done with the lying, the sneaking around, and the super lame sex."

"*Especially* the super lame sex," Naomi groaned, tipping her glass back again. With her free hand, she made an obscene jerk-off motion. "Wasn't even that good in the beginning, to be honest."

I shrugged, trying to remember. "Maybe passable."

"Maybe," she squinted.

"Except for that one thing he does where he—"

"ALRIGHT, enough!" Brian cried suddenly. "I get it already, okay? I'm the asshole."

"Oh I don't know if you're *the* asshole," Naomi purred. "But you're definitely *an* asshole. Just one of many."

She was certainly cute, I'd give Brian that. Dark hair, mocha brown eyes. The physical opposite of me, right down to being short where I was tall. As far as two-timing assholes went, my ex had good taste at least.

Naomi caught me looking her over and shrugged. "So what do we do now?"

"I dunno. Throw our drinks in his face?"

My raven-haired accomplice considered it for a moment, then shook her head. "Nah. We're classier than that." She giggled. "Besides, this wine is too damned good."

"It better be," I smirked. "It was at the very bottom of the menu."

We toasted — the two of us — and drained our glasses together. By the time we set them down on the table, Brian's face had regained all of its color and then some.

"Word of advice," I said, looking into my ex-boyfriend's eyes for what I knew would be the last time. A tiny pang of sadness threatened to rise up, but I shoved it down. "You *might* want to think about other people before you do this next time. And not just yourself."

We rose together, gathering our things. At the other end of the table, Brian looked very small and very defeated.

"Hey look, it's not *all* bad," Naomi said in consolation. "You've still got some delicious meals coming — all to yourself."

This seemed to snap our cheating boyfriend out of

his trance. "I—I do?"

"Sure," I answered, delivering my brightest, million-watt smile. "We ordered tomahawk steaks before you got here. Three of em, in fact."

We waved back at him in tandem on the way out.

"Hope you're hungry."

Two

DAKOTA

The phone rang yet again, and for the fourth time in a row my car's bluetooth intercepted the potential connection. This in turn interrupted the song, and it was a hell of a good song. Maybe even a great one, if I could only settle back into my heated leather seats to enjoy it.

Fuck off, Brian.

I closed my eyes, trying to relax as the heat from the vents washed over me. My ex had been calling me non-stop for the past five days, and today was no exception. I had no idea what he wanted. My voicemail was too full to leave a message. I'd deleted any and all texts he sent without reading them, which had been fun at first, but now it was growing tiresome.

The ringing eventually stopped and the song came back on. I rode its melody all the way to the chorus, and just when it got to the best part... the phone rang again.

Dammit!

I banged the steering wheel in frustration. It was bad enough to be stuck in a ditch on the side of the road, waiting for help. But it was even worse when that help would arrive only to chastise me for not switching over to snow tires by now.

Knock knock knock!

The sharp rapping against my window nearly jolted me out of my skin! My father's smiling face greeted me through the frosted glass and blowing snow, as I popped the door a few inches open.

"Stuck huh?"

"Yep."

He glanced down and shook his head, but it was mostly for effect.

"Should've put on the snow tires, Dakota. You know better than this."

I accepted my reprimand and stepped out into the cold Minnesota wind. The snow was mixed with sleet now, pelting the exposed skin of my face and hands like tiny daggers as I squinted into the darkness.

"Swing around," I told him, jerking my head in the direction of my father's truck. "I'll unravel the winch and—"

"I can do it, honey. You stay inside and keep warm."

I raised an eyebrow in mock disgust. "Are you kidding old man? Get back in your truck. You don't even have a jacket on!'

For as long as I could remember my mother and I were always yelling at him for going out without a coat, but my father never seemed to care. He'd wear the same flannel shirts summer or winter, day or night. You could always tell how cold it was by how many layers he had on, though.

Eventually we got the winch hooked up, and it was a simple thing to pull me free. Relief flowed through me as my car rolled back onto the road where it belonged.

"Thanks dad."

Again he'd come through. Just like clockwork.

"You sure you don't want to switch vehicles?" he jabbed, wiping his frozen hands on his dirty work jeans. "I could take it down to the shop first thing tomorrow. Get those tires all changed up for you."

"That's tempting," I scrambled, "but I really need to run. I've got work tonight."

"Ah, yes," he grinned. "Work."

My father never could — and probably never would — understand what I did for a living. But it put food on the table, whether he understood it or not.

"Plus I have groceries in the back," I continued. "And also—"

"Come by during the week," my father said sternly. "Or I'm going to tow this thing to my shop when you're not looking and do it myself."

I flushed and stared back at him, noticing the tiny changes as I always did. His cheeks were a little more sunken, his once-blond hair flecked with a little more grey. It was somewhat heartbreaking, watching time catch up to this man who raised me and loved me. Wrinkle by wrinkle, it changed him in all the ways I wished I could stop.

"Yes daddy."

My father smiled back at me warmly. "Now *there's* my ankle-biter."

He kissed my cheek before driving off, eventually leaving me to my thoughts. The ankle-biting nickname went way back to when I was a little girl, laughing and playing and biting my father's ankles to get his attention whenever he wasn't working. Unfortunately, that wasn't very often.

Another song came on, but not for long. I hadn't even put the car in drive yet when the bluetooth was interrupted by another phone call, this time from a number I didn't recognize. Most likely Brian using a friend's phone, trying to trick me into picking it up.

This time I pressed the ACCEPT button and did it anyway. Enough was enough.

"What!?" I shouted into the empty car. "For fuck's sake, what could you *possibly* have to say to me!?"

There were three of four seconds of complete and utter silence. Then: "Ummmm.... hi?"

The voice at the other end of the connection wasn't Brian's at all. It was deeper and more baritone. Velvety and delicious.

"Dakota?"

"Yes?"

"It's Jace."

Jace...

It didn't register for a few seconds. That's how long it had been.

"Jace..." I squinted, as the heat warmed my pink skin. Then, a revelation: "Oh, JACE!"

Images of my brother Tyler's best friend popped immediately to mind. I could envision his tall, slender frame. His deeply tanned skin, accented by that beautiful white smile.

"Jace!" I repeated again. "Oh, I'm so sorry! I was just —"

"Thinking I was someone else?"

He chuckled, and the visual solidified. I hadn't seen Jace for nearly a decade. I knew he'd entered the military, and I knew he was doing some very badass stuff. The last I'd heard from Tyler, his friend was somewhere on the other side of the world, getting decorated for something amazing he couldn't fully talk about.

"Yes, I thought you were someone else," I told him, before adding: "and nobody very important, believe me."

"Good," Jace answered smoothly. "Because although we teased you a lot in high school, I can't imagine you'd hate me *that* badly."

He was referring to him and Tyler, of course. When I was a sophomore and they were both seniors, they spent a lot of their time teasing and pranking me mercilessly. But that also meant I got to hang out with my older brother and his friends a lot, which was never a bad thing.

"Nah, we're good," I sighed happily. "So how've you been!? Where are you now? Most of all, what the hell have you been up to? Last I heard you were—"

"All good questions," Jace cut in, "but right now I have a favor to ask of you." He paused awkwardly. "A really *big* favor."

"I can do favors," I reasoned, saying the words slowly. "Shoot."

"Well it's actually part favor, part proposition."

I shook my head. "Can't be worse than *some* of the propositions I've been getting lately."

"And you can totally say no if you want," he went on. "But you can also say yes. At least I *hope* you say yes. Even though what I need is a little... unorthodox."

God, what the hell could it be? Jace had always been straightforward: totally cool and confident. He was a good-looking lacrosse player, with tons of friends and even more in the way of girlfriends. It just wasn't like him to beat around the bush.

Then again it had been a while, and people changed. Everything *around* you changed too, as I found out from remaining home these past several years. The changes usually happened when you weren't looking, whether you liked it or not. It was an unfortunate fact of life.

"Okay," said Jace finally. "Here goes nothing..."

I sat there with both eyebrows arched, staring into the phone. Just inches in front me, wave after wave of frozen sleet blasted against my windshield.

"How would you like a free trip to Hawaii?"

Three

DAKOTA

The descent was a little bumpy, but the views were outright spectacular. I saw fluffy white clouds and yellow sand beaches. The turquoise waters were broken by swirling, colorful reefs, and dotted with little white sailboats here and there.

Of course our landing approach also included the big city itself: Honolulu. Its streets and avenues seemed almost cast against the lush green mountains like an oversized throw-net, punctuated by rectangular hotels and skyscrapers that, oddly enough, didn't seem out of place in such a paradise.

For any Minnesota girl slogging her way through mid-December, a trip to Hawaii was a no-brainer. But a *free* trip to Hawaii, to do a special favor for one of my brother's closest friends?

Well that was an instant and enthusiastic YES.

It didn't hurt of course that I was getting over a breakup. Or that my personal life had been in a bit of a rut lately, even with all the success I'd been having at work. Getting away for a couple of weeks would definitely clear my head. It might even help soak some much-needed vitamin-D into my sun-starved skin as well, as long as I located some sunscreen and aloe plants straight away.

I'd told my parents I was taking off on a last-minute vacation, the details of which I'd fill in later. I realized trading a free trip to Hawaii for a 'favor' might not sit well with them, especially when I couldn't yet explain what that favor was. All I knew was that Jace had asked me to be his date for an extremely fancy, *very* important military dinner. Beyond that, the only other detail he promised was that it would be strictly platonic.

Besides, of all Tyler's wacky friends my father always had a soft spot for Jace. The two bonded on levels that rivaled his relationship with my brother, and I didn't want to mess that up.

Any explanation I might've owed Tyler himself was preempted by the fact he was thousands of miles away. My brother was an incredible hockey player who rocked the collegiate circuit and fell just short of going pro, but being a coach turned out to be his true calling. For the past several years he'd been criss-crossing the country with various triple-A teams.

No, everyone could learn all about my trip *after* I'd taken it. Between helping out at my dad's shop and freezing my ass off through sub-zero temperatures, for once I was finally doing something for me.

"Dakota!"

I was just through the arrival gate, and the voice

reached me before I even recognized the face. I scanned the crowd twice and suddenly there he was, standing a full head taller than anyone else in the crowd.

HOLY.

SHIT.

"Jace?"

I could barely believe my eyes. Gone was the lithe, almost skinny version of my brother's best friend. Standing in his place was a hulking, well-muscled giant in a tight green shirt and camouflage cargo pants.

"Right here!'"

We ran to each other, and he swept me up in a spinning bear hug. I dropped my carry-on and marveled at how impossibly *hard* his body felt. He wasn't just big, he was enormous! I could barely get my arms around him!

"How was your flight?"

He put me down in a daze, still blinking up at him in disbelief.

"M—My flight?"

"Yes."

"Jace... forget about my flight! Just look at you!"

"Look at me?"

"Yes!" I cried, taking a step back. "What the hell *happened* to you!?"

He laughed at my dismay, and his laughter was deep and resonant. His childhood face had matured into the strong cheekbones and angular jaw of a man, and an astonishingly good-looking one at that. He sported a well-trimmed beard that was a hundred-percent brand new. The smile beneath it however, was exactly the same.

"The Army happened to me," he answered. He dropped his gaze to his massive arms and chest, as if discovering those things for the first time. "I guess it's been a while, huh? You haven't seen me since... well..."

"Since you were some skinny beanpole punk, running around with Tyler," I jumped in. "Short-sheeting my bed. Stretching plastic wrap over the toilet bowl—"

"Oh man," he swore, "your mother was *so* mad at that one!"

"And let's not forget putting glitter all over the fan blades in my bedroom during my fifteenth birthday," I finished. "I was cleaning that up for months. Years, maybe."

Jace laughed again and held up his hand. "Guilty."

"Damn," I swore happily. "How long has it really been?"

He slung my carry-on over one giant shoulder and pointed toward the baggage carousel. "Too long."

A few minutes later we were hopping into a Ford Bronco with oversized tires; a beautiful green-and-white relic from the mid 1990's. We took off with the windows rolled down, and I gawked shamelessly at the scenery. The Hawaiian air was sweet and fragrant and pregnant with a thousand open-ended possibilities.

We made small talk at first, mainly because there was so much to say. We asked about each other's jobs, lives, and what we'd been doing since the last time we'd laid eyes on each other. Even with Tyler as common ground, the time gap was so big it seemed almost insurmountable.

"So tell me," I finally asked, as the beautiful palm trees raced by. "What kind of favor requires sending all the way to Minnesota for little old me?"

Jace bit his lip. "A... pretty complicated one."

"Really?" Now I was little more than intrigued. "Do tell."

"Well, I sort of got myself into a little white lie..." said Jace. "And it eventually snowballed into something bigger."

The big arm guiding the 30-year old steering wheel flexed casually with each turn. That arm was ripped and tan. Exquisitely wonderful. As we picked our way through the streets, I couldn't stop looking at it.

"We'll go to my place first," said Jace, "so I can fill you in. But yeah, I messed up and things quickly got out of hand. I'm in over my head now," he turned to me and smiled, "but I appreciate you coming to help."

Help. I still couldn't imagine what kind of help this man needed. He looked like he could lift the couch with one hand and vacuum under it with the other.

"As a matter of fact—"

His sentence trailed off as we pulled into the driveway of some cookie-cutter house in a cookie-cutter neighborhood. Jace killed the engine, just as one of the neighbors raised an arm cheerfully from the porch next door.

"Ah, shit."

Jace's handsome face had suddenly gone red with worry. Putting on his most plastic smile he returned the gesture, but not before circling around to help me out of the Bronco.

"Jace, what are we—"

His hands felt electric on my hips. For a split second I was weightless in his two big arms, and then I was standing on the pavement... holding his hand.

"I'm so, so sorry," Jace whispered back to me. His fingers squeezed gently as they interlaced with mine. "For now, just please—"

"JACE!"

The young woman from next door bounded over happily, now with her husband at her side. Their smiles were so big, so bright, they seemed almost painted on.

"At last!" she cried. "After all this time!"

The woman extended an enthusiastic palm my way. Still clasping Jace in my right hand, I reached out awkwardly with my left and shook it.

"We finally get to meet Jace's *wife*."

Four

DAKOTA

Wife...

The word dropped right out of the clear blue sky. I couldn't have looked more shocked if it hit me on the top of the head, which I guess it did.

WIFE?

It was another squeeze of the hand by Jace that jolted me back to reality.

"Umm, hi!" I said finally, trying to sound as casual yet cheerful as possible. "So nice to meet you. My name is..."

"Dakota," the woman interrupted with a grin. She shook my hand vigorously. "C'mon, you don't think we've already heard all about you?"

Dakota. Well that part was easy, I guess. Whatever 'little white lies' Jace had been telling, at least the name was right.

"I'm Zach, and she's Annie," the husband said,

shaking my hand next. He was young and well-built, with close-cropped hair and dark, bushy eyebrows. Another soldier no doubt. "You both need to come over for drinks. You know, once you get settled in."

"Dakota's tired I'm sure," Jace jumped in. "And probably a little jet-lagged."

"A little," I smiled.

"I'm going to rest her up for a while, but maybe in the next day or two—"

"*Definitely* in the next day or two," Annie replied. "But yes, okay. So nice to finally get to meet you Dakota!"

Zach grinned, nodding his agreement. "We were starting to think you were just a myth. Like Bigfoot!"

The neighbors turned away, leaving us to awkward looks and heavy luggage. Jace took most of it upon himself, then handed me his key. I unlocked the house and we dragged everything inside, closing the door behind us.

"What in the world—"

"Dakota I'm so sorry!" Jace interjected, his face wrought with apology. "I had no idea they'd even be home, much less come running over the moment we pulled up."

"Yeah," I quipped, "well a husbandly head's up would've been nice."

"I know, I know."

"Wife, Jace?" I said incredulously. "I'm your *wife?*"

As strange as it sounded, the word also sat like a hot little ball in the pit of my stomach. Jace stood there looking down at me, his hard, fit body not even heaving slightly from the exertion of carrying all four of my bags. I still couldn't believe how incredible he looked.

Wife...

Holy shit, the word seemed more and more exciting every second that ticked by.

"You want coffee," he asked. "Or something stiffer?"

I grinned my way through the double-entendre. "Both, I think," I replied. "But coffee for now."

He led me through an arch and into the kitchen, which was brightly decorated and immaculately-kept. For a bachelor, his house was certainly big. But Jace wasn't a bachelor anymore. Apparently, the two of us were married.

"Sit down and I'll tell you everything."

I pulled up a chair as his giant stainless coffee machine went through a noisy but delicious-smelling cycle. A few minutes later I was cradling an expertly-made latte, foam and everything.

"Wow," I offered. "This is nice."

"Yeah," he chuckled. "We take our coffee pretty seriously around here."

"We?"

He let out a low whistle. "Damn Dakota, there's so much you need to know. So much has happened."

After fixing himself a mug, Jace crossed his arms and leaned back against the counter. Which was good, because it gave me an excuse to stare at those arms.

"Why don't you start at the beginning?" I told him.

"Last time I saw you was at my house, if you remember."

He nodded slowly. "My going away party." The grin beneath his beard widened. "That whole night was pretty fucking legendary."

"Sure was."

"I passed out cold, and you all shaved my head so Uncle Sam didn't have to."

I laughed as my mind traveled back in time with him. "I can still remember plugging in the buzzer," I murmured. "I also remember being really depressed."

"What? Why?"

"Because you were a hell of a lot of fun," I told him, "all through high school. And it sucked that you weren't going to be around anymore."

Jace took a long, deep breath and let it out as a sigh. "Things always change, don't they?"

"They sure do."

He smiled again, and I felt that familiar pang of nostalgia. I could tell he felt it too.

"I remember you as Tyler's little sister, always around. Always underfoot."

"And I remember you as the tall, goofy kid who always got my brother in trouble," I replied. "I was shocked when you said you'd signed with a recruiter. But I also figured the Army would straighten you out."

"Oh, it straightened some things out," Jace nodded. As he sipped his own mug I could see his eyes were still distant, still far away. "My God, boot camp seems like a thousand years ago."

"It *was* a thousand years ago," I agreed. "Or thereabouts."

The sound of the front door unlatching echoed through the foyer, followed by cheerful voices that preceded their way into the kitchen. The first man through the archway was tall — even taller than Jace — and carried himself with a rock star's swagger. His companion was equally well-built, with sprawling shoulders and a V-shaped body that only came with long, hard hours in the gym.

In fact, both men were covered in sweat. Their shirts stuck to their hard bodies in places I would've loved to spend more time looking at, if I weren't already being introduced by Jace.

"Dakota, meet my housemates: Aurelius and Merrick."

Merrick smiled and nodded politely, then began rifling through the fridge for something. But it was Aurelius, the exceptionally tall and goateed one, who took my palm and planted a kiss on the back of my hand.

"Congratulations on the wedding," he winked.

Five

JACE

I didn't plan on overwhelming Dakota with everything at once, but keeping her in the dark wasn't doing her any favors either. It also didn't help that Aurelius and Merrick knew. Yet as my brothers-in-arms they knew everything, and always would.

"Sorry I didn't get you guys a gift or anything," Aurelius teased. "But if you give me a few days, I'm sure I'll come up with something."

Merrick dug one of his pre-made protein shakes out of the fridge and chugged it down. Wiping his mouth with the back of one arm, he jerked a thumb at me.

"Whatever you do, make sure he doesn't skimp on the honeymoon," he told her. "Jace has a tendency to half-ass everything, if you let him."

"Is that right?" I challenged glibly. "Did I half-ass pulling your *own* ass out of the fire, back in Al Fallûjah?"

Merrick grunted and went silent, as I knew he would.

It was his only option.

"Thought so."

I turned my attention back to Dakota, who was sitting there sipping her coffee. In the span of just eight or nine years so much had changed! Gone were the braces, the freckles, the last remnants of baby fat. The long-legged blonde sitting before me was a full grown woman now, and a gorgeous one to boot. She could've easily been a total stranger, if not for those piercing, arctic blue eyes I'd grown up with for so many years.

God, she's beautiful.

She really and truly was. That part might come in handy, of course. But when it came to the favor I needed, I had to push everything — including appearances — to the side.

"So two weeks before every Christmas there's an officer's ball," I began finally. "It's the most important off-duty event of the year. Especially this year, and especially for me, because I need something very specific from my CO."

She wrinkled her nose. "CO?"

"Commanding officer," said Merrick. "The big guy."

"Oh. That's right."

"See, I shouldn't even be there," I told her. "At the ball, I mean. I wouldn't even be part of this whole ridiculous thing, but for my CO who insisted I come."

"Why shouldn't you be there?" Dakota asked innocently.

"Because I'm not an officer. And I'll never be one."

I saw her avert her eyes for a moment, almost

uncomfortably. But she had the wrong idea.

"Dakota, I'm a Green Beret. Highly decorated. I've completed dozens of successful missions, across eleven different countries and seventeen conflicts."

Her eyes flitted to the others, perhaps expecting them to interject some kind of sarcastic response. There was none, of course. Both Merrick and Aurelius knew the validity of every single one of those conflicts. For more than a few of them, they were right there beside me.

"After Special Forces training I rose through the ranks fast," I explained. "In fact, I got promoted quicker than anyone in recent Army history."

"Why aren't you an officer then?"

"By choice," I replied simply. "I've been a Sergeant Major for a lot years now. I must've turned down advancement half a dozen times, most of them from my increasingly pissed-off CO."

"*Very* pissed off CO," Aurelius agreed.

"But as angry as he is that I won't accept a commission, he's also a man I deeply respect. General Burke came out of Vietnam a genuine hero. He earned two Silver Stars and the Distinguished Service Cross, plus countless other citations too. And shit, I don't even know how many Purple Hearts."

"Four," Merrick chimed in. "I think."

"He was there for Desert Storm," I added, watching Dakota's reaction. "Just as your father was. And though he's pushing past seventy, the old man's still got it."

Dakota's father was another man I respected all throughout high school, but even more now after my service. He'd been a heavy equipment mechanic throughout the conflict, working on everything from Abrams to Apaches. He served all the way through the Gulf War, and was there for the liberation of Kuwait. I knew these things because I'd looked them up. I'd seen his file.

"I still don't understand what this has to do with me," said Dakota. "Or why we're supposedly married."

The guys joined her in glancing expectantly at me from across the kitchen. Eventually, I shrugged.

"Over the past year or so, throughout all the many conversations we had about life, family, and future... I might've told the old man I was married."

Aurelius snorted. "*Might've?*"

"Okay, fine," I admitted. "I did. I told my CO I had a wife, and that wife is you. It has to be you."

"Me?" Dakota asked, arching an eyebrow. "Why me?"

"Because... well..." I winced. "I might've shown him a photo or two."

"Of me?" she asked, surprised. "Oh God, which one?"

"Just some pretty one I pulled off your Instagram account."

"You follow my Instagram account?"

"Uh... sure."

My face was turning undeniably red now, especially

31

since the guys were thoroughly enjoying this. As awkward as it was, I had to get through it.

'Which one did you take?" asked Dakota.

"That bachelorette party you went to last year? Sometime around the summer?"

"Amber's?" Now *she* was turning red. "Oh God. I got so drunk that night! Which one did you use?"

"One of the early ones," I grinned. "You were standing outside, with the lights of the city behind you. Your eyes were shining. You had the most beautiful smile."

I realized I was rambling, but I didn't care. The photo had been amazing, really — the one silent thing that bridged the gap between the girl I once knew and the woman Dakota had become. I felt shitty using it. I felt even more shitty lying. But the photo itself...

Man, I'd admired that one little photo so many times.

"Alright, that one's not bad," Dakota said, finally remembering. "I can let that one slide."

"Good."

"What else?"

I paused to pull my phone from my pocket. After swiping left a bunch of times, I held it up to show her.

"This one."

It was a photo of a photo, or maybe a scan. In it, Tyler and I stood with his sister between us. We were all so young, mid-teens maybe. The three of us had our arms draped happily around each other.

Dakota stared into my phone and slowly shook her head. "You told him we were childhood sweethearts, didn't you?" she asked flatly.

"Yes."

The kitchen went silent as Dakota and I just stared at each other. My housemates stood there innocently, watching the show.

"Look, it just came out one day," I explained. "I don't know what the hell I was thinking. The old man kept wanting to hear about my personal life, and I was floundering, so eventually I made one up. I told him I had someone from back home, someone who I grew up with. I kept building the relationship up more and more every time I talked to him, fleshing it out, giving it details. Then one day he wanted to see a photo. And I realized that this woman I'd been building up this whole time; the one who was strong, and fiery, and independent, and beautiful... this woman was *you*."

Dakota stared back at me blankly, and the complete lack of expression made her somehow prettier. It was hard to tell if she was pissed or flattered or—

"So your boss thinks I'm your wife?"

"Yes," all three of us said at once.

She bit her lip. "That shouldn't be *too* hard to pull off, I guess. Especially for just one person, over a single night."

The others exchanged sideways glances with me. Glances that were awkward enough to notice.

"What?"

"Well, like I said the whole thing snowballed," I confessed. "The general likes to talk, and for some reason he likes to talk me up."

"So?"

"So people over me, people under me, my entire company..."

"Just about everybody on the joint base thinks this guy is recently married," Aurelius finished for me. "He made up a wedding *and* a honeymoon. He even wears a ring."

Sheepishly, I held up my left hand. The simple gold band that still felt so alien on my finger glinted playfully in the dying light.

"Well then I guess congratulations are in order," Dakota declared, taking a long, casual pull of her coffee. She stared back at me again with those big blue eyes, and her mouth curled into a sardonic smile.

"I sure hope our honeymoon was a good one."

Six

DAKOTA

"Yes, you heard me right. Hawaii!"

My mother still couldn't believe me, not even the third time I told her. Probably because Hawaii was exotic and expensive and far away, and I'd never really talked about taking a trip there. But mostly she couldn't believe it because flying out here had happened so quickly, and I was never really a spontaneous person.

"I'm in Honolulu," I told her. "Yes, I'll send you the phone number for the hotel. Yes mom, I'll do that also. Yes mom..."

I nodded my way down the checklist of things she needed to tell me for her own peace of mind. When it came to travel my father was a lot more adventurous, and I'd talked to him first because I knew he'd understand. He'd wished me a great trip, told me to bring him back some Kona coffee, and promised to change my tires while I was gone.

But my mother...

"Dakota, you can't just run off somewhere by yourself," she admonished me. "Even a place as beautiful as that!"

"Who said I was by myself?"

At the other end of the phone there was a long, frightened pause. "You're not back with *Brian*, are you?"

She uttered his name like a curse word, which at this point it probably was.

"Oh *hell* no!"

"Good. Good..." I could sense the relief in her voice. "So you went with friends, then?"

"I uhhh... met some friends here."

"Who?"

"People I work with, mom. Nobody you know."

"But you haven't even *met* most of the people you work with."

"Not in person," I countered. "But I spend a lot more time with them than you realize."

I shot a glance backward, to the largest of my pieces of luggage. The square case was twice as thick as the others, and with good reason. I planned on opening it to check its contents, but hadn't yet.

"You be careful Dakota," my mother finished up. "And call us if you need anything."

"I will mom," I promised dutifully. "Love you. Bye."

Sprawling backward onto my hotel bed, I lamented

my sudden loneliness. The guys had taken me to an amazing dinner last night, at one of those places where part of the table was also a grill and you cooked your own food right there in the middle. We'd laughed, made good conversation, and had more than a few drinks together. I also got to know Merrick and Aurelius a whole lot better, and could quickly see why Jace considered them more like brothers than friends.

I learned the three of them rented the house they shared, but had been together long before that. Though they were from different branches, they'd served on joint missions that often thrust them together. Most likely due to their skillsets and specialties.

One thing immediately apparent to me was that these weren't ordinary soldiers. In the time since he left Minnesota, Jace had been to some *very* exotic places and done some incredibly perilous things. I'd often wondered why Tyler talked about his friend less and less over the years, but now I saw why. Some of Jace's duties required him to disappear for months at a time, and to keep his location a secret even if he were to call back home.

The same went for Aurelius and Merrick. I still wasn't entirely sure what they did, but Aurelius wore a SEAL patch on his leather jacket, and Merrick's sported a silver shield with pilot's wings. The trio dropped me off at the hotel Jace had arranged for me, and being five hours ahead of them I'd fallen quickly into a deep, satisfying sleep.

The sleep hadn't been dreamless, however. My subconscious kept returning to these three hulking men, each of whom was incredibly good-looking in his own unique way. Aurelius had just a *touch* of the sexiest European accent I'd ever heard, and the luscious 5-o'clock shadow on Merrick's angular jaw was something I kept reaching out for, but couldn't touch.

And then there was Jace, three times bigger than I last remembered him. The lean teenager who'd once chased me around my backyard pool with a towel had put on layer upon layer of thick, striated muscle. His once young voice was manly and deep. His steel-grey eyes, enticing yet dangerous.

I woke while it was still dark outside, feeling charged and alive. Jet lag can really suck like that. You'll want a cup of coffee at three in the morning, but nothing really opens until five or six. I'd spent the morning down on the beach enjoying the sunrise, and the rest of the day walking the city and taking things in. I planned on absorbing Hawaii from the inside out. I wanted to start with the urban, then work my way out to the unblemished countryside.

Right now though, my feet were tired. My mind was still wide awake however, so I made the command decision to get up and head downstairs. Jace had promised to call, and since he hadn't yet I figured I'd grab a drink at the hotel bar.

I should've known I'd be immediately swarmed with offers to keep me company.

"Buy you a drink, beautiful?"

I'd already ordered, but that didn't stop him. A clean-cut man slid into the seat on my left, flashing me an overconfident smile. He was dressed in the standard service uniform for the US Navy. So was half the bar.

"Sorry bud," I heard another voice say. "This one's with *me.*"

I turned, and was greeted by Merrick's chestnut

brown eyes and warm smile. My would-be suitor appeared dejected and for a moment, almost challenging. After giving my friend a second look however, he bowed out.

"You're going to get circled by sharks in a place like this," Merrick quipped, looking around. "Squids and grunts everywhere, jarheads too. Comes with the territory."

My drink arrived. I picked it up. "So you're here to rescue me?"

"Well I *am* a Combat Rescue pilot," he smirked. "But no, Jace sent me to pick you up. I was on my way to the elevator when I saw you here."

"Ah," I said, admiring his V-shaped body through his jumpsuit. "I see. Can I finish this first?"

"Sure can. I'll even join you."

He pointed, and the bartender poured him a draft. As he wrapped an oversized hand around it, I raised my drink to toast him.

"To the most beautiful place I've ever been," I smiled.

Our eyes met in the middle of toasting, causing our glasses to clink together musically.

"Just got a little *more* beautiful," Merrick winked at me smoothly.

Seven

MERRICK

I'd seen her photos for weeks now, but those photos didn't do her an ounce of justice. They couldn't convey the charm and charisma of being around her in person, or how her smile grew even more beautiful the wider it spread across her pretty face.

No, the photos Jace showed us didn't prepare us for how cute she was when she laughed, or how instantaneously sexy she looked through the simple act of biting her lower lip. They spoke nothing of her personality either, which was as warm and casual as if we'd known her for months instead of mere minutes.

It almost wasn't fair, him bringing her over like this. Super cool, perfectly matched. Breathtakingly beautiful inside and out, and yet wholly untouchable and beyond reach for any one of us.

Right now, perched on her barstool, Dakota smelled like vanilla and coconut and all things delicious. I couldn't stop staring at her legs, either. Mostly because those legs were longer and smoother than just about any woman I'd ever seen, but also because she kept crossing and uncrossing them beneath her short yellow sundress.

She grilled me about Jace, asking question after question about what he did, who he was, and how he'd ultimately arrived here. In many ways it was like she didn't know him at all, and that's when I realized she didn't know the same person I did. Her memories and recollections ended exactly at the point where mine began. She knew the boy who'd grown into the man, and I knew the man who'd grown into the selfless, unstoppable soldier who was now a brother to me.

But Jace wasn't just a soldier. He was a man whose friendship — along with Aurelius — had been forged in the fires of combat. A fearless warrior who'd risked his own life to save mine, and in doing so, indebted me to him forever.

"Merrick, can I ask you something?"

Our drinks were almost gone. Our time together, almost up. Even though I was taking her to hang out with us tonight, it felt bittersweet.

"Shoot."

"Does he like me?"

The question was so unexpected it nearly knocked me over. I paused a little too long before regaining my composure.

"Jace?"

"Yes."

I laughed nervously. "Are we back in high school?

Do you want me to pass him a note for you, or—"

"C'mon, you know what I mean," Dakota smirked. "Look at it from my perspective. I haven't seen or heard from him in years, and suddenly he's sending me a ticket to Hawaii?"

"Well he needs you," I countered. "You're his date to the officer's ball."

"I know, but look at him!" she cried. Her gorgeous blue eyes flitted over me, up and down. "Look at *all* of you, really."

I felt ten degrees warmer all of a sudden. "What are you talking about?"

"Jace could have any pick of the island," she said. "He could bring any girl to this thing that he wanted. So why send for one back home? One that he barely even knows anymore?"

I wanted very badly to order us another round of drinks, but I suspected Jace might kick my ass if I did. Or at least *try* to kick my ass, anyway.

"It's because of the general," I explained simply. ""Jace already showed him your photo. He's committed. The wife he's been pretending to have is *you.*"

Dakota stared back at me, trying to understand. Not knowing Jace as well as I did, I had to continue.

"Look, the general isn't just his CO, he's practically Jace's father, his mentor. The last thing in the world he'll ever do is disappoint this man." I maintained eye contact as I drained the rest of my beer. "It's bad enough he already lied to him about being married."

She bit her lip, once again driving me crazy. God, she *had* to stop doing that!

"So you don't think he likes me?"

"Well I didn't say *that*," I grinned back at her. "He's talked you up an awful lot, actually. Maybe a little too much, now that I look back on it."

Dakota's eyes flared. They seemed to come alive with a mischievous inner light.

"So have I lived up to the hype?"

She was staring at me unabashedly, totally unfazed. I had to give her credit.

"Actually, you have," I admitted. "But there are a couple of reasons he *can't* like you. Very good ones."

There was a moment of silence as she stared straight ahead, numbly.

"It's because I'm Tyler's sister."

"That's one for sure," I told her truthfully. "You don't go messing around with your best friend's sister, at least not without his blessing."

She nodded, seeming to understand and accept this. Shoving her empty glass away, she looked up at me.

"What's the other reason?"

I froze again, and this time it was a little more obvious. For several long moments, I was a drowning man scrambling for flotsam.

"Merrick?"

I stood up abruptly, shaking my head. "C'mon," I

told her. "I've already said too much."

"But you haven't said anything!"

"Yeah, and that's probably for the best," I smiled, tipping the bartender. "I've always had a pretty big mouth. That's why I fly choppers instead of working in Intelligence."

"But—"

Her sentence died as I reached for her hand, pulling her in the direction of the exit.

"You hungry?" I called back.

"I—I guess so," Dakota admitted.

"Good," I told her. "When we get back to the house, I'm gonna need you to help me talk Aurelius out of ordering pizza."

Eight

DAKOTA

It turned out we couldn't talk Aurelius out of pizza, but that was okay. The flatbread "pizza" that arrived was still pretty delicious, made even more delicious by the fact I'd barely eaten all day.

Together we washed it down with whatever beer the guys had in their fridge, while lounging around and talking about life in general. We'd originally planned to go out and walk the city for a while, but just as we finished dinner a tropical storm abruptly rolled in.

"Monsoon season," Merrick grunted, peering out through a window. He glanced back at me. "You're in for a real treat."

I looked on, watching the shadows of the distant trees bend toward the ground. The wind was so fierce that the rain came sideways, obliterating any chance we had of leaving the house.

"Stay in I guess?" Jace had eventually offered. "Listen

to Christmas songs, like we used to?"

I grinned back at him, remembering all the times we'd done that together as kids. Our parents had an extensive collection of strangely-cool Christmas music. It had become something of a tradition for Tyler and his friends to spend at least one night getting drunk on my parent's booze, listening to Christmas carols. Usually while mom and dad were out at one of their overnight holiday excursions to Minneapolis or St. Paul.

A few hours later I was feeling no pain, and the party had moved to the living room. Aurelius and Merrick were dancing merrily to Holly Jolly Christmas, while Jace began mixing some kind of Kahlua-based cocktail I was sure would give me an instant headache.

Take it slow, Dakota.

I frowned, bitterly. The voice in the back of my head sounded more and more like my mother each day. I wanted to tell it that I was in Hawaii, and on vacation. I wanted to tell it I was having fun for once, and I had everything under control.

All of this was something I knew already, so I turned my attention to the tiny, three-foot Christmas tree centered against the wall of the living room. Brightly lit with evenly-spaced lights, it was too perfect. Too plastic.

"Who's responsible for this?" I pointed egregiously.

"That would be me," Aurelius grinned proudly. "You like?"

"Are you kidding? It's a plastic tree!"

"So?"

"That's sacrilege!" I moved closer, sniffing the air. "And what's that weird smell?"

"Pine-scented spray," Aurelius replied, raising his drink proudly. "It's called 'Just Like Christmas.'"

I wrinkled my nose. "They should call it 'Just like Chemicals.'"

Merrick laughed, and Jace joined in too. I whirled on him, theatrically.

"How the hell could you let this happen?"

"Hey, we're in Hawaii," he shrugged. "Even if we went out for a real one, they don't have the same trees we have in Minnesota. They're all leafy and weird."

I was busting chops of course. I could picture them huddled around this tiny perfect tree, exchanging whatever gifts military roommates might give each other at a tropical island Christmas. As totally alien and different from all the Christmases I'd spent at home, it still seemed like fun.

"You ready for tomorrow?" Jace asked, handing me something that looked like a glass of milk with chocolate streaks.

Outside the wind howled fiercely, causing the very walls to groan. Inside though, the house was calm, cozy, and toasty warm. The drink smelled creamy and wonderful, and tasted even better. I followed the first sip with an immediate second, letting the alcohol warm me from within.

"The better question is, are you ready for two days from now?" Aurelius interjected, smiling broadly.

"For the last time, she's not going to your stupid

SEALs thing," Jace grumbled.

His goateed friend looked wounded. "And why not?"

"Because she's here for *this*," Jace replied. "She's here for me."

"Yeah, quit trying to piggyback," Merrick quipped, poking Aurelius in the ribs. "Go out and find your own best friend's sister."

I had no idea what in the world they were talking about, but I knew the deal I'd made with Jace. I'd come to the officer's ball, all primped up and hanging off his very nice arm, and for the rest of the trip I'd be free. I could spend the next week or more hopping puddle-jumpers or taking boats to other islands. I could explore Kauai, Lanai, Maui... literally wherever the wind took me.

"I promise I'll be ready for tomorrow," I conceded finally, looking back at Jace. "Anything I should know about being your wife?"

The last word put a smile on his face. A good one, at that.

"Only that it's been hard, being away from each other all this time." His eyes narrowed pointedly. "My CO could barely believe it when I first told him I was married. But when I told him it was to my childhood sweetheart, I could see him soften up a little."

"That's how he did it too," I guessed.

Jace nodded. "His wife's name is Meredith. They've been married for more than fifty years."

"Damn."

"My reaction exactly," Jace replied. "But that's what I mean when I tell you the guy is old school. He's all about adherence to tradition. Loyalty and respect."

"He's also expecting you to charm the pants off him," added Aurelius with a chuckle. He nodded toward Jace. "This guy has talked you up so much, you'll practically need to be Superwoman."

Jace glanced back at his friends and frowned. "Don't listen to either of them," he said dismissively. "Just follow my lead and everything will be fine."

The music changed, and a new song came on. Bells and horns preceded Perry Como telling us it was Beginning to Look a lot like Christmas.

"You mentioned you wanted something from your CO," I said. "Something specific."

"Yes. That's the whole point of the night."

"Mind letting me in on what it is?" I smirked. "As your wife, I feel like I have the right to—"

"I want *out.*"

My brow furrowed. "Out?"

"Yes," Merrick took over. "We're all getting out, actually. My contract is up in a few months, and I'm not renewing it. And Aurelius already has his own exit plan."

Aurelius nodded in agreement. "Everything you see here is temporary," he said, looking around. "But the place we're already building together, up in the mountains outside of Denver?" His face lit up with new satisfaction. "Now *that's* permanent."

"You're all moving to Colorado?"

My question was met by more nodding and crossing of arms. I could see there was still a lot I didn't know.

"We've got plans together," Jace said. "A new partnership. The three of us have already done more than most, when it comes to our service. We've put in our time. We're looking to start something new."

"Something *ours*," Merrick agreed. "Something—"

Three quick knocks turned our attention in the direction of the door. Aurelius made his way over and peered through the peephole.

"Shit. It's *them*."

I blinked, even as the other two groaned. "Who?"

"The neighbors."

I still didn't get it. "Zach and Annie?" I said, adding a chuckle. "What's wrong with that? They're harmless."

"Yeah, right."

"No, seriously," I said. "Why wouldn't you—"

"There are still a handful of people on the base that aren't buying the idea of me being married," Jace said quickly. "We're pretty sure our neighbors are among them."

"Oh."

I took a step back as the couple knocked again, this time even more loudly. Aurelius rolled his eyes.

"I guess we can't just leave them out in the storm," he

sighed.

"You sure about that?" asked Merrick.

"I mean we *could*, he reasoned. "It might make things awkward the next time we run into them at the mailbox, though. Or the driveway. Or at the pool. Or—"

Jace stepped into me, shielding my body with his. He was close enough that I could smell his scent, all virile and strong. Taking my hand delicately in his, he pressed something hard into my palm.

When I opened it, I was staring down at two beautiful wedding rings.

Whoa.

"They're only gold-plated," he lamented gently. "And of course the diamond's not real. Even so..."

He helped me slip them on, and somehow they fit perfectly. The wedding band matched the one Jace was already wearing. Real or not, the engagement ring was absolutely stunning.

"For appearances only," he said, adding a smile.

The door opened. The neighbors came in, shaking rain everywhere.

"For appearances only," I winked back, before sliding my arm around him.

Nine

DAKOTA

Zach and Annie were initially as pleasant as the first time I met them, maybe even more so. But as the minutes ticked by, and I got to really know them?

Well, that's when it was more obvious what they were trying to do.

"You're crazy for running over here in the storm," said Jace. "You know that, right?"

"Yes," Annie said breathlessly. Her dark eyes — which were shiftier than a normal pair — flitted momentarily to me. "But like I told you before, we weren't letting you go until we had that drink."

This time it was Merrick behind the bar, trying his best to get a quick drink order out of them. After stalling and ignoring him for several minutes, the couple finally gave in and ordered whatever it was *we* were drinking.

"Right," said Merrick.

Aurelius on the other hand wasn't exactly so subtle about his own thoughts and feelings. He muttered several colorful phrases under his breath, and refused to take our guests' coats because they 'wouldn't be staying long.'

"So..." Zach said, turning toward me. "You finally managed to land this fish, huh?"

He was referring to Jace, who already looked miserable.

"It was a long fight," I said sweetly, "but yes, I eventually got him in the boat."

"You're wearing your rings now," Annie nodded toward my hand.

I held out my arm proudly. "Sure am."

She tried on her best expression of mock disinterest. "You weren't before, though."

"Oh, I always take them off on the plane," I said smoothly. "My fingers swell at altitude."

"Your fingers *swell*..." she repeated flatly. "At altitude."

"Yup."

Whether she believed me or not, I really didn't care. I couldn't see how Jace cared either, but apparently he did and that was good enough for me.

"So you guys met as kids?" asked Zach. "In Minnesota?"

"North Star forever," I smiled.

Annie squinted harder, this time not even trying to

hide her skepticism. "And you've been dating since..."

"Well as kids we were always *around* each other," Jace said truthfully. "But it probably wasn't until—"

"—he finally came to his senses and asked me out," I finished happily. I pulled Jace even closer now, feeling the warmth and heat of his body against mine. "One day we realized the attraction was just too overwhelming. From there, the rest was history."

I leaned up to show him some affection, and Jace bent down to kiss me back. Our lips touched for the first time, and an electric jolt rocketed its way through my body.

Holy SHIT.

Not willing to shatter the illusion with a quick kiss or platonic peck, I remained on my tiptoes. Together we continued evolving the kiss into something bigger and deeper, rolling our mouths hungrily against one another while the others looked on.

Oh wow.

The sudden ball of heat in my belly hit me unexpectedly, although I couldn't see how. For a split second our tongues touched, and I felt myself go almost totally weightless. With Jace kissing me back every bit as much I was kissing him, it seemed like an eternity passed between us.

Then, just as quickly as the whole thing began, our lips parted and we broke away.

Gulping hard I downed the rest of my latest drink — the second such cocktail handed to me by Merrick. He was doing his best not to look stunned from his position behind the bar. Neither he nor Aurelius were doing a good job, though.

"Weird," said Annie, still staring. "We've served with Jace for more than a year now, and until recently he's never even mentioned you."

"That's funny," I shot back. "He's never mentioned you, either."

I let my eyes shift over to Zach, who by this point looked utterly miserable. Whatever shit his wife was trying to pull, he didn't seem to be all that sold on it.

"You know babe," I yawned, "I'm getting sleepy. Wanna take me to bed?"

Jace squeezed me possessively with the flex of one big arm. I had to admit it felt amazing.

"Yeah," he agreed. "Let's go up. I'm tired too."

He broke away from me, but only long enough to show our guests the door. They hadn't yet finished their drinks, but Aurelius plucked them from their outstretched fingers anyway.

"Always nice to have you guys over," Jace muttered, a little sarcastically. "We'll have to do it again sometime."

The door closed behind Zach and Annie, and for a few long seconds, silence reigned. The only sound was the constant patter of the rain outside.

"That was... pretty convincing," said Merrick.

Aurelius scratched at his chin. "Yeah. No shit."

I was still a little woozy. Some of it was from the drinks, but a lot of it had to do with everything that else transpired.

My God. Just look at them.

Much of it was because of Merrick, with his boulder-like shoulders and whiskey brown eyes. It was Aurelius too, his long, lean body stretching his much-too-tight T-shirt over a full set of scrumptious-looking abs.

And of course it was Jace, looking more like a dark, dangerous stranger than the innocent boy I once crushed on throughout my sophomore year. Jace, who'd brought me here to play the part of his wife.

Jace, who so thoroughly kissed me...

Or did you kiss him?

I sank into the nearest couch cushion, not even sure anymore. The music started up again. The room filled with warmth, camaraderie, fun.

"Got any more of these?" I asked, holding my empty glass out.

The three handsome grins spreading across their faces were all the answer I needed.

Ten

AURELIUS

"Finally!"

She stumbled into the kitchen, trailing the blanket behind her. Even bedraggled she looked incredible, all sleepy-eyed and bed-headed and dragging her feet.

"W—What happened?"

Dakota's voice cracked as she rubbed the sleepers out of her eyes. Her makeup was everywhere. Contrary to what most women think they look like with smudged mascara, I'd always found it adorable.

"You crashed here last night," I told her. "Between the jet lag and the white Russians you passed out mid-sentence."

"I did?"

"Yes."

Our sleepy blonde house guest grunted. "So attractive," she yawned.

"Very," I agreed. "Jace carried you up to his room and gave you his bed, then took the couch." I pulled down a coffee mug and poured until it was full. "Milk or sugar?"

"Both, thank you." She paused, looking around. "Where are the others?"

"Working all morning, on base. They'll be back early this afternoon though."

"Oh."

She sank into the nearest chair. I slid her the mug, looked up at the wall clock, then made for the doorway.

"Drink that, then shower fast." I pointed back to the staircase. "I left you towels in the upstairs bathroom. There's aspirin in there too, if you want some. Your clothes are in the guest room, third door on the left."

Confusion crossed her face. "My clothes?"

"Yeah, Merrick and I kinda took the liberty of lifting your hotel key and retrieving your stuff for you. Since we didn't know what you needed, we brought it all."

She stopped the mug halfway to her pretty lips and blinked. "My stuff is *here?*"

"Everything that was in there," I smiled. "By the way, what's in that square box? It's heavy as hell."

She took a long pull from her coffee mug, her eyes closed the entire time. When she opened them again they looked clearer, much more lucid.

"I'll show you later."

"Fair enough," I told her. "Now hurry, because we're already late."

"Late for what?" she squinted.

"You'll see. Dress casual, and meet me outside when you're done."

I began walking the seven blocks it would take to bring the car around, taking my time with a leisurely stride. It was another gorgeous, seventy-two degree morning. The kind of morning where the sky was so blue it didn't even look real, and the clouds were so stark by contrast they seemed painted on.

I'm going to miss skies like these, I mused silently. *But definitely not the rain.*

I breathed deeply, trying to remember my time in Greece. I was only seven when we left. The clear, dry summers were something that still stuck out in my fondest childhood memories, especially when compared to the never-ending rain of Washington state.

Growing up in America had been tremendous! Living in and around Seattle, even more fantastic. There was so much hustle here, so many people moving so quickly and with purpose as compared to back home. I grew to admire it, even emulate and revel in the aggressive work ethic. By seventeen I was a US citizen working the shipyards of Tacoma. By eighteen I was enlisted in the Navy, excelling so far beyond my basic class I was immediately shipped off to BUDS training.

But now...

Now my whole family was back in the 'motherland' – a place I only vaguely remember. As it turned out, it was a place they couldn't resist. A place they still somehow expected me to return to, once I finish my service, of course...

59

"Hey."

I pulled up to the curb and she was already there, looking bright and alive and heartbreakingly beautiful. With her wet hair pulled up into a makeshift bun I got an even better look at the high cheekbones of her lovely, porcelain face. Her stark blue eyes, accented by fresh eye-shadow, were almost cat-like in their femininity.

"*Now* will you tell me where we're going?" she asked again. I noticed she was still clutching the mug from the kitchen.

"Well first," I took the mug and dumped it unceremoniously over my shoulder, "we're stopping to get much better coffee than this whipped foam crap. Jace has gone *way* overboard with that latte machine."

That reaction drew a short, musical laugh. "Seems like a good start."

"And then," I smiled back at her, "I'm taking you dress shopping for tonight."

Her well-manicured eyebrows came together. "But I already *have* a dress for tonight."

"That black thing we found hanging in your hotel room?"

She stared back at me wordlessly.

"Yeah, that's okay for a funeral maybe, but not for the officer's ball."

Eleven

DAKOTA

The afternoon was a whirlwind of fun and excitement and breathtaking weather, as we shot through the city beneath a flawless blue sky. Aurelius was my steadfast chauffeur. My saint and savior and ever-knowledgeable tour guide, and as a shopping partner, he was any girl's best friend.

He plied me with addictively decadent coffee, then took me to shops and boutiques I would've never found on my own. I tried on various dresses in four different stores, until I found the one perfect gown that he swore was going to knock every man at the officer's ball 'square on his ass.'

It wasn't that my original dress was bad, it was that the ball had a reputation for being over the top. The last thing I wanted was to underwhelm Jace's mentor with some lackluster outfit, so if I could start off the night swinging a home run it might definitely help his cause.

Through it all Aurelius wasn't just a trooper, he was a fantastic and charming date. He'd made me laugh dozens of times everywhere we went, sometimes with old stories at Jace or Merrick's expense. I got to learn how he ended up here all the way from Greece, and that he'd met the others while running joint missions involving his SEAL platoon. The specifics of his service were vague, maybe even intentionally hazy. But the humility made him all the more mysterious. And let's face it, all the more attractive, too.

We shared lunch on the water together: Mahi Mahi with grilled oysters, washed down with Bloody Marys so spicy they made my eyes water. Then, with the sun finally getting lower in the sky, we headed home.

Home.

It occurred to me that I might spend another evening at the guys' place, especially if they had a guest room. I decided that scenario was fine by me. It sounded like a lot less lonely way to end the night.

"Wait! Pull over."

Aurelius obeyed, and even miraculously found a spot. Two minutes later I was leading him by the hand into yet another dress shop.

"I thought we decided on the dress we bought earlier?" he said.

"We have."

"Then what are we—"

"I saw something in the window."

Walking along the front of the store, I pointed to the display. The red dress I'd seen from the street had a wickedly plunging neckline. From this angle, it had an open back, too.

"That dress is hot," Aurelius admitted, letting out a

low whistle. "But it's not the kind of thing you'd wear to the officer's ball."

"Maybe not," I agreed. "But what about your SEALs thing?"

His expression went utterly blank. It was the first time all day I'd seen him at a disadvantage.

"Did you still want me to go to that?" I asked.

"YES!" he replied enthusiastically. "Then again, I don't think Jace—"

"You let me worry about Jace," I stopped him quickly. "Besides, I agreed to be Jace's wife for a night. After that, according to the deal we made, I'm on a solo Hawaiian vacation."

Aurelius's fierce brown eyes came suddenly alive. His smile was back, too.

"You are, huh?"

"I most certainly am."

"And you'd be willing to do date night with the rest of my platoon?" he asked. "Let me show you off a little?"

"Well what kind of night is it?"

He shrugged his gorgeous shoulders, as his eyes shifted from side to side. "Well, it's a lot less formal than the officer's ball."

I chuckled. "Go on."

"We grab some food, some drink, some merriment..."

"Sounds good so far."

"Then we all throw on Santa hats and do a good old American bar crawl, playing whatever games we find in the pubs along the way."

I pictured a dozen or more men like Aurelius stumbling happily from bar to bar, each with a beautiful wife or girlfriend on his arm. It sounded fantastic.

"Could I go wearing this?" I pointed again.

"Are you kidding?" he laughed. "I'd take you *anywhere* in that dress!"

I spent the next few minutes in the dressing room, trying it on. I couldn't help thinking about what it would be like to wear it out, surrounded by deadly warriors sporting festive Santa hats. Boisterous warriors who were most likely drunk. Throwing darts. Playing pool...

But mostly, I thought about what it would be like to wear it for Aurelius.

The dress was daring, scorching hot, totally sexy. Rather than step out into the shop's main floor, I pulled him into the dressing room instead.

"What do you think?"

I was standing there looking into the mirror, with Aurelius just behind me. He'd pulled the door to the dressing room closed behind him.

"I think you're the hottest fucking thing on two feet."

He took another step closer, until our bodies were practically touching. I could feel his heat now, smell the sweet, minty scent of his hot breath. The big SEAL towered over me, but he bent forward just enough so that his face protruded past my left shoulder.

"It's a shame you're off-limits," he whispered softly. "A travesty, really."

He brushed against me from behind, either intentionally or not. Cold shivers ran down my body from head to toe, followed immediately by hot tingles.

"W—Who says I'm off-limits?"

The words just sort of spilled out. They caught in my throat on the way past my lips, that's how dry everything was.

"Well, for one thing you're Jace's girl," he said with a hint of genuine sadness. "And before you try to tell me you aren't, you'll *always* be Jace's girl."

Aurelius stood tall again. Clearing his throat, he let out a long, wistful sigh.

"So what's the other thing?" I asked.

I locked eyes with him in the mirror. This time I wouldn't let him go.

"Merrick already told me there's a reason Jace *can't* have me, and it had nothing to do with my brother." I whirled to face him. "Is this the same reason?"

He paused. "Merrick really said that, huh?"

"He sure did."

Aurelius shook his head slowly. "Well Merrick always did have a big mouth. That's why he's not in Intelligence. As a matter of fact, he once—"

"Forget all that," I cut in. "Come on, tell me. What's this big secret?"

For a moment I thought he might turn away. That he might take with him any chance I had of ever knowing. But then I saw his eyes.

Oh my God...

His eyes — usually so innocent and honest — were dark and smoldering now. Those eyes were hungry. Full of lust.

"We're looking for something specific," he said, and his voice somehow didn't sound like his own. "Some*one* specific, really."

"Who?"

Aurelius swallowed hard. His body stiffened as he placed his hands on my shoulders and spun me around again. Maybe because he couldn't face me.

"Dakota, listen, we can't do this with you. And the reason we can't do this with you is because Jace, Merrick and I..."

His jaw went tight. In the vast abyss of the full length mirror, his eyes somehow found mine again.

"We like to share."

My eyebrows knitted together. I wasn't sure I'd heard him right.

"Share?"

"Yes."

I cocked my head. "You mean..."

He didn't say a word. He only nodded in the reflection, looking back at me stoically.

"Oh."

His hands were still on my shoulders. They felt like they weighed a thousand pounds each.

"Oh, wow."

"Yeah."

The room was twenty degrees hotter all of a sudden. Like I'd just walked into a sauna.

"I should probably get you back already," Aurelius said abruptly. "If you're even a second late for this thing, Jace is going to—"

"H—How long has it been like this?" I stammered. All of a sudden I had a million questions. "And... all three of you? Jace too?"

Aurelius merely shrugged. "I know it sounds crazy, but it's a part of who we are. We're extremely tight-knit. Partners in everything. And the three of us have shared before. We've shared before and we liked it."

"The same woman?"

"Yes."

The lump forming in my throat felt like a bowling ball. I found just enough oxygen to keep breathing.

"Look, it's not something we broadcast," Aurelius went on. "But we've had relationships like this in the past. We've shared girlfriends during deployment, and we found that it suited us."

He paused, and I saw the hint of a smile curling its way upward at the very corners of his mouth.

"The women didn't seem to mind it either, to be honest."

Shared. I repeated the word over and over in my mind, almost until it lost its meaning.

"So you only date women together?"

Aurelius's hands slid downward casually, like they'd somehow done it before. They settled on my hips.

"Well, no," he admitted. "I mean, we each have *needs* too. It's not like we don't satisfy those needs when we want to, but those one-on-one relationships are purely sexual. We consider them placeholder relationships, until we find the one."

"The *one?*"

"The woman we all fall in love with. Someone strong and fierce and open-minded, who can accept three husbands instead of one."

"So basically you're looking for a unicorn," I couldn't help but chuckle. "At the end of a rainbow."

"Maybe," Aurelius smiled. For a brief instant he squeezed my hips, scanning me up and down. "Maybe not."

He let go, and once again I turned to face him. Everything around me had faded away at this point. The entire rest of the world was forgotten.

"You already know we're looking to get away, to start over in this new place we're building together," he went on. "That also comes with sharing a woman together. We don't want three wives, we want one wife between us. We want to make her happy. We want to make her the queen of our world."

I was silent for a few moments, as my brain struggled to process everything I'd just heard. My shocked expression must've been hard to read because Aurelius shook his head.

"You probably think we're assholes now," he said miserably. "I've completely ruined your opinion of—"

"No!" I cut in quickly. "No, it's not that at all. I'm just... surprised. I never imagined something like this was even a thing."

The big SEAL folded his massive arms, shifting from one foot to the other as he towered over me. With his dark hair and sun-bronzed skin he looked like a Spartan warrior.

"Whether it is or not, we're going to *make* it a thing," he said definitively. "It's what we want."

His eyes flared dangerously.

"And we *always* get what we want."

Twelve

DAKOTA

The old general was witty, charming, and funny as hell. Throughout the night, he had the best comebacks to anything that was said, by anyone who said it. He commanded the room, and when there was a question at the table he held all the answers.

All this, and the man was almost seventy-five.

"And do you remember the first time you saw each other?" he asked, swiveling the question my way. His eyes, which appeared to have once been brilliant blue, were going a milky grey from the outside in.

"Yes," I told him with a smile. "I sure do."

Even so, those eyes were sharp and piercing. Still totally full of life.

"Please tell me about it."

I snuck a glance at Jace, who was dabbing at the corner of his mouth with a napkin. It was just one of five predetermined signals that I had free reign to make up whatever answer I wanted.

"It was summertime," I said, smiling wistfully. "My friends and I had some pocket change, so we took our bikes up to the corner store for some candy."

On the other hand, if this were something he'd previously made up a story for? I'd get a quick kick under the table that would let me know to defer.

"Not many kids on bicycles these days," General Burke grunted.

"No," I agreed. "Not nearly enough. But then again I always had parents who pushed me outside. Summer time, winter time, it never really mattered. I was expected to go swimming, take a hike, make a snowman — didn't matter what it was, as long as I did *something*."

"Good parents," the general smiled. "Go on."

I jerked a thumb Jace's way. "Your golden boy here started throwing rocks at our tires. That's my first ever memory of him."

"My *friends* were throwing rocks," Jace jumped in defensively. "Not me."

I smiled and leaned into the general conspiratorially. "That's a decades-long point of contention," I whispered softly.

The man laughed, eyeing Jace over my shoulder. "You always throw rocks at the ones you like," he said. "That's how I know he's lying."

"Oh yeah," I agreed. "But in the end, he did the

right thing. He followed me back to my house on his own bike, and that's where he apologized. And so I shared my candy with him."

"So it was love at first sight?" one of the Lieutenants at the table — a blond-haired man by the name of Dietrich — asked.

"Yes and no," I smirked. "I mean, at first I was wary. We were still very young, and I thought boys were icky."

"Boys *are* icky," another officer chuckled.

"Well they become *less* icky in junior high," I agreed. "They're a whole lot cuter after their growth spurts." I placed my hand over Jace's, interlacing our fingers. "Especially this one."

The CO's gaze followed mine, dropping to where my big cubic zirconia flashed brilliantly on my ring-finger. I smiled happily at my pseudo-husband and pulled him close.

"So general," I said, pausing until he looked up at me. "Are you ready to give him back to me?"

The man leaned back in his chair, pursing his lips as he considered me carefully. He was calculating, I knew. Weighing pros and cons and everything else a general might weigh, especially one who'd been through so many, many battles.

"I mean, you've had him for so very long," I pressed. "He's done everything that you asked."

"And then some," the man agreed.

"And then some."

Every Army officer in the building was dressed to the

nines, all decked out in their blue dress uniforms. Table after table, each came complete with black ties, epaulets, and gold-gilted buttons, along with colorful service ribbons pinned high on each person's chest.

The general's gaze drifted to Jace's chest now, where a massive array of multi-colored bars were stacked in rows and columns above his shiny Airborne lapel pin. Multiple oak leaf clusters and metal stars were pinned to some of the ribbons, meaning he'd been awarded that particular medal or commendation more than once.

As a Sergeant Major, Jace wasn't even an officer. Yet he still had more medals, ribbons, and awards pinned over his heart than any other person in the entire officer's ball.

Anyone except for General Burke, of course.

"So you need him for a few missions of your own, I suppose?" the general quipped.

"A couple, yeah," I smiled back.

"I'm assuming they're no less dangerous."

The man's soft eyes and kind face made me chuckle. "Depends on how much longer he makes me wait. I've loved this man since he threw rocks at me. And now he's throwing grenades at *other* people, which of course makes me a little jealous."

General Burke's face broke into a broad, white-toothed grin. He let out a long, gruff laugh that sounded far younger than his seventy-five years.

"She's a keeper, this one," he told Jace.

"Don't I know it."

The old man's smile eventually faded, his laughter turning into something a bit more serious.

"You're finally ready to start that family, are you son?"

The general directed the question at Jace this time, not me. He nodded respectfully and squeezed my hand.

"Yes sir. We've been putting everything off for a long time now. Even the wedding." He looked back at me lovingly. "But that one I couldn't wait on any longer," Jace said. "I've kept this poor woman waiting long enough."

The general stared at Jace for what seemed like a very long time, studying him up and down. Somewhere in the background the music changed to something slow and melodic and very, very old.

"Well I can't say I blame you," the man finally replied. He turned to face me, and his expression softened. "And if we've kept him much too long, it's only because of his value. Rocks and grenades aside, your husband has been of incredible service to his country. Well beyond most."

I smiled sweetly and nodded.

"You'll never truly know the full scope of the things he's done," the general went on, "but know that I've never commanded a man more brave, more loyal, and more unwavering than this one."

Rising, he patted Jace on the shoulder before dropping his napkin to the table.

"One thing I have to insist upon however," he smiled, "before you run off to start an all new life?"

The general extended an open palm my way. I took it happily.

"Is that you indulge this old soldier in a dance."

Thirteen

DAKOTA

My dance with General Burke was slow and sweet and downright beautiful. For a wily old veteran the man still had a few great moves left in him, and he didn't mind showing those moves off as we glided together across the ballroom floor.

Dancing with Jace however...

"So do you think he bought it?"

My 'husband' and I were on the other side of the floor now, swaying gently to another old song. He had one arm pinned firmly around my waist, with the other holding my hand.

"Maybe," Jace shrugged. "Where'd you get the rocks thing from? That was brilliant."

I laughed softly. "That was another boy. Another time."

"You really shared your candy with him?"

"No, I made that part up."

Our bodies were close now, and drifting closer with every few steps. I didn't mind at all. In fact, I might've been guilty for some of the drifting.

Gotta keep up appearances, right?

My gaze crawled over Jace's big arms, his broad shoulders, his hard chest. I breathed deeply as I pressed my face against that chest, inhaling his sweet, cologne-infused scent.

Sure. Whatever you need to tell yourself.

"I think you did fantastic," he told me. "Burke's not an easy man to impress, and an even harder man to bullshit. Somehow you pulled off both."

"Yeah, well I think he might also have a soft spot for smiling young women."

Jace rolled his steel-grey eyes and grinned back at me. "Don't we all."

I punched him playfully in the arm, then slid my face back against his chest. Being against him felt so *good*. So totally and completely safe.

"Hey, remember that night we were in the pool together," Jace asked, "after everyone left? And somehow we ended up sort of wrapped around each other, floating in the water, face to face?"

I nodded against him. "Yes. Of course I do."

"We stared at each other for like a full five minutes without saying anything," he went on. "It should've been awkward, but it wasn't. It was actually one of my favorite childhood memories."

I thought back, calling up memories of that night. I could remember how incredibly lucky I'd felt at the time. Lucky, but also warm and safe and protected... just like now.

"I wanted to kiss you so badly that night," Jace admitted. "But I couldn't, because of Tyler."

I pulled back to look up at him. We were staring again like last time, and it still wasn't awkward.

"I wanted you to kiss me too," I breathed. "But I was afraid, and not because of my brother."

"You were?"

"Sure. You were a pretty big catch back then. Tall, strong, funny. Captain of the lacrosse team. But we were around each other so much, I was terrified that if things got screwed up..."

"... it would be weird between us, from then on."

"Yes."

I couldn't believe he was saying this. Now, after all this time.

"I was an idiot," Jace went on. "I really should've kissed you."

My heart was beating faster now. I shrugged one shoulder.

"Yeah, well when opportunity knocks, you have to let it in."

Our bodies touched. His eyes searched mine.

"Opportunity, huh?"

"Yes," I agreed. "Opportun—"

Jace's lips came crashing against mine, rolling softly but firmly as an all-consuming heat washed over us. This time we went for broke. There was no one to stop us, no one to tell us what we were doing was wrong. As far as everyone knew we were husband and wife, reunited at last after a long, desperate tour of duty.

HOLY FUCK.

Our tongues continued to surge, sliding hotly into each other's mouths as our kiss melted the rest of the world away. Everyone around us was gone in an instant; replaced by the all-consuming need to mold our bodies tightly together and devour each other, even as our hands continued to roam. Suddenly I was back in the pool again: breathless, weightless, deliriously happy. Floating in the warmth and wetness of that hot summer night, my bare legs wrapped around his long, lithe body.

Jace broke the kiss still cradling my face in his two big hands, the tips of his fingers lingering affectionately on my cheeks. As he finally pulled back we tilted forward again, so that our foreheads touched.

"Holy shit you *were* an idiot!" I gasped when I could speak again.

"Oh yeah?" he chuckled. "How do you figure?"

I brought my face back to his, hovering my lips over his mouth until every breath he took was mine.

"Because we could've been kissing like this all these years," I said, and kissed him again.

Fourteen

DAKOTA

We floated home, dancing on cloud nine. The car service dropped us right on the guys' doorstep, and Jace kissed me one last time before ushering us through the front door.

We were greeted immediately by Merrick and Aurelius, relaxing in the living room watching a movie.

"You're back early?"

"It's past midnight," I countered. "That's early?"

"Depends on the night," Aurelius grinned.

Jace began peeling off his uniform layer by layer, then hanging it neatly in true military style. It was distracting as hell, watching him unbutton his way downward, laying the upper half of his chest bare.

"You look amazing in that dress," Merrick whistled. He eyed me up and down now, his gaze lingering unapologetically as he tossed back the last inch of a glass of whiskey. "I'll bet you totally slayed."

The compliment came with a sly wink that made me feel even warmer inside.

"These shoes are definitely slaying my feet," I smiled, kicking them off. "But thank you."

My head was spinning, and not just from all the champagne. I'd spent the entire night thinking about the guys — all three of them. Throughout the whole time I was kissing Jace, I couldn't help but fixate on every smoldering, gut-churning word of what Aurelius had told me about them.

We want to make her happy.

I'd fantasized all day about what he'd said. And while drowning in the depths of those fantasies, *I* was the one they wanted.

The queen of our world.

I couldn't help but picture these three incredible men, closing in around me. Approaching me from all sides, as their hands moved to touch my shivering, quivering body...

"Dakota?"

Jace was standing before me, removing his cufflinks. Even that little action seemed overtly sexual. I knew it was all in my head, obviously. I'd been thinking so much about all the wickedly hot things these men had done together, I was practically in heat.

"Are you okay?"

"Yes," I nodded, trying to swallow. "I am."

"Do you want a drink?"

I thought about slipping into Jace's bed, instead of the guest room. It could happen. With the kissing we'd done early it would be easy, maybe, except that—

"I don't want a drink, no," I said, my heart pounding. "I want *you.*"

Jace's face flushed immediately red. His eyes shifted to the left and right.

"But that's not all I want."

I walked to the center of the room, not stopping until I was standing between all three of them. It felt like someone else's legs were carrying me.

"Share me."

The room was suddenly blanketed with a dead, stunned silence. I could've announced I was holding a live hand grenade, the faces surrounding me would be no different.

"W—What?" Jace stammered.

"Don't pretend you don't know what I'm talking about," I said, feeling an abrupt surge of confidence. "I want you to share me. All of you."

I stood there trembling with excitement, gauging their reactions. Jace and Merrick's eyes both shifted to Aurelius.

"Oh don't be mad at him for telling me," I chuckled. "At least he's the honest one. Merrick dropped a sly hint about it, then played it off as some kind of big mystery. As if a girl like me wouldn't get to the bottom of it."

Aurelius and Merrick dipped their chins, but it was

Jace's expression that concerned me the most. It seemed to be a mixture of anger and confusion and panic. But beneath that outer layer, I could sense other more amorous emotions too.

"Look, I know it's your rule, your goal, your fantasy," I told them matter-of-factly. "I know you're looking for one woman to share between all three of you."

"But—"

"I'm not saying I'm that woman," I told them quickly. "But I *will* say the whole idea of it makes me hot. I've been thinking about it all day. Wondering what it would be like if you boys... well..."

I turned in a slow circle, looking at each of them in turn. My eyes settled on Jace's intentionally last.

"Listen, I want this. I *need* this. I have to try it, and I know you've already tried it, and I know that no matter what happens it's going to be so fucking *good*."

I pulled my hair back slowly, seductively, then shrugged my dress over my shoulders. The guys gawked silently as I pulled it down, first over one arm then the other. With a quick shimmy of my hips, it dropped straight down my body and to the floor.

"I'm giving myself to you," I said softly. "You have my permission. I want to experience all three of you in every way."

I should've felt naked before all three of them, dressed only in my satin red bra and matching thong panties. Instead I felt exhilarated and empowered — and yes, hot — beyond anything I could've imagined.

Jace finally took two steps in my direction. I slid my arms over his shoulders, but his face was still serious.

"And Tyler?" he asked.

I shrugged. "Tyler never has to know."

His handsome face contorted into a frown. It didn't seem to be the answer he wanted.

"He's my *friend*, Dakota. And you're his sister!"

"And Tyler's a big boy who can take care of himself," I countered, letting my eyebrows knit together. "We're not kids anymore, Jace. We're all grown up. Tyler has his own life, just like we do. I don't interfere in anything he's doing, and I don't remember my brother ever seeking my approval for anything that he did."

With that I kissed him, swirling my tongue through his hot mouth. With each second that ticked by I could feel his resolve weaken. The tension slowly drained out of his shoulders, and the hands on my hips finally began to wander.

Holy shit this is actually happening...

My heart thundered away in my chest as Jace began kissing me back. And then there were two sets of hands on my body. Three sets...

Oh my GOD.

I had Merrick on my left, pulling me in his direction. His big hand was gentle as it guided my mouth away from Jace's and onto his own. Once again my lips parted, and a second hot tongue plunged inside. I whimpered softly as he kissed me over and over, practically melting into his arms as someone else pressed against my mostly-bare ass from behind.

Aurelius.

The SEAL's hot mouth dropped sensuously to my neck. And then he was kissing me too, his goatee brushing against my skin with a delicious tickle. I was shivering all over. Shuddering with lust. Every inch of my exposed skin broke out in goosebumps as they passed my lips back and forth between them, taking turns exploring my mouth. By the time Aurelius's hands slipped around me, cupping my breasts from behind, I was practically drenched.

"You have to *want* this if we're really going to do it," another voice whispered in my opposite ear. "I need to hear it again, Dakota. From your own lips."

I pulled back for a second, turning to face Jace again. His expression was calm, rational, placid. But his eyes, like mine, were swimming with lust.

"Look, I know you boys are trying to be good," I said gently. "But I'm here for another nine days. I can spend them alone, drinking from coconuts and doing touristy bullshit. Trying to find some cute, meaningless fling to unleash some of this pent-up sexual tension on..."

I unhooked my bra, letting it fall. Three sets of eyes dropped accordingly.

"... or I can spend it here with you, men I already enjoy and respect," I finished breathlessly. "Laughing and playing and making you boys very, *very* happy..."

Fifteen

DAKOTA

I don't know who put the music on, but it was certainly a good idea. It broke the ice even more. Made everything we were about to do that much easier, as something soft and melodious began playing in the background.

In the meantime, the guys played with *me*.

Very quickly it became obvious they were as hot for me as I was for them, and maybe even more so. I was kissed and made out with until I was absolutely breathless, then passed to the next pair of strong, cable-like arms for more. Back and forth these men traded me between them, drinking from my lips as their hands roamed my body more boldly with each passing minute.

Holy—

They'd unmistakably done this before. That part both frightened and thrilled me at the same time. There was a kernel of deep-seeded envy somewhere in the pit of my stomach; a smoldering jealousy that they'd shared other women, in other places, at other times. Still, that jealousy burned with a raw, primal heat that also thrilled me to think about. I got butterflies just envisioning those lucky women and the things they'd experienced, all the while knowing those same things would be done to *me*.

Easy, Dakota...

And then there was the Jace factor. I realized now how much I'd wanted him for so long. How I'd pushed him to the back of my mind as wildly unattainable all those years ago, when in reality he'd been one of my very first fantasy crushes. And now I could have him — wholly and completely. And not just him, but him and his two hot *friends*...

"God, just feel her. Right... here."

A hand slipped between my thighs and cupped my thong, two fingers pressing hard against the slick satin fabric. Right now I was hotter than I'd ever been. I was wetter and more excited for this than anything else in my entire life.

Ohhhh...

In many ways I knew I was being too eager. I was too thrilled to be racing toward that finish line, when I really should be enjoying the ride.

"Sit back," I said abruptly.

I stood again, and watched as the guys did exactly what they were told. Jace and Merrick dropped to either side of the long couch, looking up at me eagerly. Aurelius sat in the center of the loveseat on the opposite side...

"My turn."

I spun in a circle then pointed to Aurelius, who smiled as if he'd won the lottery. Looking him right in the eyes I slowly rolled my thong down my thighs and bent to step out of it, simultaneously giving Jace and Merrick a perfect view of my bare, beautiful ass.

"Fuck..." one of them said.

"Eventually," I chuckled. "But right now, you boys sit there and enjoy."

The song changed. I rolled with it, swaying my hips slowly and rhythmically while backing up against Aurelius and settling down into his lap. I gave him my best rendition of a lap dance, grinding my ass against his rapidly-swelling shorts. His hands slid to my hips. I closed mine over his for leverage and squeezed them encouragingly, while staring straight ahead at the others.

"You boys are wearing entirely too many clothes."

I laughed as Merrick began stripping feverishly. Jace on the other hand took things more slowly. He locked eyes with me as he undid the rest of his shirt buttons, then worked his belt as he mirrored my own sly smile.

You've wanted this for a long time, haven't you?

His eyes spoke the words that his mouth didn't have to. There was no use denying it. I nodded at him slowly, grinding even harder into Aurelius's lap. His hands were growing bolder, the knot in his shorts bigger and more intimidating with every turn of my hips.

And through it all, Jace sat there and watched.

Shit, I thought to myself. *This isn't just about fucking me.*

My brother's friend's eyes were following my every lurid movement. They crawled hungrily over my body as Aurelius slid his hands through the warm valley between my thighs.

He loves to watch.

Aurelius was rewarded with a flood of wetness. He applied pressure, prying my legs open for his friend. It left me spread wide. Exposed and dripping.

Oh my God.

I sighed in contentment as I leaned back against his hard, sculpted body. My hands slid backwards so I could run my fingers over his incredible abs, which were every bit as hard and wonderful as I'd imagined they would be.

With our gazes still locked Jace slipped to the floor, unable to watch any longer. His two big hands went to my thighs, spreading them further as he lowered his mouth against my hot, dripping entrance...

OHHHHH...

Throughout it all, he never looked away. He maintained unwavering eye contact as his beard brushed my thighs and his tongue slipped straight past my folds and buried itself achingly deep in my eager, throbbing channel.

"Fuuuuck..."

I drew the word out in a whimper, as Aurelius's hands played with my tits. My thighs were spread over his now, my back arched along the broad expanse of his chest. Our heads were side by side and he turned my cheek to begin kissing me, his tongue rolling hotly over the inside of my mouth just as his friend's tongue was busy doing the same thing down below.

This is out of fucking control.

It was for sure, but in all the best ways. I was being attended to by more than one mouth, more than one body. More than one set of eager, questing hands that—

"Oh!"

Another warm mouth entered the game, this one settling over my right breast. Merrick had stripped down to his boxer briefs and approached from the side. His sculpted body looked magnificent as he bent down to nuzzle my chest, and a third hot tongue began tracing wet, wonderful circles around my exposed areola.

This is unbelievable...

I gasped into Aurelius's mouth as Jace slipped a thick finger inside me. He curled it inward delicately, dragging it over my G-spot as he continued to devour me with his hot, questing mouth.

Totally fucking UNREAL.

It was the only way to put it. The only way to come even close to describing the sensation of taking on three men at once. Three hot, hard, Special Forces soldiers, hellbent on making me their sole mission because it was what they liked, what they wanted, what they did together...

And of course, exactly what I'd *asked* for.

My hands went frantically to Jace's head, plunging my fingers through his hair as I pulled him into me. Bucking my hips forced his questing tongue even deeper as I arched backwards against the ripped, well-honed body of my beautiful Greek god.

Between Jace's finger and all these mouths it didn't take long. I came explosively, moaning against Aurelius's beautiful lips as I writhed through an earth-shattering orgasm that rocked me all the way to my very core. I floated through nirvana for a long while, weightless in their strong arms. Drifting along in a sea of euphoria, my eyes eventually fluttered open and I realized I was no longer where I once was.

And that's because Jace was carrying me into his bedroom... with the others trailing just behind.

Sixteen

DAKOTA

It took forever for the kissing to stop, and forever was fine by me. They were all so different, yet in some ways the same. Each of them handling me in such uniquely hot ways, as I was stretched naked and made out with in the middle of Jace's soft, king-sized bed.

Eventually I was left kneeling there, watching anxiously as the guys finished disrobing. Whatever clothes they still had on were peeled off slowly, deliberately, to enhance my enjoyment and prolong the agony. Their hard bodies were brought into stark, glorious view as my eyes crawled every last inch of their tan, muscle-bound flesh.

And then they were in their boxer-briefs... and nothing else.

Fuck YES.

For a moment I imagined I was a helpless animal, trapped by three powerful predators. And that they were about to devour me whole, showing me absolutely no mercy.

Fuck, even *that* made me hot.

It was Jace who moved first, kissing me hard while pushing me backwards onto the bed. The huge knot in his boxers was bigger and thicker than the outline I remembered from years ago, when I stole glances of him in his swimsuit whenever we were by the pool.

Halfway through kissing him I took that knot into my hand. It was impossibly hard. Incredibly, wonderfully thick and warm and—

"You sure this is okay?"

Jace whispered the words into my ear, while chewing on my shoulder. All the while I kept working him with my hand.

"Yes."

"Because if it's not," he warned sullenly. "If it's something that might affect things between Tyler and—"

"Jace," I interjected.

"What?"

I took him by the cheeks and turned him to face me. "Shut up and *fuck* me."

He kissed me one last time, eyes open, looking at me as deeply and meaningfully as he did while we were floating in the pool. I nodded breathlessly as he pushed his way between my thighs. I spread even wider for him, as he shoved his underwear down his hips and kicked it off the foot of the bed.

Here we go.

Together we glanced down, to where his incredible-looking cock hovered against my throbbing, honey-coated entrance. Pushing his hips forward, it parted my folds and slid through the heated shallows of my pussy.

"Inside me," I groaned, kissing him some more. "I want you insi—"

I gasped the second part of my sentence into his mouth as Jace shoved himself home. He drilled me in one long, deep, satisfying thrust that made my eyes cross and my toes curl...

YESSSSS!

We were finally whole. At long last, our circle complete. I took his face in my hands as he bottomed out, his swollen balls pressing tightly against my gyrating ass. Our eyes were still locked as I kissed him again, this time with sensual slowness. This time as *lovers*, and not just friends.

"We're *both* idiots," he murmured, causing me to laugh.

"Why? Because we could've been doing this for years?"

"Because we *should've* been doing this for years," he growled, grinding into me slowly as we continued kissing. He sighed lustily, rocking forward on his two big arms. Flexed beneath the weight of his massive body, those arms looked more like bridge cables than biceps or triceps. "Dakota, this is fucking *amazing...*"

Jace rolled forward and back, screwing me exquisitely deeper on every thrust. The sheer size of him stretched my thighs so wide on either side of his body it felt like I was being torn in half!

But oh, what a way to go...

"God, your brother would *kill* me," he grunted, still holding my face. I could feel him throbbing deep inside me, as he planted kisses on both my cheeks.

"If he saw how much muscle you put on," I chuckled, "I'm pretty sure he—"

"You know what I mean."

Of course I knew what he meant. Jace and I had been around each other so much while growing up, it felt strangely taboo screwing Tyler's best friend. But deep down in a place I didn't like to admit, maybe that was also part of the appeal.

"This is for *us,*" I murmured, kissing him back. "We wanted this. We made it happen."

"Yeah, but—"

I pulled him in, and somewhere in the heat of my core I squeezed hard. I saw his eyes flare with pleasure.

"This has nothing to do with Tyler," I smiled up at him. "I'm a big girl, Jace. I do what I want..." We brushed lips again as our eyes searched each other. Our kisses were fire.

"And what I want is *this,*" I whispered hotly.

The others had hung back during our intimate little reunion, giving us our time together. But now apparently, their time on the sidelines was over. I smiled as they collapsed onto the bed, gliding up on either side of me. I spread my arms now as well as my legs, reaching to touch them wherever I could.

"You sure you're sharing this one?" Aurelius poked his friend.

Jace didn't even reply. He leaned back and kept sawing away at me, putting me through the paces.

"Oh he's definitely sharing," I chuckled, sliding a hand up the SEAL's thick, corded thigh. "I... can't wait... to feel what it's like to..."

Something warm touched my face, and that something was Merrick's palm. He cradled my cheek gently as he bent to kiss me, then took my hand and placed it somewhere else entirely.

Oh!

My God, he was *thick!* So big I could barely fit my hand around him. I lolled my head to one side to get a better look, and that's when he straddled my face and pushed the smooth, bulbous head right up against my wet, eager lips.

Holy fu—

And just like that I was blowing him. Stroking the thick shaft up and down with one hand, while taking him as far into my throat as I could.

Mmmmmmmmmm...

Merrick tasted sweet and musky at the same time, with an arousing hint of salt on his skin. I moaned shamelessly around him as Jace continued fucking me, all but crushing me between them as I took on two men for the very first time.

Wow.

There was no preparing for the magnitude of such a

moment. No amount of daydreaming or fantasizing could ever do it justice.

Just... wow.

Being plundered at both ends felt sinful and wicked and wrong... but in all the right ways. It came with an exquisitely vulgar heat; an inherent naughtiness and wanton debauchery you could never hope to put your finger on, unless of course you were actually the one writhing and sucking and fucking your way through the glorious act itself.

I whimpered and moaned, screwing back and forth between my two sexy new lovers. It all felt so warm and safe. Totally comfortable and somehow even familiar, although I'd never come close to anything like this in my life. All of these things let me relax even further, allowing me to open up and really enjoy what was happening to my body, as well as anticipate what would happen next.

Then I didn't have to wonder, because I was being rolled onto my stomach... pulled backward...

Oh my God—

And I heard Aurelius let out a huge sigh of contentment, as he entered me from behind.

Seventeen

JACE

Sharing a stranger was one thing, but sharing a girlfriend was something entirely different. We learned the difference because all three of us had done both over the years, and each scenario came with its own set of drawbacks and rewards.

The drawbacks of course were jealousy, but that one we'd gotten over quickly. Watching your girlfriend's eyes go wide as another man enters her turned out to be a searing hot thrill, lending to the excitement of realizing her enjoyment while fighting down that white-hot envy in the pit of your stomach. Over time, the envy turned to excitement as well. And that's because you could draw upon that feeling. Use it to push yourself that much further down the twisting path to this type of arousal, as you circled around to kiss, touch, and even feed yourself to this woman you loved or cared about.

We'd shared Beth first; one of my longtime girlfriends who got tipsy enough to invite Aurelius into our bed. From there we called in Merrick because I wanted no secrets between us. We'd decided long ago and in far-flung places that we'd share our life's path together, and somehow this translated to this situation as well.

It could've been a one-time thing. A spur-of-the-moment fantasy, fulfilled. Instead it went on for weeks, then months, then all the way until Beth and I broke up amicably, to follow much different goals. The only thing was, the three of us immediately agreed we weren't finished with that type of arrangement. Pandora's box had been opened, so to speak.

In other words, we liked it *way* too much.

From there we shared Kelli, the field nurse Merrick had dated a few times, and Aurelius's "friend" Jaana from the motor pool. Both those relationships burned hot and fast, and although they eventually flamed out, it showed us that we could ultimately be happy sharing just one woman between us.

If only we could find *that* woman.

Right now though, this situation seemed entirely different. Dakota wasn't some girl we'd met and played with together, nor was she some ex-girlfriend of mine having a little more fun than she bargained for. No, this was Tyler's *sister*. I'd laughed with her, played with her. Enjoyed growing up around her. Together we shared memories of my childhood that were both sacred and sacrosanct; recollections I couldn't possibly share with the others.

She wanted this, though.

I suppose she did. She certainly made a good enough case for it.

But YOU wanted this too, Jace. For yourself.

99

I had to admit it. Right now I was realizing my own deep-seeded fantasies. Fulfilling the unspoken dream of finally taking this girl — no, this *woman* — in ways I'd never hoped or dreamed were possible. All because as my best friend's sister, I'd been required from the beginning to write her off.

But now...

"*Unnnffff...*"

Now she was riding me slowly, eyes closed, head thrown back so that her long blonde hair shimmered like strands of gold against her naked back. I was achingly deep inside this woman I'd wanted for so very long, and it was nothing but amazing. Totally beyond magnificent.

As I watched, Aurelius stood up to feed himself to her again. Her mouth opened eagerly, her tongue sliding wetly along the underside of his manhood to guide him in. Merrick stood with his hands on his hips, awaiting his turn on the other side. Dakota's hands had been pumping them both, but now they were splayed desperately across my chest for additional leverage.

And that's because she was about to come.

Her gaze drifted over to lock on mine, and after one more whimper she popped my friend from her mouth. Those eyes were blue and beautiful and filled with awe. But there was an admiration too. A special connection we both felt whenever we looked at each other, that ran all the way back to our shared origins.

"Come," I smiled up at her, sliding my hands to her gently swaying breasts.

"Come *with* me," she countered, curling her mouth into a devilish smile.

In a flash of alarm I realized how perilously close I was. How long we'd been fucking her, and how many times we'd traded her off between us. By now my balls were heavy and swollen and begging for release. Just those three simple words nearly pushed me over the edge, especially considering how hotly they'd dropped from her beautiful lips.

But there was another reason for the alarm, too. One that I hadn't considered until now.

"It's okay," Dakota murmured, reading my mind as she bent her body down to mine. We were chest to chest. Eye to eye. She kissed my forehead and let out a little giggle, while simultaneously rolling her hot little ass in a slow, deep circle.

"I'm on the pill."

She kissed my mouth now, doing things with her tongue that I wouldn't ever have imagined Tyler's little sister could do. But yes, she was doing them. And she was doing them while fucking me and grinding into me and telling me to come inside her, which was all the more strange yet perversely wonderful.

"You sure?"

My screaming balls kicked myself for even asking, but I had to double check.

"Yes," she hissed, as her eyes came alive with excitement. "After everything else, I think we're *owed* this."

I slipped a little deeper in love with this strange new woman who used to be Dakota. With every word, every phrase, I found myself sinking even further into my own little world.

"Jace..." she said frantically, and I realized she was getting off on the word itself. Her eyes fluttered closed. Her hips rolled like a dancer's, swallowing me deeper as she kept gyrating and twisting and—

"*Jaaaaaaaceeeeee!*"

Dakota didn't just climax, her whole body erupted. Her back arched, her legs stiffened, and then suddenly her insides were molten lava.

Fuck!

That lava somehow clamped down on me, milking me to orgasm. It sent me sailing blissfully off the edge of a really tall and wonderful cliff...

"FUCKKK!"

I filled her up with my own lava now, spurt after heavy spurt until she was so full it threatened to spill out and run down her perfect, porcelain thighs. My hands cupped her breasts, my fingers rolling against her ever-stiffening nipples as Dakota's chin tilted back, her mouth opened, and she howled like a sexy werewolf at some unseen moon.

This can't be happening.

Oh, but it was. I was shooting my very soul into Tyler's little sister. Forever altering the lifelong relationship between all three of us, whether he knew it or not.

I didn't come down until it was all over, and our bodies were making obscenely wet noises as we continued our grind. Aurelius was watching the show with renewed interest.

Merrick's eyes were similarly locked, patiently waiting his own turn.

Because we're sharing her...

That little detail hadn't fully hit me yet, but it eventually would. Because as much as I could try to defend myself for giving in to the irresistibility of my friend's beautiful sister, I couldn't possibly rationalize all three of us making her every last fantasy come true.

"That..." Dakota breathed, wrapping her arms behind my head. She squeezed me again internally, leaving the sentence open-ended.

"Was totally ridiculous?" I finished, feeling the same way.

She nodded happily. "Yeah."

"Well if you think *that's* ridiculous," I bragged, as the others gently pulled her in their direction.

"Wait until we've done it two or three more times..."

Eighteen

DAKOTA

I woke naked and alone, sprawled face-down in a *very* disheveled bed. It took three tries to sit up. When I finally did, my arm immediately went up to shield my face from the sunlight, which streamed in through an open window off to my left.

But the window was on the right. *Wasn't it?*

Squinting into the offending light, I looked around. I was in a different bedroom. Not Jace's, but similar.

Merrick.

Memories from last night crashed over me in waves, each one more incredible than the last. I could remember my time in Jace's room, being the complete center of attention. My three hard-bodied lovers ravaging me to the point of joyous tears, taking turns on me over and over again until I passed out in a warm ocean of pure, unadulterated sex.

I could remember waking up to Aurelius kissing my face. Taking me by the hand, he'd led me silently through the hall and into his own darkened bedroom, where the bed was just as big, just as soft...

Aurelius! Holy shit, YES.

My shredded Greek god had been an incredible lover, spreading me open and burying himself deep between my thighs. We'd screwed slowly and lazily in his bed, kissing and nuzzling and saying things to each other that only the most familiar of lovers say. Yet somehow it all felt *right.* The intimacy was deep and genuine. The connection I felt with him, absurdly instant and natural.

I could remember turning sideways as he scissored me from behind, holding my leg up as he pistoned in and out of me with the smooth, near-effortless motions of a well-oiled machine. As a Navy SEAL, I supposed he was exactly that. A man sculpted to peak physical perfection and honed to a razor sharp, dangerous edge.

And God, I took full advantage of *that.*

Spinning my legs sideways, I finally set my feet on the floor. My clothes were nowhere in sight, but there was a soft-looking bathrobe and a pair of oversized slides arranged beside me. I slipped them on and stood up, stretching my tired body into the gorgeous Hawaiian dawn.

My memories of Merrick were less hazy, and that's because they were most recent. After passing out in Aurelius's bed, I remembered being awakened by a formidable presence and lifted into two gargantuan arms. Merrick had carried me back here to his own room and cuddled me beneath the blankets. There we'd made out hotly, staring into each other's moonlit eyes and grazing each other's bodies with our fingertips beneath the warmth of his down comforter. It was nearly dawn by the time he finally pulled my naked body over his, impaling me one last time on his wondrously thick shaft.

HOLY

FUCK.

I crossed the room, soberly aware of both how sore I was and how much I needed a shower. It turned out the latter was something easily remedied, because just inside the main bathroom I found a fresh bar of soap, a bottle of shampoo, and a small stack of towels.

I spun the hot water to max, then eased it back only a little. As steam filled the glass enclosed stall, I shrugged off the robe and stepped into blissful oblivion.

For the next five minutes I tried letting my mind go utterly blank, as the soap and hot water washed the more physical aspects of last night away. It wasn't easy. I kept wanting to go back to the absurdity of my whole situation. Less than a week ago I was freezing my ass off, cursing like a truck driver as I skidded into an icy ditch. Now I was in sunny Hawaii with *Jace* of all people, having just experienced the sexual adventure of a lifetime. Enjoying a deliciously hot shower that was soothing my aching muscles, accented by the underlying aroma of what promised to be really good coffee.

Coffee!

I toweled dry and put the robe and slides back on, then re-entered the hallway. For a second or two I thought about dipping into the guest bedroom to get dressed, or at least returning to Jace's room for my undergarments. In the end though, I found myself in the brightly-lit kitchen.

"Hey!" called a deep, resonant voice. "Back here."

I followed that voice onto a sun-kissed patio, where Jace rested casually at the other end of a round metal table. He wore a faded green T-shirt, cargo shorts, and mirrored sunglasses that looked sleek and sexy against the clean-shaven sides of his head. He rose, hugged me sweetly, then pulled a chair out for me as well.

No sooner had I sat down than a steaming mug of coffee was being held out to me. I wrapped both hands gingerly around it, and for a brief moment our wedding rings touched.

"Good morning, husband."

I gave him a very wifely kiss on his bearded cheek, then took a long sip. The taste nearly caused me to melt into my chair! The coffee was every bit as amazing as it smelled from the shower.

"Not bad?" Jace asked.

I shook my head in awe. "Did you run this through God's own coffee maker, or—"

"The beans are from Molokai. They were roasted this morning, while we slept."

I sighed into the cup, taking another long pull. Once finished, I flashed him a contented smile.

"Slept might not be the word I'd use."

Jace stared back at me, giving me the once-over. "No," he admitted. "Probably not."

Was he being sullen? Or just tired? I couldn't tell.

"Are you okay?"

He sat up straighter. "Seriously? I should be asking *you* that, no?"

"Why?" I shrugged happily. "I'm fine. I just had the best night of my life."

"I know, but—"

"Jace, don't worry about me. I'm serious. I *wanted* this. I was the one who asked for it."

His mouth twisted sideways, like he was thinking about something. He'd been doing it for as long as I could remember.

"You didn't drag me into anything I wasn't ready for," I continued. "And in fact—"

"But Dakota, you're Tyler's sister!" he cried. "And I didn't just sleep with you, I... I..."

"Shared me with your two closest friends?"

His shoulders slumped guiltily. He said nothing.

"Friends who are comrades in arms?" I went on. "Men who are more like brothers to you than Tyler ever was?"

Jace's eyebrows crashed together. "Don't go diminishing my friendship with your brother."

"I'm not. It's important to you, I can tell. Tyler too. But what I *am* saying is that it's been a long time, Jace. Things aren't the same. You and Tyler took radically different paths, and have different lives now."

In the pit of my stomach I was just as worried about Tyler as he was, but it pained me to see him like this. At the same time it also felt good knowing this bothered him. It would be worse if it didn't.

"You'll always have Tyler's friendship," I told him solemnly. "That'll never change. And I appreciate how loyal you're being to my brother."

I rose slowly, moving to his side of the table. Pushing my leg through the slit in the bathrobe, I straddled his lap and kissed him.

"But I'm my own person, Jace," I said gently. "I never asked my brother's permission for anything. And I never will."

His hands slipped around me, settling somewhere down near my bathrobe-covered ass. Just touching him brought back memories of last night. It made me shiver.

"This is something I could've never done with just anyone, you know," I told him truthfully. "Not with ex-boyfriends, and certainly not with strangers. Only with someone I really loved and trusted."

Jace pushed his sunglasses down his nose to look at me directly. "Loved?"

"Of course!" I smiled. "I've loved you all my life, Jace. In my home, you were practically family."

I thought back to Jace's absentee father, and his constantly-working mother: a functioning alcoholic if there ever was one. Jace had spent so much of his childhood at our house because his own home was empty.

"I felt like family," he eventually admitted. His gaze drifted somewhere very far away. "You *all* felt like family."

"Exactly," I agreed. "And we always will be."

I screwed myself even deeper into his lap. Maybe it

was a negotiating tactic. Maybe it was something else.

"Hey," I murmured, tilting his chin upward again. "What we did last night was pretty next level, I'll admit that. But we didn't do anything wrong, Jace. We merely shared an intimacy we couldn't before."

I took his glasses the rest of the way off, then set them on the table.

"Now... where are the others?"

His eyes came into focus again. The question seemed to bring him back from wherever it was he'd gone.

"Merrick's on base all day. Aurelius had some errands to run, but he said he'd be back early afternoon."

"Good," I smiled, kissing him again. His lips felt impossibly soft, especially in contrast to his hard, masculine jawline.

"After the gauntlet you three put me through last night, I think you owe this girl a big breakfast."

Nineteen

DAKOTA

"Go on," I urged. "Open it."

Aurelius undid the double-latch of the big square box. He took the top corners in both hands, then paused again.

"You sure it's not a bomb or anything?"

"Pretty sure, yeah."

"Because I've held disarmed IED's that weighed less than this," said Aurelius.

"He's held live ones too," Jace added, chuckling. "But they didn't always tell him that."

The Navy SEAL frowned playfully, then opened the reinforced box. The gleaming silver instrument was exactly where I'd left it, packed securely in egg crate foam on all sides.

"What the hell is *that?*" Merrick demanded.

"That," I said, pausing triumphantly, "is a Neumann

large-diaphragm condenser mic with shock mount. The holy grail of microphones."

"Whoa," Aurelius whistled. "You're a *singer?*"

"No," I laughed. "Not even close. Although sometimes I like to *imagine* I'm a singer, but that's usually several drinks in on karaoke night."

He lifted the microphone from its protective housing, hefting it again before handing it to me. I began the process of setting it up.

"This is a hell of an expensive mic though," Jace went on. "I mean it looks like it, anyway."

I nodded. "Everything in this case amounts to almost six thousand dollars, so yes."

"And you brought it all the way out *here?*"

"To do a little bit of work," I told them. "I have a few gigs I need to get caught up with, so I figured I could sacrifice a couple hours of vacation time." I glanced around, then pointed. "That corner over there would be perfect," I said. "As long as the house is quiet and I'm not disturbed."

The guys were even more in the dark now than before. I smiled and let them in on my 'secret'.

"I'm a voice actress," I told them. "Have been for a few years now."

"Really?" Jace asked. "That's your job?"

"Yup."

"That's awesome!" swore Aurelius.

"Thanks!" I grinned. "I do commercials, voice-over

work for videos, and I narrate audiobooks when I can. I even scored a few cartoons."

Merrick folded his two big arms. "Like what?"

I thought for a moment. "Hmm. This is kind of a long shot, but have you ever watched Princess Peyton and the Candy Castle?"

Aurelius snapped his fingers loudly. "My little niece watches that! She loves that show!"

I turned and smiled. "Well I'm the voice of the lead mermaid, Sapphire Swirl."

The SEAL's handsome face went abruptly serious. "You're shitting me."

"Would a mermaid really shit you?"

"I don't know if a mermaid *can* shit," offered Jace. "Seems physiologically impossible."

"What?" Merrick cried. "Of course they can shit!"

"Oh yeah? Have you ever seen a mermaid's asshole?"

The chopper pilot thought for a moment. "No," he admitted reluctantly. "I guess not, but—"

"There you go."

I giggled, letting the boys continue their debate as to whether mermaids had 'holes' or not. It got pretty graphic and absurdly silly, and they took the conversation in several different directions by the time I'd finished setting up the microphone and syncing it to my laptop.

"So I can use this room?" I asked.

"Of course," said Jace.

"Good. I'll start tomorrow, if that's okay. Because tonight..."

My sentence trailed off awkwardly. Aurelius picked it up however.

"Tonight," he grinned, winking at the others. "She's all mine."

I watched as he ducked out of the bedroom, presumably to go get ready for our night out with the rest of his platoon. Merrick was still examining the microphone from all sides as I pulled Jace away.

"Listen," I murmured, once we were on the other side of the bedroom. "You sure you're okay with me going out with Aurelius for his SEALs thing tonight?" I asked. "Because if you aren't—"

"No, no, of course I am," he cut in. "Why wouldn't I be?"

"Yeah, well you sort of put him off before..."

"That's because I didn't want to take advantage of your hospitality," he replied. "You were already doing *me* a huge favor. I couldn't ask you to do favors for my friends, too."

"Your friends are my friends now," I smiled. "And then some."

"And then some," he agreed.

I looked into his smoky grey eyes, searching for a hint of jealousy. I still couldn't believe there wasn't jealousy. It just didn't make sense.

"You guys really are like brothers, aren't you?" I

114

asked.

Jace stood for a moment, then nodded solemnly. "More than you'll ever know."

"But I *want* to know," I told him. "I... I missed out on so much with you. We lost touch for so long."

"I know."

"I'd love to fill in those blanks. Bridge the gap between this Jace and the old one."

"The old one, huh?" he smiled.

"Yes," I grinned back at him. "Old Jace was a hell of a lot of fun."

"And new Jace isn't fun?"

I took his hands in mine. They were so much bigger and thicker than I remembered them.

"New Jace is fun in much different ways," I said slyly. "And trust me, it's an improvement."

I stood on my toes to kiss him, feeling the instant electricity as his lips crushed mine. My body reacted, melting into his arms. Pleading with him for more of last night, even though I had other plans.

"Have fun with Aurelius and his squid friends tonight," he said with total and complete sincerity. "I'll see you when you get back."

"If you're even up when I get back."

He smiled with our lips still touching. "You don't think a husband should wait up for his wife?"

Jace held up his hand and wriggled his ring-finger. I

laughed into his mouth.

"If you do," I whispered, kissing him again. "This wife promises to make it worth your while."

Twenty

DAKOTA

"Go in! Go in! Go INNNN!"

The buzzer sounded, and the lights flashed. My last shot bounced off the backboard and went straight through the net, not stopping to touch the rim as a cheer went up behind me.

"Did it count!?"

My eyes shot to the scoreboard, which displayed a giant dot-matrix 37. We'd won by two points. On my last basket.

"Holy fucking shit, you did it!"

Aurelius picked me up and spun me around, causing my dress to flare outward in a wide red circle. The dress had been a hit so far, but now it *really* caught the attention of the half-dozen or so other SEALs waiting their turn at the arcade-style basketball game.

Oh, and it also matched my Santa hat.

"I think the more you drink the better you play," said Aurelius, slipping his arm around me. "Let's go get you another before we're out of here."

It was our fifth bar, and our eighth competitive game. So far we'd won at pool, lost at darts, got killed at pinball, and somehow I'd slaughtered everyone I faced at the Ms. Pac-Man machine we encountered at the place we'd just come from.

Whatever you wanted to call it: a holiday party, a Christmas pub-crawl, or just a platoon of elite Navy soldiers dragging themselves from one drink to the next, I could see why Aurelius's group had kept up their annual tradition. Between them and their significant others, they practically took over every bar they went to. But upon entering, the very first thing they did was order eight pints of beer to be placed in front of eight empty chairs, smack dab in the middle of their revelry.

I didn't ask who the drinks were for, or the names of the men they'd lost. I knew only that they'd been brothers-in-arms, and whether they were there or not they each got a beer and a seat in every single bar we went to.

And all that was good enough for me.

As for Aurelius's comrades, I got a quick rundown of the bigger names and more animated faces. There was Boombox, who'd gotten his nickname after bringing a giant radio into camp one day, and Magellan who was infamous for always getting lost. The biggest guy in the room was called Tiny, and the shortest SEAL there was named Legs. One of my favorites though was a tall, platinum blond giant who they just called Teflon, because apparently he'd never been shot, wounded, or even scratched. In even the heaviest of firefights he hadn't taken a single piece of shrapnel, causing several other platoon members to stick near him whenever things got hairy or out of control.

Accompanying most SEALs were their wives and girlfriends, who all turned out to be way cooler than I could've imagined. I started thinking being cool was probably a requirement in order to date such radical men.

"These are from Traci," a dark-haired warrior told us, before handing us a pair of amber-colored shots. I located Traci not far away in a group of three other girls, then raised my shot-glass in salute. She returned the toast and together the entire lot of us threw back what tasted like smooth, single-still whiskey.

"So... how many bars do you generally make it to?" I chuckled, feeling no pain.

Aurelius reached out with one hand to take my empty shot-glass. With the other, he righted my crooked Santa hat.

"I think my personal record is eleven," he said, thinking back. "Although by then things get kinda hazy, and we start looping back around to the first few bars again."

"Eleven," I swore. "Whoa."

"Yeah. Last guy left standing with a drink in his hand gets the trophy."

The trophy, I'd learned earlier, consisted of a dented bronze drinking cup mounted roughly — and not squarely — on some lacquered mahogany base. The general premise was the last guy conscious would do his final shot from the cup, throw his Santa hat in the air, and retain bragging rights for the entire year.

"Of course we can peel off whenever we want," Aurelius offered. "Voodoo and his lady are long gone, and I noticed three or four others dipped out at that last place."

"But what about the trophy?"

The dark-haired SEAL's eyes crawled my body beneath my tight red dress. I noticed they lingered on all the same places he'd so thoroughly enjoyed last night.

"Dakota, *you're* the trophy."

I laughed nervously, fighting off a strange inner heat. "That's a damned good line."

"I'm serious," said Aurelius. "I've done this thing a half dozen times, but I've never brought a smarter, funnier, more beautiful woman than you."

Now I did blush. Between our proximity and the crowded bar, it felt like my whole body temperature went up a few degrees.

"What is it?" he asked, smiling.

God, he had the most amazing smile! It lit up his ruggedly handsome face in ways that made my stomach explode with butterflies.

"Nothing," I shrugged sheepishly. "It's just... I guess I'm just flattered."

Aurelius stepped into me and reached out for my hand. He held it close, pinned between our bodies. Dangerously close to the veritable playground of his flat lower abdomen.

"This will be my last one, too," he added wistfully. "We kept this thing to enlisted only. This time next year I'll be in Colorado, with the guys."

"Starting your security company?"

The three of them had told me something about their post-enlistment plans, but not much. Everything I'd heard so far was intriguing, though.

"Already the house is half built," said Aurelius. His smile broadened. "Dakota you should really see it. It's amazing!"

I want to see it! I wanted to say. Hell, I wanted to see everything.

"So the three of you are really close," I murmured. It wasn't a question.

"We've saved each other's lives," Aurelius said plainly. "We also shared a lot of tough missions together. The kind where you're unsure if you'll even make it back."

He looked around the bar, at his friends. Maybe even at the eight sweating pint glasses huddled around a table nearby.

"That sort of thing tends to bond you," he said. "You end up sharing things you never thought you would."

With that he bent to kiss me, gently cradling my face in his hands. It was slow, deep, beautiful. And of course, enormously hot.

Somewhere in the middle of it I pulled back, nervously scanning around.

"What?" asked Aurelius. "You don't want to kiss

me?"

That hint of a Greek accent was making me melt again. Among other things.

"Oh I *want* to kiss you!" I assured him quickly. "Very badly, too. But I'm supposed to be Jace's *wife*. I just wanted to make sure there was no one around who could—"

"Joint Base Pearl Harbor-Hickam is a melting pot of different branches for sure," Aurelius agreed. "But there's no one here right now who would recognize you in that way."

"You sure?"

The tall SEAL thought for a moment and shook his head. "You can never be *totally* sure about anything," he admitted. "That's one of the first things the military teaches you: managing risk."

He took the hand that was between us and squeezed it.

"Would you like to manage this risk outside then?" he asked. "On the way home?"

His touch, his voice, his mocha brown eyes — they were a package deal, all driving me crazy. I could still feel the tingle of his lips on mine.

"Maybe after we hit one last bar," I said. "One more drink."

Pulling his body closer, I smiled up at him and winked.

"Right now I'm having too much fun."

Twenty-One

DAKOTA

We took the scenic way home, walking along the palm-lined streets and down near the waterline. Holding hands beneath a calm night filled with twinkling stars, and the most gentle of breezes carrying up from the ocean the scent of salt, and sea, and spray.

It was warm and romantic. Beautiful beyond my wildest dreams. We'd ducked out of the last bar somewhere near Kaimana Beach, and were moving north and west along the shore of some magnificent, unnamed lagoon as our buzz carried us into the night.

"Cut through the park?"

I smiled and nodded, eager to follow Aurelius literally anywhere. We'd laughed and talked all night, and now my handsome date was content just to walk beside me, letting me enjoy the silence and breathtaking views.

It was well past midnight. Probably closer to two in the morning. The grass-kissed pathways tracing their way through the park side of Waikiki Beach were soft and cool beneath my feet, as Aurelius had been carrying my shoes for the past half mile.

"I can't believe you get to live here," I said.

He squeezed me close. "It wasn't always this way. For years I did tour after tour, visiting place after place. Stopping here only sometimes between assignments."

I stopped at a stone wall, where one of those pay-to-view metal binoculars were mounted. I swiveled the heavy instrument toward the ocean as Aurelius came up behind me.

"Got a quarter?"

He fished around in his pocket for a moment, then dropped one in. The lenses clicked open, and I was treated to a shimmering nighttime view of Mamala Bay.

"So you've seen a good chunk of the world," I breathed, focusing on a couple of sailboats anchored nearby.

Aurelius didn't answer. Instead his arms slid around me from behind, his strong fingers flexing as his hands went to my hips. They felt like they belonged there.

"What's the most exotic place you've ever been?"

I felt his palms slide lower. They lifted the hem of my dress upward, gliding it along the backs of my thighs.

"Oh, I don't know..." he murmured softly. "The Colombian rainforest was pretty wild. I've scaled cliffs in Croatia. Done rescue ops in Cambodia, Queensland, Fiji..."

"You've been to Fiji?"

His hands moved again. My dress inched higher.

"For a hot minute I was assigned to a Marine Recon Unit at an Ice Station in Antarctica."

I blinked. "What was that about?"

"Can't talk about that one," Aurelius whispered, as his lips dropped gently to my shoulder. "Classified."

He began planting tiny kisses against my exposed skin, sending a wave of goosebumps washing over me. As his hot mouth traced its way along the flesh of my neck, I arched my body into him.

"But the most exotic place I've ever been?" he repeated softly. "Hmm..."

His vise-like hands had brought my dress all the way up now. I could feel the cool night air against my naked ass. The tug of my thong as he pulled it downward, then stretched it off to one side.

"That one's *easy,*" the big SEAL whispered hotly, directly into my ear.

I gasped as his hand slipped downward, melting into my thigh gap. Two thick fingers began rubbing my mound, probing the pleasant soreness I still felt from last night.

Oh wow...

I was already wet. Already tingling. I sighed into his mouth as he began kissing me from behind, while the distinct jangle of a belt buckle shattered the nighttime silence.

"Here?"

I whispered the word breathlessly, already knowing the answer. Aurelius responded by kissing me harder, while navigating a button. A zipper...

A moment later I felt the heat of his two big thighs, causing me to bite my lip in anticipation. I was standing on a slight rise, eliminating the height difference. Our bodies spooned perfectly into each other, as he dragged his growing hardness through my tender, glistening folds.

And then he plunged into me, burying himself all the way inside in a single thrust. My gasp was a sharp intake of breath laced with a whimper, swallowed quickly by the stillness of the night.

OOOOhhhh...

I couldn't believe I was doing this! Rutting around four thousand miles from home, with someone who was practically a stranger. Fucking in *public* of all things!

But my God, it felt so fucking *good!* So hot and naughty and romantic, all at the same time. I still gripped the cold metal binoculars with both hands as Aurelius continued thrusting into me, pounding his hard abdomen against my naked ass over and over again, as his hands screwed tightly into the curve of my hips.

This isn't real.

Was it? Everything had happened so fast it was hard to tell. In the blink of an eye, I'd gone from snow and ice to sun and surf. From zero romantic prospects to having three hot, beautiful boyfriends at once... even if that situation were only woefully temporary.

I began gasping uncontrollably at the end of my lover's thrusts, which were coming harder and faster now. I was losing the battle of restraint, and was now on the brink of surrender. I'd been holding out, trying to come *with* him as I had with Jace.

Jace...

I couldn't believe I was out with Aurelius with Jace's full permission, probably even knowing something like this would happen. Then again, Jace was okay with it. Merrick also. They'd not only made their peace with sharing the women in their lives, they actually got off on the very idea of it. It turned them on, and if we were being honest it turned *me* on just knowing that little fact. I loved the idea of being watched. Of looking into the eyes of one man, while being taken by another.

My orgasm threatened to crash over me again, and this time I didn't resist. I tilted my head back. Stared up through the palm fronds into the star-filled sky, when suddenly—

Aurelius stopped all at once, pressed tightly into my body. Voices floated in from over my shoulder. Footsteps...

Shit!

A couple wandered by, cuddled together arm in arm. They skirted a few steps around us, as the big SEAL pulled up the back of his slacks and folded himself even tighter against my body.

I pretended to look through the viewfinder of the coin-operated binoculars again. But this time around, Aurelius was *inside* me. Buried deep. I could feel his chest thundering away against my back, even as his shaft thrummed in perfect rhythm against my insides. It pulsed magnificently up and down with every beat of his strong, warrior's heart...

And then I came, unable to hold it in any longer. Gripping the cold metal binoculars so tightly in my trembling fists, I feared I might rip it right off its steel mount.

Pinned between the instrument and Aurelius's hard, chiseled body, my climax was almost violent in its intensity. My eyes screwed shut as my lips parted and a gasp threatened to escape... and then a big, calloused hand clamped itself over my mouth.

YESSSS...

I bit down into the meaty part of his palm as I climaxed around Aurelius's cock. Everything else disappeared. All that existed was the sheer ecstasy of my orgasm, and the feel of that throbbing, pulsating shaft buried so deeply inside me.

I whimpered, moaned, even cried out loud – and all of it was captured by his hand. And then suddenly he was coming too, filling me from within. I could feel his thickness jumping and pulsing inside me, shooting my womb full of his hot, life-giving seed.

HOLY–

It was hotter than hell. The craziest feeling in all the world. At this point I didn't care who saw, or who might've heard. There could be a hundred people circled around us, watching us grind and writhe and buck into each other. None of it would matter even the tiniest bit.

When I opened my eyes and looked back the couple was gone, and we were alone again in the park. Aurelius's handsome face was painted the most blissful expression of satiation, as he went about righting himself and re-buckling his belt.

I was still breathless as he reached down to slide my thong back into place. Already he was leaking out of me, staining the sleek satin fabric an even darker shade of wetness.

"Think they saw?" he asked, smoothing my dress back down.

I spun and kissed him, so deeply and soulfully I could feel my heart wanting to leave my chest.

"God I hope so," I grinned back, realizing it was the truth.

Twenty-Two

DAKOTA

"So... what *else* are we doing this week?"

I walked up from the ocean, squeezing my hair out as the guys lay sprawled in a line before me. They were three long, hot, hard bodies, stretched out on lounge chairs in the afternoon sun.

"Besides what we've *been* doing?"

Merrick's eyes crawled me hungrily as he asked the question, lingering on the scant fabric of my white string bikini. I'd packed it a little self-consciously, not knowing if I could bring myself to wear something this skimpy in public. But the guys had gone crazy the moment they saw it. In fact, they'd insisted.

Not that they hadn't seen me naked anyway, so...

"I've maneuvered the rest of the week off," said Jace. He stretched his big arms overhead, flexing those wonderful shoulders and biceps and triceps. "So I'm up for whatever."

My pulse started racing again. A little while ago, I'd spent a good half hour rubbing oil over every inch of their three sculpted bodies. Now that oil was pooling in every beautiful crack, every breathtaking crevice. It gleamed brilliantly in the sun, making every muscle stand out in stark, incredible contrast to the next one.

"I'm off too," said Merrick. He tilted his aviator glasses down over the bridge of his nose and looked up at me. "You still wanna do the touristy thing?"

I was in a trance now. Just looking at the wings of striation beneath their V-shaped rib cages was making me lose my train of thought.

"W—What?"

"I mean, if you still want to see the other islands we can arrange that," said Merrick.

Beside him, Jace nodded. "But we're thinking a more personal tour could be a little more fun."

Personal tour...

I nodded mechanically. "Uhh... yeah. I'm totally in."

The guys glanced at each other. So much passed silently between them, it made me jealous of the closeness of their connection.

"You wanna see Maui?" Merrick eventually asked. "Tonight?"

The question snapped me from my self-indulgent daydream.

"Are you kidding?"

"Nope."

"Of course I do!"

"Then pack warm," Merrick smiled. "It gets cold on the beach sometimes."

"Sometimes," Jace agreed.

I glanced at Aurelius, who still hadn't said anything. Sullenly, he shook his head.

"I can't make it tonight," he said, "but the three of you have fun. And hey, make sure to keep our girl warm." He winked and smiled. "Like I did last night."

The others' faces reflected wry smiles. Aurelius had delivered me home at three in the morning, still soaked and dripping from our tryst in the park. Merrick wasn't up, but Jace had stayed true to his word. He'd led me into his bedroom and screwed me in the same red dress his friend had just ravaged me in, depositing a second batch of hot seed deep inside me before stripping me down and collapsing into bed with me.

I'd woken tired and sore, but still a very happy, happy girl. I'd even logged in and gotten a little work done after breakfast. I finished a couple of chapters for one of the books I was voicing, and did a few re-records on lines from a radio commercial a client had requested.

Score one for my 'working' vacation.

"Let's pack up," said Merrick. "I've got to reserve some wings right now if we're going to do this."

The guys began picking up our stuff, just as my phone rang. I looked down at the screen and froze.

It was my brother Tyler.

My gaze shot straight to Jace, who was busy repacking the cooler we'd had lunch from. I walked a few paces toward the ocean before pressing the green button.

"Hello?"

"SIS!"

Tyler's chipper voice carried faintly over the sound of the wind. I shielded the phone with my other hand.

"Hey bro. What's the word?"

"The word is you're in Hawaii!" he shot back.

Mom. The confusion on my face faded into grim realization. *Shit.*

"Are you?" Tyler went on. "Or is that just something you told mom to throw her off your *real* trail."

I laughed, trying not to make my laughter sound nervous. "No, no. I'm definitely here. In Honolulu."

"Honolulu?" my brother repeated incredulously. After a short pause. "You know what? Jace is probably there!"

"He is?"

The words came out before I could even think. I was committed to playing stupid now. Stuck in a lie, when I probably could've told him the truth.

Or at least *some* of the truth.

"Yes!" Tyler went on. "I mean the Army's got him running all over the world, usually. Most times I don't even know where he's been until he's back. But he's stationed over there, somewhere. I know he's got his own place in the city."

"Wow," I breathed. "I'll uh, have to reach out to him."

I took another few steps backwards, watching as the boys departed the beach. Jace shouldered the big cooler. He glanced back at me and I held up one finger.

"Need his number?"

"Umm, sure."

"You know what? I'll just shoot him a text. I'll tell him my sister's in town, and that I insist he take you out."

"O—Okay."

"Not take you *out* out though," he said with a brotherly laugh. "You know, he's still *Jace* and all."

Jace's big legs were pumping magnificently through the beautiful Hawaiian sand. My gaze lingered on the curve of his ass.

"I'll bet he is."

"Cool," said Tyler. "Where are you staying?"

I fumbled for a moment, then cleared my throat and gave him the name of the hotel I'd crashed at for barely one night. At this point, I even stumbled over the room number.

"Alright good enough," my brother said. He let out a jealous sigh. "Hawaii! Damn. And here I am stuck in Lewiston."

"Lewiston?"

"Yeah," Tyler confirmed. "The ass-end of New York. We've got a three-day tournament here, and our goalie has bronchitis."

"Damn," I commiserated.

He chuckled. "Dakota you don't know the half of it. I'd give anything to be there with you and Jace right now. I haven't seen him in... oh man. I can't even remember."

I felt bad now. My brother didn't exactly sound depressed, but he was definitely down. I'm sure the mention of Hawaii had him missing his friend. Or at least missing out on the old times we'd shared together.

"If you run into him, give him a hug for me," said Tyler.

My stomach dropped. I felt terrible.

"I will," I promised.

"A good one, too," my brother added. "I kind of... well, we kind of lost touch with each other a couple years back. Which is probably my fault as much as his."

"Go ahead and text him then," I smiled. "I'm sure he'll be thrilled to hear from you."

We said our goodbyes, and I hurried back to where the guys already had the Bronco running. I hopped into the back seat alongside Merrick, just as Jace threw the truck into reverse.

"Your phone's about to go off," I told him, as he looked over his shoulder to back up.

Jace paused, stepping on the break. Right on cue, his phone buzzed.

"It's Tyler," I told him, watching his eyes go wide.

"Tyler?"

"Yeah," I smiled weakly. "Apparently you're supposed to hook up with me and take me to dinner."

Twenty-Three

DAKOTA

The view was nothing short of astonishing; the spectacular orange sun setting beneath an impossibly purple sky. Like a golden coin it sank slowly into the ocean, as Merrick guided our little aircraft through the lush green mountains at the far end of the beautiful island.

My God, it's gorgeous!

We drifted in slowly, floating past Hana, gliding effortlessly down to the sea. There were many tiny inlets on the north face of Maui, but the guys had one particular cove in mind as the pontoons of the seaplane finally skidded against the glass-like surface of the rapidly-deepening water.

I was a total spectator. An honored guest. Every offer to help was politely refused as Merrick taxied our aircraft-turned-boat as close to shore as he dared, and Jace threw the anchor that would moor it in place.

A few minutes later we were wading ashore, and the guys were busy setting up camp. Until the tent actually went up I didn't realize we were sleeping on the beach, but the idea thrilled and excited me as I wandered out to gather driftwood for the fire.

"Look for anything dry," said Jace. His expression reflected my own happy smile. "We've still got a couple of bundles of our own, though."

The place we'd landed looked wholly inaccessible from above. We had our little private cove. A black sand beach where the sky opened directly above us and cliffs surrounded us from three sides.

And of course the fourth side: the gentle crash of tiny waves from the ocean.

In no time we were sitting on blankets, feeding a humble yet growing fire. A spacious-looking tent has been staked out nearby. The boys had raised it quickly and with military efficiency.

"This is insane," I said for the third or fourth time. "I can't believe this place exists!"

"It only really exists if you have a boat," Jace explained.

"Or a seaplane," said Merrick, adding a handsome grin.

As if all of this wasn't romantic enough, they began pulling things from a canvas rucksack. First blankets, then a bottle of wine. A bottle of whiskey, too.

"We can just set up here?" I asked.

"Yup."

"And stay the night?"

Jace laughed. "Does it *look* like we're staying the night?"

I shook my head, not fully accepting the situation for what it was. It was just so unbelievably awesome, it felt like someone would come along and spoil it.

"Here."

I looked up, and Merrick was handing me a couple of long wooden skewers already speared through various foods. I saw chicken, shrimp, vegetables...

"We've got to cook our own meal tonight," said Jace, grabbing the next batch from his friend. "But this still counts as 'hooking up with you and taking you to dinner.'"

I crossed my legs on the blanket, scooting my ass a little closer to the fire. "I'll be sure to tell my brother," I said sardonically.

"You do that."

We sat there slow-roasting our modest meal over the fire. I drank from a glass they thoughtfully provided, while the guys passed the whiskey bottle back and forth.

"You've been here before," I asked nonchalantly.

The guys glanced at each other, then nodded. "Found it a couple of years back while fishing for Marlin," Merrick said. "We try to get out here once or twice a year, ever since."

I bit into a roasted red pepper, then washed it down with a gulp of wine.

"Ever bring a girl with you?"

This time they didn't have to look at each other.

Both men shook their heads.

"You'd be the first," said Jace.

"I'd be fine if I wasn't," I added quickly, although the honor *did* feel admittedly special. "It's just obvious by how familiar everything is for you."

The sun had vanished entirely, but a faint violet haze in the sky still remained. I stared into it wistfully, waiting for the piece of chicken at the end of my skewer to finally stop steaming.

"It's nice having someone here who appreciates this the way you do," said Jace.

"It's December," I chuckled. "This is paradise compared to what it's like in Minnesota right now."

"Or Boston," added Merrick casually.

I crooked an eyebrow. "Is that where you're from?"

The big pilot nodded. "Originally, yes. We lived a little too close to Hanscom Air Force Base. I was always watching the jets fly overhead, and that's how I got bit by the pilot bug."

"That's cool," I shrugged.

"Not according to my father," Merrick smirked. "He hated the idea of me joining the service. Forbid me to even apply. Of course I did anyway, and signed on with a recruiter after just one semester of college."

"What did you study?"

"Beer and women," laughed Jace.

"I didn't even get the chance to do *that*," Merrick

lamented. "My father is a surgeon — has been all his life. Apparently I was supposed to follow in his footsteps. He had a whole path laid out for me, with friends and contacts that would get me to wherever I needed to be."

"And so you took off for the Air Force," I smiled, reaching for the bottle again.

"Yes."

I poured another half glass. I did it slowly too, hoping it would help him relax.

"Did your father disown you?"

"For a while he did," said Merrick. "He told me I was wasting my talent rather than using my 'gifts' to their fullest potential. What he wanted was a carbon copy of himself. Instead, he got a Rescue Flight Officer with six commendation's worth of combat experience."

Merrick picked up a stick and threw it into the fire. He wasn't even looking at us anymore.

"In the end, who's the asshole, though?" he continued. "He's sitting at home with my ice cold mother, and I'm here in Hawaii drinking whiskey with my best friends on a moonlit beach."

I raised my glass and he toasted with me, and together the pair of us drank. Jace was resting back on his two big arms, just soaking everything in.

"I'll never push my kids to do anything," Merrick added at the end. "They can be whatever the hell they want to be."

"Kids, huh?" I smiled coyly. "Just how many are you

having?"

The question forced both men to look at me, then turn toward each other. Merrick stayed silent while Jace only shrugged.

"Depends on the kind of woman we end up with," Jace said. "After all, she's going to have a pretty big say in it."

I tried to picture this woman; the fantasy unicorn they'd been searching for all this time. Depending upon how many kids they'd want, she'd be pregnant an awful lot. At least one time by each of them, if I knew anything about how competitive these men were.

"You guys really *do* want to share one wife, don't you?" I asked casually. "I mean, you've totally thought this out?"

"Yes."

The answer was simultaneous. Unhesitant. Entirely genuine. Their determination intrigued me even more.

"Think you'll find her?"

I felt a pang of unwanted jealousy, just talking about their future-mate. I tried imagining what type of girl would be serious about marrying three men at once. And not just for the combined affections or the obvious sexual benefits, but someone who really knew these guys. Who really *loved* these guys...

"I think with some luck and a little patience we will," Merrick answered.

"Or maybe we don't have to find her at all," said Jace.

"Oh no?"

"No," he said, studying my expression. I noticed his lips curling into the tiniest sly smile.

"Maybe she'll be the one to stumble across *us.*"

Twenty-Four

DAKOTA

The evening ended exactly as I'd hoped it would, with the three of us lying side by side beneath the vast expanse of the nighttime sky. I was in the middle of course, flanked by my two strong, military men. Their bodies were physically warm and comforting. The presence of their conversation and laughter, even more so.

We stared up into the heavens as the fire dwindled beside us, letting the additional darkness bring out the shimmering canopy of bright, twinkling stars. As it got cooler they snuggled into me, spooning me from either side.

And thank God, that's when the make-out session began.

I'd been anticipating it all night, and was eager to get started. I couldn't get enough of kissing these men; of breathing my arousal into their hot, waiting mouths. Of drinking my fill from their firm but supple lips, as their hands roamed my spread, eager body beneath the blankets.

My mind soared as they took turns touching me, gliding their thick fingers in and out of my molten pussy. I was flat on my back, eyes half-lidded with lust. Floating through the cosmos with a joystick in each hand, pumping them slowly up and down like an oversexed space-traveler from some distant, perverted future.

"Wanna try something cool?"

Jace breathed the words hotly into my ear, causing me to shiver as I nodded.

"Come into the tent with us."

As reluctant as I was to lose the spectacular view, I was even more eager to enter the world of blankets and pillows and sleeping bags that awaited me just beyond the zipper of the canvas tent. Besides, the fire was all but out by now. With the wind picking up, it was getting cold.

Jace carried me to the entrance, where Merrick swept my feet clean of any lingering black sand. I giggled because it tickled, but my laughter died as they deposited me in the center of our sleeping arrangements and began stripping down on both sides of me.

"You boys be careful," I teased. "I've never done anything like this before."

I giggled again. It was fun to role-play, and the wine was certainly helping.

"Really?" Merrick grinned. "Because you sure don't look that innocent."

"Oh I'm a good girl," I assured them. "A *very* good girl."

Merrick peeled his long-sleeved shirt over his head, revealing every swollen muscle of his V-shaped body. His chest was as wide as a farm field. His shoulders were smooth, deeply-tanned mountains.

"Fine," said Jace, going along. "We'll play just the tip, then."

I chewed a finger innocently. "Just the tip?"

"Yeah," he smirked. "Get those panties off. Let us show you."

They pounced on me together, laughing and grunting and nuzzling their way between my arms and legs. I was getting the tip, that was for damned sure. The tip and *then* some.

"Easy," I chuckled. "I'm just an innocen—"

My sentence died in a gasp of pleasure, as Jace's hands pushed my thighs apart and his tongue plunged inside me. He was facing away from me, and in the opposite direction. By the time he rolled onto his back and pulled me with him, I knew exactly what he was doing.

YESSSS.

My knees settled to either side of his broad, beautiful body, as we settled into a hot sixty-nine. I engulfed him immediately with my mouth, taking him as deep as I dared go, while his hands slid to my ass and his mouth kept devouring me from underneath.

"Ohmy*God.*"

I mumbled the words around the iron spike of his erection, gripping it by the base as I bobbed up and down on the smooth, warm skin. My lips were tight, my tits pressed firmly against his hard, Green Beret's stomach. Our bodies somehow molded perfectly together, writhing as we went down on each other hungrily.

"This sure as hell doesn't look innocent," chuckled Merrick, somewhere off to the side. I could see him in my peripheral vision now, stroking himself as he watched us.

The tent fell relatively silent, filled only with the heated sounds of Jace and I pleasuring each other. The wind howled faintly outside. And just beyond that, the rhythmic lapping of waves kissing the shore.

This is beautiful.

I picked my head up, trailing a line of saliva down to Jace's pulsing shaft. Merrick caught my eye and winked.

So fucking beautiful.

I closed my eyes for a moment, thinking about the cliffs, the beach, the sea. Realizing where we were made the whole experience so much more surreal. We were castaways in the middle of nowhere, camped out on some cold empty beach, surrounded by darkness.

Inside though...

Inside the tent, everything was warm and safe and comfortable. I had these two incredible men, who could protect me from anything. Their bodies generated enough heat to make me more than comfortable, especially considering what we were currently doing.

"Give her over."

I felt Merrick's hands on me, and suddenly I was

rolling again. This time I did a full rotation and ended up sprawled chest to chest with his hairless body, facing an all-new shaft while another hot mouth closed over me down below.

Holy shit.

A different pair of strong arms wrapped around my body from beneath, pulling me firmly against Merrick's hungry face. For several minutes we feasted upon each other, my eyes crossing more than once at the exquisite pleasure of his mouth, his lips, his talented tongue.

It was like that for a long while, until I was screwing my thighs against the sides of Merrick's head and gasping around his incredible thickness. I could come, but I didn't want to come. Not yet, not now.

Right now, I just wanted to be *fucked.*

"Take me."

I whimpered the words around him, while pumping him with a slick fist. Merrick responded by burying his tongue deeper, and squeezing my ass even harder in his two big hands.

"Please..."

Locked tightly against the broad expanse of the pilot's hard body, there was nothing I could actually do. I was delirious with want. Drunk with desire, and the overwhelming need to put one or both of these men inside me.

But I was also completely at their mercy.

"I need—"

Just as quickly as he'd seized me, Merrick spun me around again. This time he stopped the motion when we were face to face. Our eyes met, as my legs straddled his massive torso. Then my whole body shuddered as I sank down, impaling myself all the way to the hilt.

"*Ohhhhhhh...*"

It made me feel so full, so *taken*, like everything was right in the world again. I rode him slowly, spreading my hands across his chest. Feeling the size and power of the enormous pectorals that lay coiled beneath my palms, as I rubbed my aching clit along the slippery length of his raging thickness.

"Now comes the cool part," I heard Jace murmur.

A hand slid up my back, pushing me forward and downward against Merrick's chest. Before I could even react, a very warm, very slick thumb crept downward to hover over my tight little asshole.

I jumped and gasped. But Jace only pulled my hair back, so his lips could reach my ear.

"We'll save this for another time," he whispered wickedly, rolling the ball of his thumb forward with just a moment's worth of pressure. "But tonight..."

He maneuvered me forward a tiny bit more, until Merrick's shaft completely slipped from my body. I wasn't empty for a single second, though. And that's because Jace took my hips and shifted forward, plunging into me from behind.

Mmmmmmm....

I rocked forward and back, taking him doggie-style as

Merrick smiled up at me from beneath. He dipped three fingers into my mouth, turning me on as I chewed them wetly. A moment later those fingers were on my nipples, rolling circles around the areola as the saliva-coated surface left little in the way of friction.

He went ten strokes, maybe twelve. Then they switched. It happened effortlessly, easily, like they'd practiced it a thousand times. It didn't take much to realize that maybe they even had. They loved doing this, therefore it made sense they'd be good at it.

After all, this is what they wanted.

What do you *want, Dakota?*

Long term, I had no fucking idea. Right now though, I wanted nothing more than to be sandwiched between these two gorgeous men. I wanted them to take turns on me all night, using my body over and over until I was sweating and screaming and coming all over them. I wanted to fuck them until I was delirious... until our little cocoon against the elements was a hot, filthy mess of blankets and pillows and canvas walls, and the air was thick with the combined scent of our sex.

Again they switched, and again after that. Jace would hold me from behind, his strong arms pumping my body steadily up and down on his friend's thick shaft. Then Merrick would withdraw, screwing his hands into my hips and guiding me forward and back against Jace's long, beautiful member.

The area below my navel filled with a rising heat, as I could sense the inevitability of my upcoming climax. When I couldn't take the pressure anymore I finally let loose, rocking backward with Jace buried deep inside me. Screaming as loud as I could because there was no one to hear me, no one within miles to even worry about.

And *nothing* to be quiet about anyway.

Twenty-Five

MERRICK

We pumped her full, the both of us, within seconds of each other. That part wasn't planned, but it wasn't unexpected either. Controlling her body was just way too hot. Between that, the noises she made, and all the switching back and forth inside her, erupting together was an inevitability.

And fuck... she was just so damned *sexy*.

As Aurelius and I had already discussed in private, it was a double-edged sword just being around this woman. On one hand Dakota was everything we'd been looking for: someone who was smart, funny, and indescribably beautiful. Someone who could slip seamlessly into our lives, and who fit in perfectly when it came to personality, interests, and even ambitions.

On top of all that, she fit effortlessly into our bedrooms as well. As a lover she was fun, exciting, voracious... always hungry for more. She was up for anything, and never afraid to teach a few tricks of her own.

Our unorthodox arrangement hadn't scared her off one bit, either. In fact, she'd gone out of her way to take full advantage of it.

No, Dakota was everything we were looking for in a lover and a friend. She was the feminine version of us; the perfect companion to round out our group. The more I looked at her, the more I could envision her filling that final void between us. She'd be the one that would give us that sense of love. Of family. Of future...

It was wholly fucking unfair that we couldn't have her.

For so long we'd been looking for a woman like this, and now here she was, practically serving herself up to us on a silver platter. And still Jace steadfastly refused. At first it was easy to accept her as off limits. As the kid sister of his best friend, we hadn't even thought about flirting with this girl, much less falling for her in ways we could never expect.

And then Jace fell for her himself, whether he could admit it or not. Especially when she asked us to throw our rulebook over our shoulder, at least for the remainder of her vacation.

In the end, that was the only outcome I could accept: that Dakota's appetite for us was finite, and our arrangement had a legitimate end date. But if the whole thing were really just a fling, why did it *feel* like it wasn't? How come every time I looked into the eyes of this beautiful blonde goddess, it seemed like I could see past the sex and beyond the lust. How come every time we breathed each other's breath I could feel her falling that much deeper in love with me... and me with her.

"My *GOD*..."

I thought about these things as we collapsed sideways into a naked, tangled heap. Dakota's skin was pink all over. She was breathless and sated and happy.

And judging by the wetness running down the insides of her delectable thighs, very, *very* full.

She faced Jace first, kissing him softly and slowly as I molded my body into hers from behind. Her ass felt like fire against my pelvis. My spent, contented manhood was still semi-firm between her beautiful cheeks.

She's insatiable.

That part was extremely important. Especially with three of us.

But she's not yours. She can't be.

My frustration rose. I pushed it down, unwilling to let it shatter such an awesome moment.

"Hey..."

Dakota's beautiful voice accompanied the twisting of her body. Two delicate hands went to either side of my face, and then her lips were brushing gently against mine.

"You're amazing, Merrick."

The ensuing kiss was apocalyptic. It was so slow, so sensual and poignant, it blew me emotionally away.

The smile that came afterward made my life complete.

"Thank you so much for bringing us here."

Dakota shifted one sexy leg upward, sliding it over

mine as she kissed me deeply, eloquently, with both purpose and meaning. My heart physically ached. I hadn't felt like this since... since...

Since ever.

She continued kissing me slowly, eventually working her full lips down my face and along one side of my neck. I held her there, enjoying the electricity. Feeling the warmth of her long, feminine body, and the wetness of her slowly trailing tongue...

God, I want her.

Dakota started dragging her fingernails up and down my arms.

No. I need *her.*

Over her smooth naked shoulder, Jace's gaze locked on mine. He looked strangely as if he could read my thoughts.

We have a problem, I murmured wordlessly, hoping he could read my lips as well. To my surprise, it turned out he could.

A big problem, he agreed, mouthing his answer.

Twenty-Six

DAKOTA

The whole next week was beyond legendary. A sun-kissed, sex-soaked wonderland of lips and tongues and delicious bronzed flesh, plus a few other more hard-hitting parts of the male body as well.

And every last drop of it was for me.

We returned from Maui relaxed and refreshed, where Aurelius greeted me with open arms. The guys had been making plans in the background I didn't know about. Arranging things to do both for and with me, including spending as much time with me as possible before I had to go back to my frozen land of darkness.

I cut through crystal blue waters on a sleek white catamaran. Shared a gourmet breakfast at sunrise, on the rim of a volcano. We went snorkeling in turtle canyon, then watched the most unbelievable cotton-candy sunset while Humpback whales swam by, in a pod.

The pinnacle of the whole trip was on Kauai, where

the boys took me on an ATV waterfall tour that ended in a remote bamboo bungalow. There we stripped naked beneath an outdoor shower, where I took my sweet time washing the mud from their hard, rippled bodies. They cleaned every inch of my body as well, but not before surrounding me on three sides and ravishing me right there, beneath the spray. One by one they screwed me absolutely senseless, each of them taking turns holding my body open for the others.

That night was warm and amazing, especially with the bungalow all decked out for Christmas with long strands of beautiful lights. Relaxing with a glass of wine beneath those colorful strands of twinkling lights was the first time it actually felt like the holidays for me, at least since I'd left Minnesota. But with Christmas itself still a few days away, a sad thought suddenly occurred to me:

I'd be celebrating without them.

I didn't have much time to dwell on the negative, because the guys were so sweet and attentive to me. We talked about life in general, about family, about our futures. Jace and I reminisced about some of the blizzard-like Christmases we'd spent back home, while Merrick and Aurelius told funny stories about their own experiences and traditions.

We baked cookies together in the little kitchen, then stretched out on couches in the almost-darkness. There we listened to Christmas music while I gave out shoulder massages, sipping more wine and eventually dancing my way toward the pile of blankets and pillows they'd strewn across the bungalow's living room floor.

Unreal.

I didn't have to open my arms for them to converge

157

on me, but I did it anyway. I wanted to embrace each one of them individually. To spend a long time kissing and caressing their bodies with the tips of my fingers, lips and tongue; tracing their muscles, their curves, their best and most amazing spots. In short, I wanted to derive every ounce of information I could and burn it into my brain. That way no matter what I did for the rest of my life, I could always remember this ten-day stretch of absolute bliss.

They made love to me slowly that night, which was an amazing and welcome change. Because as much as my body loved and even craved the unmerciful plundering they'd been giving it each night, there was a part of me that desired the emotional connection that came with kissing them, caressing them, and taking them one by one.

I don't know when I passed out, only that I woke up curled against Merrick. Aurelius wasn't far off, snoring blissfully away at arm's length. My third lover however, was nowhere to be found.

Jace...

I got up and searched the bungalow, padding naked through its quaint little rooms. When I still couldn't find him, I quickly threw on some clothes and grabbed a blanket.

The back deck of the place had a little bench that looked out over a lush, tropical garden. I found Jace there staring straight ahead, his legs pulled up to his chest.

"Hey stranger."

My words caused him to turn, and eventually smile. I was still trying to determine if the smile was forced when he slipped an arm around me.

"Sorry if I woke you."

"You didn't," I told him. "So don't be."

I pulled the blanket across the both of us, then leaned into the warmth of his body. It was cool outside, but not cold. I had no idea what time it was, but we were probably an hour or so before dawn.

"I'm finally adjusted to the time difference and now I'm leaving," I chuckled.

"Ain't it always the way it happens?"

"Sure," I agreed. "I don't get many vacations, but I guess so."

Jace chuckled gruffly. "Pretty sure you just had the mother of all vacations though."

"This one should keep me for a while," I laughed. "Yeah."

We sat quietly for a moment, as I marveled at the gorgeous red and yellow flowers that bloomed just about everywhere. The more time I spent here, the more strange and wondrous everything seemed. Even the sound of the insects buzzing around us was different.

"You worried about Tyler at all?" I asked abruptly.

"Nah."

"Why not?"

Jace shrugged. "Because as you pointed out in the beginning, this is a vacation fling. That's all it is."

"Yeah," I murmured softly. Something in the pit of my stomach didn't feel right. "Probably the most intense vacation fling ever, though."

"Maybe," he agreed. "But it's not serious. You said it yourself: you're unleashing sexual tension. Having fun wiling away the days with us until it's time to go back to reality."

The flowers faded and another series of images flashed before my eyes. I saw snow, darkness, my lonely apartment. My father's garage. Brian's betrayal.

Reality...

Did such words even hold meaning in a place like this? Everything here was so amazing I'd shoved the past into the nearest closet so I could focus on the present. But also, the future too.

What happens when I get home?

I hadn't thought about my previous life for so many days it actually felt foreign now. Like it belonged to someone else, and that someone wasn't me.

"Merrick joined the Air Force because he wanted to fly," Jace said suddenly. "And Aurelius got recruited while working the shipyards as a kid." One of his arms was still folded across his knees as his head swiveled to face me. "Know what made me want to serve?"

I tried to think; to remember back to when Jace first sat down and told us he'd signed with some Army recruiter. Slowly, I shook my head.

"It was your father, Dakota. He made me want this life."

My lips parted as my mouth dropped slightly open. "Really?"

"Tyler and I used to hang around the garage a lot," he went on, "and your father told us stories about being in Desert Storm. He used to fix tanks, Humvees, all kinds of things. He was a heavy equipment mechanic, but he was inserted into forward columns that also saw action. Lots of action."

I nodded slowly. I knew all this of course, but I didn't know that Jace knew it too.

"He inspired me to join the service, Dakota. To get out and see some of the things he did."

"Wow," I smiled. "He'd be thrilled to know that."

"Yeah."

"He'd also love to hear about some of the things you've seen."

The smile on his face was genuine now, instead of forced. A step in the right direction.

"My father adores you, Jace," I told him. "He always has. Out of all Tyler's friends, you were the only one he considered... how do I put this..." I elbowed him and grinned. "Not a total fuckup."

My words elicited a distant, hollow laugh, but a laugh nonetheless. "That's your father, alright."

I slipped my left arm from beneath the blanket and stared down at my beautiful rings. It had been a lot of fun, pretending to be married. Now that our time was almost over, I loathed the idea of taking them off.

I wish we really were married, I thought absently.

The thought flashed alarm bells in my head. Not

161

because the idea was crazy, but for another reason entirely:

Actually, I wish I were married to all of them.

I swallowed hard, trying to keep my stomach in check while I searched my feelings. There was so much to process, so much to reconcile. I'd been pretending this whole time, but also not pretending. And maybe, just maybe, I'd been lying to myself about something really important.

Something to do with the word 'fling.'

Twenty-Seven

AURELIUS

"Good morning princess!"

I'd rushed home from a six mile run, having spent the pre-dawn hours prepping info for a variety of classes. Imparting my wisdom before leaving would turn out to be a big chunk of my last few months. Just one more favor I had to do Uncle Sam, before he'd cut me loose and grant me my freedom.

Dakota was sitting on her bed looking melancholy, folding the last of her things into her biggest suitcase. There were tears in her eyes still. According to Jace and Merrick, they'd been there all morning.

"Don't be sad," I said, sitting down next to her. "This isn't goodbye, it's—"

"See you later?" she sniffed.

I wrapped my arms around her and squeezed as tightly as I dared. "Of course!"

The sobbing began immediately, as I suspected it would. But I had to choke back tears of my own, too.

"Dakota, listen," I told her. "It's not like you'll never *see* us again..."

She didn't want to be consoled. At least not right away. Her tears ran down my neck and onto my shoulder, as I did my best to maintain my own composure.

"You know where we'll be," I went on. "Colorado's not that far, and you can always come visit."

She pulled back, bleary-eyed, and shook her head miserably.

"It'll never be the same," she said softly. "It'll never be like this."

I leaned forward, placing my forehead against hers. Very carefully, I kissed away her tears.

"Everything changes," I admitted gently. "But no matter what happens we'll always have this place. We'll always have our time together."

She lowered her face, so I took her chin in my hand. Bringing her back to eye level, her eyelashes kissed my face like butterfly wings.

"Hey..." I said pointedly. "I got you something."

Dakota sniffed again, clearing her throat as she sat up straight. After drying her eyes with the hem of her shirt, I handed her the small white box.

"Go on. Open it."

She undid the ribbon and pulled out the long, gleaming chain. As the charm dangled before her eyes, she looked at it curiously.

"It's your name in Greek," I smiled. "There's a street vendor who crafts these not far from here. He twists them with pliers from precious metal wire."

Dakota's lower lip quivered. Her eyes were glassy.

"I know it's a little silly, celebrating a name," I laughed. "Hell, my name is originally Roman, not Greek. But my parents—"

The rest of my sentence was lost forever, as she pressed her beautiful lips to mine. I could taste the salt of her tears. The distinct strawberry flavor of her ChapStick that would, for the rest of my life, remind me of her.

"Dakota—"

She put a finger to my lips, shushing me. When it was obvious I'd remain silent, she slowly drew it away.

"Just hold me," she said, and this time she didn't cry. "Don't say anything. Don't try to talk me down from the ledge."

I did exactly as she asked, pulling her down into the softness of the bed. With her head on my chest we just laid there, staring up at the ceiling for what felt like a long, long time.

Inhaling deeply, I concentrated on remembering her scent. I focused on the feel of her body, and how amazingly perfect she fit all curled up against my right-hand side.

Forever. That's how long I could stay like this. If only we had forever, instead of the three paltry hours she had left before her flight.

I wanted to tell her I'd come to her. That I'd visit her in that magical place Jace always referred to whenever he talked about his childhood, and she could show me around that frozen northern wonderland.

But I couldn't. And the reason I couldn't was simple: it went against everything we were trying to do.

I sighed softly, hoping she wouldn't notice. As much as I wanted and needed Dakota, she was still strictly off-limits. There was no way she wanted all three of us, and zero chance of Jace letting such a thing happen anyway. In that respect, we were lucky to have gotten her at all.

You get what you get... and you don't get upset.

It was my father's stupid saying — or at the very least, he'd borrowed it from somewhere. He broke it out whenever I wanted something he wasn't willing to give to me, which was often.

Right now however, I really didn't want to hear any of it. Having Dakota for a little more than a week had been beautiful and intense and amazing.

But it was also the biggest tease of our lives.

Breathing deeply, I let my fingers sift slowly through her long, honey-blonde hair. As much as we told ourselves we were having fun, I knew it went well beyond that. Somewhere during the week the mask had slipped and true feelings spilled out. Both on her side as well as ours.

It was good. It was bad. It was heartbreaking...

Still, I regretted absolutely nothing.

"You guys ready?"

We shook ourselves from our half-sleep to find the others standing over the bed. Jace looked down expectantly, his keys already in hand. Merrick was gathering Dakota's bags together.

"I'm not even close to being ready to leave this place," Dakota sighed, eventually pushing herself to her feet. She looked at each of us in turn, then smiled wistfully and shrugged.

"But let's go anyway."

Twenty-Eight

JACE

I'd never been nervous before, being called into the old man's office. Then again, I'd never had this much at stake. Right now the halls seemed smaller, more claustrophobic. The subordinates milling around seemed busier than ever, like a bunch of worker bees buzzing around a big old hive.

"Ah, Sergeant Major."

The general's gravelly voice was pleasant enough, which I took as a good sign. But there was something else there too. Something in his vocal timbre that I'd never heard before.

"Please, come in and have a seat."

I saluted and entered his office, sitting carefully in the chair across from him. General Burke didn't seem overly formal, as he sometimes was. Nor did he seem overly friendly either.

In fact, he seemed somewhat nervous. And that

made me feel worse than anything.

"You wanted to see me, sir?"

He waved a hand dismissively. "Relax, Jace," he ordered. "I want none of this 'sir' stuff between us right now."

I watched as the man spun in his chair to face the bar behind his desk. After the pop of a cork and some musical clinking he spun back again, this time returning with two glasses of 21-year, single malt Glenfiddich.

"Here."

I was even more nervous than ever. And that's because they were two very *full* glasses.

"We need to talk about something... difficult," the general said. "Something that won't be easy for either of us."

I stared into the man's blue-grey eyes, searching for answers. I could usually read him, but for the first time I was actually stumped.

"Are you denying my discharge request?" I asked respectfully.

General Burke sipped his whiskey and squinted down at me. Without saying anything, he bit his lip.

"Because if you are, I'd like to say—"

"Jace, I don't know how to say this, so I'm going to just come straight out with it." The old warrior sighed heavily. "Your wife is cheating on you."

I was stunned now, too stunned to speak. Not only because I didn't *have* a wife, but because the last thing I expected when I came in here was—

Oh.

Realization dawned all at once. I just sat there in the stone silence, blinking.

Oh SHIT.

General Burke had been studying my expression carefully. He shook his head, then pushed the glass of scotch whiskey even further my way.

"Drink, son," he said gently. "That's an order."

I took the glass and finally brought it to my lips, moving slowly to keep from seeming too anxious. I figured the less I said the better, so I said nothing.

"Seems your wife was spotted at a local bar with someone else," the general said solemnly. "All *over* someone else by the sounds of it, and that someone happens to be your roommate."

He looked at me pointedly, waiting for my reaction. I put on my best mock-wounded expression, and his gaze turned sympathetic.

"Now I know this might be hard to believe," said Burke, "but I wouldn't even bring this up if I hadn't verified the source. But I know it likely comes as an even bigger shock hitting this close to home..."

I looked down now because I couldn't look up, couldn't face this man who'd been such a mentor to me. But my expression was all wrong. The general knew it, too.

"Sergeant Major?"

His eyes squinted. He peered back at me.

"You picking up what I'm putting down, here? I said

your wife is—"

General Burke stopped abruptly, mid-sentence, and his whole countenance changed. A look of enlightenment crossed his face.

"You knew, didn't you?"

I couldn't answer. I couldn't lie to this man who'd been a mentor for so long, nor could I tell the truth.

"This is some kind of a love triangle, isn't it?" he asked, leaning forward to steeple his fingers together. "It's not cheating. It's something... else."

Once more I didn't know what to say. Burke was a traditionalist, a steadfast husband, a family man. I couldn't very well tell him anything remotely close to the truth.

And then he told *me*.

"Look, I've lived through the 70's, son," he said, as if that explained everything. "I've seen my fair share of 'free love'." He paused. "Hell, maybe a little more familiar than you know."

His eyes softened. He was still expecting something, though.

"It's... complicated," was all I could finally say.

Awkward seconds passed, but eventually I could see the man behind the rank. I could imagine him young again. Free. Torn from his last year of high school or maybe college, and thrust into the jungles of Da Lat, or Nha Trang. He was a person way before he was a legend. Someone who was rash. Impulsive. Someone who made his own mistakes, and followed his own heart.

"Look son, what you do in your personal life means nothing to me," the general said. "What matters here are a man's deeds. His accomplishments."

He pointed to the desk with one withered finger. His expression was stern, but admiring.

"Everything you've done has been without hesitation, or even the slightest hint of anything but bravery," Burke went on. "I know the type of man you are, because I know your deeds. And as far as I'm concerned, you've already paid far more debt to society than you can ever owe."

I sank further into the chair, feeling a chill go through me. Our ranks were gone all of a sudden — stripped away by the complexities of shared experience across multiple generations. It left us sitting there as nothing more than two men. Two grizzled warriors who shared the same love of country, of duty, and of respect.

"I couldn't hold you back even if I wanted to," General Burke said. "And I don't want to. As much as we need men like you, we also need to recognize when someone wants a different life, a different path."

His face, withered by time, broke into what looked suspiciously like a young man's smile. He pointed toward the door.

"So go, Jace," he finished. "Live that life. Enjoy... whatever."

Now he did smile, and the smile warmed my heart.

"You don't need my blessing because you've always had it," the general finished. And with that he grunted, nodding firmly. "And you always will."

Twenty-Nine

DAKOTA

I stared at the doorway to the little cafe, not sure what I was doing there at all. There was a queasiness in my stomach that wouldn't go away. A general unease that made me wonder if I were even hungry, or just too frazzled to eat.

And on top of that my lunch date was late.

It was the first time in a long time I'd actually been this nervous about meeting someone. Each time the door opened a fresh blast of cold Minnesotan air swirled through the front half of the restaurant, and that was with two separate doors acting as a double entranceway. I'd chosen a table near the back. Well out of earshot of the lunch counter and pickup area.

I can't believe I'm doing this.

It was a wild idea, but I really needed to talk to someone. Preferably someone who wouldn't judge me, so that eliminated friends or family or—

"Hey! Sorry I'm late!"

Naomi swept in with the latest arctic blast, the festive sleigh bells attached to the door jingling and jangling. She gave me a warm hug hello in her puffy Patagonia coat. We exchanged pleasantries and sat down at our empty table, just as we had with Brian.

"How've you been?" the pretty brunette asked. Eyeing me up and down, she shrugged off her coat and adjusted the sleeves of her sweater. "Wow. You look amazing!"

"Thanks," I blushed.

"Wherever you went, you got a *hell* of a lot of sun."

It had been a few days since I returned home from Hawaii. I'd spent them buried in my recording studio, making up for all the lost time. As it turned out, having three simultaneous boyfriends tended to keep a girl busy. In more ways than just one.

"I was in Hawaii," I told her. "It was... spur of the moment."

I must've seemed nervous, because Naomi squinted at me skeptically.

"With Brian?" she asked.

"Hell no!"

Relief flooded her face. "Oh, *good!* For a minute I was worried you were backsliding."

"Trust me," I assured her. "Even for a trip to paradise I wouldn't be backsliding with *that* asshole."

Naomi laughed and ordered us a pair of coffees. Christmas music drifted down to us as we waited for them to arrive, settling back into our chairs.

"Has he called you?"

"Of course," I replied. "A few times in the beginning, at least. I didn't take the calls, though."

"Me neither," Naomi admitted. "Although he's still trying from time to time."

Together we let that conversation die and be buried. Satisfied that I hadn't called her down here to discuss our shared ex, Naomi relaxed a little.

"So... what is it then?" she smiled, looking a little devious. "You're obviously not here to talk about Brian. And as much as I think you're lovely, our whole little alliance centered around confronting and dumping that cheating shithead. So we're not really 'friend' friends, are we?"

Our coffees arrived. Naomi began pouring enough sugar in hers to jump-start three diabetic comas.

"Number one, we *are* friends," I countered. "Or at least we can be. We'll just be friends with a shared disaster."

She laughed, reaching for the cream. "Like survivors of the Titanic?"

"Sure," I shrugged. "I'd like to think some of those people ended up as lifelong friends, don't you?"

"I guess so."

"Good," I declared. "Number two, I really need to talk about something. Something I can't really tell my existing friend group, because... well..."

"They'll cast judgment?"

My face lit up. She understood.

"Yes."

Naomi brought her milky-white, sugar-filled mug to her lips and took a long, satisfying sip. If she could stir it with a rock-candy stick, I knew she would.

"Was this something that happened in Hawaii?" she asked.

"Oh yeah."

"Something juicy?"

Her eyes flashed in a way that told me she was hungry for gossip. I knew right then and there I was going to like this girl.

"Juicy enough that you're going to need a bib and a raincoat," I teased.

For the next hour or so I settled into my seat and went over the whole, sordid tale. I started with Jace, and our relationship growing up. I went on to explain how he'd called to ask me to play the part of his wife, and even pulled my faux wedding rings from my pocket to show her.

"You still carry the rings around?" she asked.

It was something I hadn't even thought about. "Umm... yeah. I guess I do."

"That's fine," Naomi smiled. "Go on!"

I told her about Jace, about Merrick, about Aurelius. I described each one in jaw-dropping, panty-soaking detail, too. Like a schoolgirl gushing about her latest crush.

Crush? That's funny.

It felt amazingly cathartic to talk about them again, even to what amounted to a total stranger. Maybe it was even *because* she was a stranger, although not for long. Naomi wouldn't judge me for what happened. In fact, I had a feeling she'd egg me on.

When I got to the really juicy parts, I left nothing out. I gave her *everything,* leaning in and lowering my voice so that she could experience every sensual thrill, every life-altering sexual moment, by living vicariously through me.

Thirty

DAKOTA

By the time I finished we were huddled together, our faces so close we practically looked like a married couple ourselves. Naomi was six shades redder than when she'd first walked into the place. Her mouth hung all the way open.

"Oh my God..." she breathed, when I was finally finished.

I nodded numbly. "I know."

"Oh my *God,* Dakota!"

Adrenaline pumped through my veins, even as my shoulders slumped with something akin to relief. Having finally unloaded the tale to someone else, I felt physically and emotionally drained.

"And have you heard from them?" Naomi asked.

I shook my head. "When they kissed me goodbye at the airport, Jace said something about letting me decompress. Since then, only Aurelius has reached out. He sent a single line text-message telling me they missed me."

"And what did you do?"

"I sent back a heart emoji," I shrugged. "Actually, I sent three of them."

In a lot of ways it was sad, not speaking to the guys or even hearing from them at all. But I knew where they were coming from. After all, I'd been the one who'd downplayed the seriousness of our time together. I'd been the one who told them I wasn't "that woman" — the one they were ultimately looking for — and I was the one who used the words 'meaningless fling.'

"So they *really* want one wife?" Naomi was asking. "Like, they're actually serious about it?"

"Dead serious."

"How do you know?"

"Because I *know* them," I told her easily. "These aren't just men, they're soldiers. Heroes. They've been bonded in ways you or I couldn't even begin to imagine, and they've relied on each other for so long that—"

"So why not you?"

Naomi's question stopped me dead in my tracks. It was four simple words. But four words with an insane impact.

"What do you mean, why not me?"

My new friend smiled and rolled her eyes. "Dakota, look at you right now. You're happy, you're animated, you're all lit up. It wasn't like this when I first walked in. This all happened the minute you started talking about them."

The door to the place kept jangling with every new customer. The holiday songs kept playing merrily on the speakers, overhead. But I couldn't hear any of it anymore. Christmas was in three days, and still nothing mattered.

Nothing but *them*.

"You're even carrying the rings around for shit's sake," Naomi pressed. "So in the end, what's stopping you?"

It was the last thing in the world I expected, being talked into it. My other friends would've shoved each other aside to talk me *out* of something this crazy.

"I can't do *that!*" I gasped.

Naomi chuckled. "Seems like you might've already done it."

"I mean long term! It's not feasible. It's not something people do."

"But they're doing it, right?" she pointed out. "Or at least they're trying to. And you don't see a problem with *that*, do you?"

I pondered her point. "A problem? No. Not a problem."

"Then they have your blessing?"

I shrugged. "Yeah, sure, of course. Whatever makes them happy."

Naomi leaned forward, smirked, and pointed a finger into my chest.

"Dakota, *you* make them happy. Can't you see that?"

It was like a bomb went off. My mind was suddenly reeling, spinning with possibilities. Voices in my head — greedy voices, conservative voices — all began arguing pros and cons. Ifs and whens. Logistics. Benefits. Impossibilities...

I thought about Tyler and my parents and the full, bustling house I grew up in. I also thought about Jace and his empty home. I remembered all the times I crushed on him in high school but didn't do anything about it. All those missed opportunities like the one in the pool, because neither of us took that leap.

Tyler.

It wasn't just Tyler, though. I could see that now. I was using my brother as an excuse — a shield against the fear of a rejection. A fear of change. Of going outside my comfort zone, when I was already in a safe, cozy place.

But not *the* place. The place I really wanted.

"Here's a question," Naomi said, after a long bout of silence. "What if you *tried* it?"

"T—Tried it?"

"Yeah," she grinned. "I mean shit Dakota, you've already tried it! You know you like it. *More* than like it, if I'm not mistaken."

I nodded numbly. "You aren't."

"It's radical as hell, but it's not like you haven't already dipped your toes in the water," she continued. "For the last week and half, you've been swimming in the pool without a lifeguard." She paused for a second and grinned. "Or with three very yummy lifeguards, depending upon how you look at it."

I bit my lip. *Could I? Really?* Nothing made sense anymore.

"This isn't the advice you wanted," she chuckled. "Is it?"

"I don't know what the hell I wanted," I said truthfully. "It's definitely not what I expected."

"Yeah, well..." Naomi unscrewed the cap off a tiny flask and poured some into her third cup of coffee. She held it over my own mug and I waved her on.

"Sometimes opportunity knocks," she said. "Other times it shatters your door with a battering ram and comes crashing into your living room."

The image

"Now you can scramble out the window and escape it," she continued with a shrug. "That's one option."

Her eyes shot up to meet mine. There was mischief in them, maybe even a little envy.

"Or you can sit down on the couch with it and see what the hell it wants."

I took a sip of my newly-spiked coffee. The much needed rum was delicious.

"I asked what was stopping you before," said Naomi, "and maybe that was a little backwards. Because if these men truly love you — and it sure sounds like they do — I have an even better question."

I glanced up just in time to watch her pretty eyes flash dangerously.

"What's stopping *them?*"

Thirty-One

DAKOTA

"You're not giving them enough dough. Cut more dough!"

My father elbowed me playfully, as I rolled the next couple of cocktail wieners into slightly wider strips of Pillsbury crescent rolls. Carefully, I placed each one onto the greased cookie sheet.

"They're called pigs in a blanket for a reason," my father smiled. "If you don't give them enough blanket they're not nearly as good."

My mother was her frantic, usual self, running around the well-decorated house like a chicken with its head cut off. She'd already cleaned, prepped, cooked, and then cleaned again, but as always she was checking on every last detail before people started getting here.

"How many do we have this year?" I asked, just to slow her down.

"Counting all your aunts and uncles, your cousins,

the boyfriends and girlfriends of cousins, plus the children of the boyfriends and girlfriends and cousins?"

I rolled my eyes as I rolled my next pig into its blanket. "Yes, mom. Everyone."

"Then sixty-eight."

My father laughed maniacally, then dumped a pot of boiling water through a steel colander in the sink. Steam exploded through the kitchen, billowing against the ceiling until only a pile of ziti shells remained.

"It's a new record," my mother added, and not without a measure of pride. "But it's Christmas Eve, so..."

Christmas Eve. Traditionally it was the biggest day of the year in my house, and with good reason. It was roughly five times more important than Christmas day, and was bigger than Thanksgiving in terms of the sheer number of people in the house at once, if not quantity of food.

Thank God for Italians.

"Oh my God!"

I whirled at the sound of the deep, yet mocking voice. My brother's voice.

"You're letting *Dakota* make the pigs in the blanket?"

I frowned as my brother was enveloped in hugs, first from my mother, then from my father as well. Still wearing his oven mitts, the old man patted him on the back gruffly.

"You know she never uses enough blanket," Tyler grinned.

I hugged him anyway. I hadn't seen him in weeks.

"Nice to see you too, big bro."

His long arms enveloped me aggressively yet lovingly. "Hell yeah."

Tyler pushed back from me for a moment, then stepped aside. Behind him, another figure stepped up.

"And you're not gonna *believe* who I bought with me!"

The smile on my face faded into pure, abject shock. My heart all but stopped.

"Hi, everyone."

Jace stood in the entrance to the kitchen, wrapping his two big arms around my mother. She hugged him for so long I thought she might keep him, and then finally he was shaking hands with my father. Their grip was so tight, so vigorous, for a moment I thought he might keep him too.

"Welcome home, Jace!"

Jace's expression was a mixture of excitement, emotion, and nostalgia. He hugged the rest of the way through the kitchen until he was eventually standing before me.

Looking at him was the most awkward thing in the world.

"Umm... hi!"

He put his arms out and I fell into them.

"What's up, Dakota?" he smiled. "How's things?"

"Hectic."

With my face momentarily shielded from the rest of

my family, I closed my eyes and inhaled the Green Beret's musky, masculine scent. My body recognized and reacted to it instantly. So did a few other... parts.

"I heard the two of you were in Honolulu together!" my mother exclaimed. "I still can't believe you missed the chance at hooking up."

Hooking up. Yes, that's what she said. Jace looked down at me and winced.

"I really wish I hadn't been so busy," he called over his shoulder, "or I would've taken her out for sure. It would've been so great to catch up on things. Dakota and I could've had the best time over there."

Still facing away from my family, his smile widened into a shit-eating grin. My stomach dropped as I couldn't return it.

"Ah well," my father said. "You're here now and that's what matters."

"Yeah."

"Maybe the two of you could get together while you're here in town," my mother offered. "And catch up then."

"Yeah," Jace said, looking down at me. "Maybe."

He was still holding me. A little too long for Tyler's liking, too.

"My sister and my best friend going out together?" he chided. "Not a chance." Clapping Jace on the back, he spun him away. "No one's going anywhere without *me.*"

My brother pulled his friend into the working part

of the kitchen, where he would invariably be given a half-dozen tasks. Tyler had seen Jace intermittently throughout the years, but my parents hadn't seen him in God only knew how long. They had a thousand questions for him, which would probably be asked as he was cutting up onions.

Jace.

All of a sudden my mouth was dry as a desert. I looked around for my wine glass, which I'd set down before I started prepping appetizers.

Here.

Tyler's friend hadn't showed up in so many years, since just after being enlisted. And now here he was, standing in my kitchen. Telling my father how good his cornbread was, while my mother tied an apron around his trim, beautiful waist.

This can't be a coincidence.

Suddenly I regretted not keeping in touch after Hawaii. Memories of my impromptu vacation came rushing back — all the same feelings and butterflies and gut-churning desires. Jace's lusty, heartfelt laughter boomed through my parent's kitchen, as he licked icing off his finger and stole a sly glance over his shoulder at me. My father was talking a mile a minute, asking a billion questions. My mother kept feeding him from various trays, as my brother uncapped a fresh round of beers.

In many ways it was like he never left. Like Jace was always a part of our family; a second brother maybe, all fun-loving and jovial and making everyone's holiday better just by being there.

Yet all I wanted to do was steal him away.

Nobody noticed me uncorking a new bottle of wine, knowing I'd need several glasses to deal with this incredible new development.

By the same token, not one of them noticed me pouring all the heavy cream straight down the drain.

Thirty-Two

DAKOTA

I rose up on my knees, shifting my ass backward until I felt the mushroom-like head push its way inside me. Jace's hands slid to my hips as I sank down, taking him all the to the root with a slow, glorious hiss of ecstasy.

Ohhhhhhhhh....

My breasts bounced against his face as I rode him. They'd been freed from my shirt and bra five minutes ago, during our frantic make-out session.

"God I missed this," Jace breathed, rolling his tongue against one pink nipple.

My mother had gone completely berserk upon learning we were out of cream; the kind of level ten freak-out associated only with not having everything precisely ready on a holiday this big. I volunteered quickly and was out the door in a flash, dragging Jace with me while my brother was upstairs getting something.

He jumped into my car and we sped off, tires

spinning, like we'd just committed a crime.

"Is this the part where we catch up?" he'd joked.

Eight minutes later we were parked behind the old boarded-up bank, making out like teenagers, steaming up the windows. There was little time for words. Conversation could always happen during the party, with all the other guests eating and drinking their faces off.

No, right now there was only one thing we wanted. One thing we both needed...

"Fuckkkk..."

I bounced across Jace's lap in the front seat, grinding into him as his hands slid to my ass. He felt enormous inside me. All swollen and throbbing and beautiful.

"Heavy cream, huh?" Jace quipped. "The irony."

The quart of heavy cream we'd picked up from the mini-mart lay on its side in the back seat, completely forgotten. With my hands locked behind the back of his neck, I began kissing him some more.

"You know your mother's going to kill us," Jace chuckled. "If we don't get back soon."

"I don't care," I murmured into his mouth. "Her cheesecake can wait."

Last night she'd spent more than two hours beating together eggs, sugar, cream cheese and everything else in my grandmother's recipe, while baking the crust from scratch. But if she didn't have fresh whipped cream to slather over her cheesecake tonight, someone in my house was going to die.

Jace's hands curled tightly into my supple flesh, as he

lifted his ass to drive into me even deeper. I could feel my climax building quickly. My mouth dropped open in a perfect, silent 'O'.

"I can't believe you're here," I whispered softly. "I can't believe you *came*."

I expected a joke about how he hadn't come *yet*, but we were past jokes for the time being. Our bodies writhed with familiar rhythm. The sounds and scents of our combined sex permeated the warm, enclosed world inside of my car.

"God, it's been too long," I sighed happily, still bouncing. "*Way* too long."

Jace grunted sexily, while screwing me back. "It's only been a week," he replied. "Not even."

"Yeah, well have you ever gone from having sex every day to not having it all?" I questioned him.

He smiled and winked. "As a matter of fact, yeah."

"What about going from three partners to zero?" I pressed. "Three men constantly taking care of your every need on a daily basis, to being a celibate, indentured servant to your mother's everyday holiday whim?"

His smarmy grin only made me love him even more. As my impending orgasm took full control of my brain, all thoughts of Tyler, my parents, and my mother's cheesecake went straight out the window.

"Well when you put it *that* way..."

I came hard, exploding spectacularly around him. Screaming like a banshee against the fully-steamed windows, in the confines of the old bank's parking lot.

"OOooHHhhOOooHHhh..."

Jace grabbed the back of my head and pulled me close, pressing my face into one hard, rounded shoulder. I bit down on him as I cried out, grinding him in circles throughout my orgasm.

FUCK!

It felt soooo good! So incredibly, life-changingly good that for a full minute afterward I just stared into his gunmetal eyes, rolling my hips to elicit every last ounce of pleasure while enjoying the beauty of his flawless, ruggedly-handsome face.

"Come..." I whispered softly. "Please, come for me."

"In a minute," my sexy soldier countered. His fingers sifted my hair, admiringly. "I'm enjoying this way too much. And besides, there are way too many people at your house."

I sighed contentedly, then went back to kissing him.

"You know you're the sixty-ninth guest, right?"

"Ohhh," he grinned. "Sounds like that should come with some sort of prize, no?"

"Yes. You get to come inside me."

His hands were on my hips again. They were guiding me faster at times, but also slowing me down periodically, to maintain control.

"Dakota, I need to tell you something."

My blonde hair bounced about my cheeks, creating

two shimmering walls of gold that further separated us from the world. The nagging voice in the back of my head told me that if my mother served dessert without her standard topping, she might literally disown her only daughter. That if Tyler caught wind his sister and best friend had been gone for this long, he might start putting two and two together.

But the other voice — the louder one, coming from deep in my heart — told me the only thing that mattered was right here, right now.

"I love you."

The words were sweet, beautiful, amazing. Still buried so way up inside me, I thought I felt him swell.

"I love you too," I whispered.

Jace's eyes changed. They pierced even deeper, reaching all new levels of intensity.

"No, you don't understand," he said softly. "We've *always* loved each other, for as far back as I remember. We're practically family. But that's not what I'm talking about."

His lip quivered, which was weird. I'd never seen him do that before.

"Dakota, I'm *in* love with you."

The words reached my ears, and for a few seconds they were meaningless syllables. Then the realization hit. It crushed me like a ton of bricks.

HOLY—

I couldn't breathe. Couldn't get enough oxygen into my lungs to process what he was saying.

Jace...

He was staring back at me expectantly, our bodies still connected yet all but stopped. The car was silent. The world, at a standstill.

Then a giant wave of conflicting emotions crashed over me.

Love.

Our foreheads touched, and an overwhelming sensation of joy surged upward and outward from my core. It made me feel warm. Safe. Ridiculously happy...

"I— I feel—"

He kissed me, and for the duration of the kiss everything else melted away. It was one last chance to bail out. One final opportunity to get off this runaway train, before it ultimately derailed.

But I knew with all my heart I didn't *want* to get off.

"I feel the same way," I breathed, and my heart soared as I said the words. "Jace, I... I don't want to be without you."

"Then don't."

I swallowed hard. "I don't want to be without Aurelius. Or Merrick. Or—"

"Then *don't.*"

He smiled, and that smile was everything I'd ever wanted. He began rolling his hips again. Screwing me slowly, tenderly, as his lips brushed mine and our tongues danced and the entire world was nothing more than heat between our bodies, fusing us together at the most primal and intimate of all places.

"Three weeks," Jace murmured quietly. "We'll all be in Colorado. The three of us."

He whispered the words, even as his eyes told the story. But there was love in those eyes too now, as well as lust.

"I told them I'd bring you," he went on. "I told them you'd come."

An hour ago, I could've come up with a dozen reasons why I couldn't fly off again to see Jace and others. Right now, I couldn't think of a single one.

"*Be* with us," Jace offered. "Come down and see the future we're building together."

His hands grabbed my ass again. They were desperate this time. Frantic.

"Please, Dakota. Tell me you'll—"

"I'll come."

His whole face lit up. His hands squeezed possessively, furiously, causing me to cry out.

OH my GOD—

And then Jace was shooting hard, blasting off like a rocket. Spewing great jets of white-hot plasma everywhere, as he fired away inside me.

Mmmmm...

Collapsing around his body, I came again.

Thirty-Three

DAKOTA

At one point in my life, the week between Christmas and New Years was a magical, mythical world of sleeping late, playing with toys, and never really stepping out of my pajamas. There was no school, no homework, no responsibilities. All the family craziness was pretty much over, leaving a peaceful, week-long marathon of board games, leftovers, and late-night movie-watching in its wake.

Unfortunately, as a kid no one really tells you how badly adulthood obliterates all that.

Sure, there was still time to have a little holiday fun here and there. But for the most part I spent the week working, marketing, and promoting myself online to score even more jobs. I'd neglected all three of those things since before leaving for Hawaii, so playing catchup was an uphill battle as the year slowly drew to a close.

Three weeks.

Jace's invitation still made my heart race, as did the

nightly text-messages and sometimes even phone calls between me and all three of the guys. My trip to Colorado was already booked, already planned. As far as I was concerned it couldn't come fast enough, yet it was probably a good thing I had time to get my work taken care of first.

Christmas Eve had been incredible, but unfortunately it had also been a one-shot deal. After screwing our brains out we'd returned heroically in time for dessert, just before my mother was ready to put a hit out on me. We made up some bullshit excuse about the stores being out of stock, and endured a few sideways glances from my aunts, uncles, cousins... even Tyler himself. Jace spent the rest of the night laughing and joking and partying with everyone in my house, while the two of us stole hot, knowing glances from across crowded rooms.

As the night wound down we even managed a little make-out session, somewhere in the darkened corner of the yard. The kissing was fiery hot, the touch of his fingertips totally electric. And it was made all the more exciting and forbidden, knowing we could get caught at any time.

After that Jace sped home to spend an obligatory Christmas with his family, then caught a military flight back to base that same night. I was left dreaming about what would happen in Colorado, and wondering how long I could keep our relationship a secret from Tyler and the rest of my family. Still, for once I was pretty damned sure of something. I didn't doubt for a single second that I was making the right decision, in agreeing to go.

I thought about all these things as I sipped cheap champagne, watching the ball drop in Times Square on my modest thirty-six inch television. Spending New Year's Eve alone in my apartment didn't bother me one bit. In fact, the solitude allowed me to get the rest of my work done, and made my reflection upon the past year — and especially the last month — even more in-depth.

Also, the guys had promised to call me at midnight.

One week to go.

My excitement was building fast. I'd seen glimpses of the place the guy's were building and now living in, on what looked to be the most beautiful, scenic piece of property. I'd always loved Minnesota and its wide open spaces, but the mountains surrounding the countryside they'd chosen were absolutely breathtaking.

And that was just on a Zoom call.

I'd been thrilled to learn that Jace was finally free, and the general had given him the honorable discharge he so richly deserved. I was looking forward to spending time with all three of them. To getting to know them better as men. I wanted to learn more of their history together. I wanted to hear their stories—

KNOCK KNOCK.

It was well past eleven o'clock, and normally a knock like this would've been out of the ordinary. But with everyone in the world still awake, and the ball dropping in just half an hour, I didn't think twice about opening it. Especially since my neighbor had come down earlier to borrow a corkscrew, and was probably just returning it.

"Hi, baby."

My body froze, as my breath caught in my throat. Standing before me, of all people, was Brian.

"Wha—"

"I wanted to talk to you," he interjected quickly. "Actually it's more like I *need* to talk to you." He lowered his gaze a little, looking sullen and guilty. "Besides, I couldn't stand the thought of us starting the new year apart."

My eyebrows came together, as my face twisted into a frown.

"Brian—"

"You used to call me baby," he cut in. "Remember that? Remember when we first got together, how good everything was? How much you really loved—"

"That was before you decided to stick your dick in other people."

It came out harsh and abrasive, but I didn't care. I was angry as hell. Pissed off that he'd just show up like this.

"I— I should never have done that," he apologized quickly. "It was always *you*, Dakota. It still is. There's nobody I'd rather—"

I laughed loudly, shutting him down.

"Spare it," I snapped. "Naomi and I talk regularly, and I know you've been trying to get back with her, too. You're playing both sides of the fence again."

"You're the only side of the fence that I want," Brian countered.

His mouth curled into that once-charming smile I used to fall for so easily. Now it just made me sick.

"Brian go away. Enjoy your life."

He looked down at his feet again. If the gesture was meant to garner sympathy, it wasn't working.

"Do you really mean that?"

"Yes," I replied. "I mean, no. I mean, I really don't care, to be honest. I have no feelings left for you whatsoever. You can do whatever you want, it means nothing to me."

I closed the door. Or rather, I *started* to close the door, but something stopped me.

Glancing down, I saw that he'd jammed his boot inside.

"Brian, don't even—"

"You blocked me," he said coldly. "You blocked my calls, my texts, my—"

"Brian, move your foot."

My whole body was shaking by now. My voice was dripping with acid.

"No."

A cold feeling stole over me, starting at my feet and sweeping all the way up to my shoulders. It wasn't anger, it wasn't rage. It was worse than either of those things.

It was total helplessness.

"Let me talk to you," he pleaded again. "Dakota, if you just let me in and hear me out—"

"MOVE. YOUR FUCKING. FOOT."

I shoved again, this time as hard as I could. When I looked down, Brian's foot hadn't moved a single centimeter. Neither had the door.

Fuck.

I wanted to call out, to scream as loud as I could. Maybe my neighbors would hear. Maybe someone would come running over.

Or maybe Brian would get desperate and push even harder, shoving his way inside...

"Dakota—"

My mind raced, trying to calculate whether I could talk my way out of this or if I should go a different, more desperate route. If I invited him in, I might be able to bullshit long enough to concoct some kind of an escape plan. But then I'd be trapped inside, and it might also go the *other* way. The wrong way.

My eyes were glazed, as tears welled up. I couldn't tell if I was actually crying or if it were just the extreme cold seeping in from outside.

"Dakota, listen—"

He pushed and the door bowed, hurting my foot. The pressure was too much. There was no way I could hold him.

And then I didn't have to hold him, as a hand clapped itself over Brian's shoulder and yanked him violently backwards into the frozen darkness.

Thirty-Four

DAKOTA

Fists rained down again and again, pummeling my ex-boyfriend into the frozen sidewalk just outside my apartment building. I screamed out loud, not knowing what else to do. It was a scream of alarm more than anything else, but as the blood flowed and fists kept coming the screams turned into pleas for the madness to end.

"STOP! STOP!"

The man standing over Brian's limp, bloody form whirled in my direction. The look on his face was so savage, so primal, I almost didn't recognize my own brother.

"Tyler!?"

He threw one last punch that connected hard with Brian's stomach, eliciting a final, strangled gasp. Then he lifted my ex by his shoulders and pulled him to his feet.

"Tyler, let him go! Please."

My brother snarled into my ex-boyfriend's face, and

for a second I thought he might even spit. Then he kicked him hard in the ass, sending Brian sprawling down the icy, salt-strewn pathway leading up to my front door. With his arms pinwheeling wildly out in front of him, he somehow regained his footing and kept on going out into the street. It was a true miracle he didn't go face-first back to the cement.

"Are you okay?"

I nodded with my arms crossed, shivering against the cold. Tyler looked back one last time, and apparently satisfied, ushered me back into my apartment before closing the door.

"Holy shit Dakota, what happened?"

I couldn't immediately answer. My teeth were chattering as I hugged him tightly.

"I thought you were finished with that asshole?"

"I—I was finished," I stammered. "I mean I *am* finished. With him, I mean."

"Thank fuck."

I looked down and saw my brother's bloody fists. My mouth dropped open.

"Oh my God, Tyler!"

I dragged my brother bodily to the kitchen sink. He didn't wince as I shoved his hands beneath the cold water, or when I used a paper towel to dab away the last remnants of blood.

"You didn't even get cut," I marveled. "Considering how hard you were pounding him, that's pretty amazing."

"The asshole deserved it," growled Tyler. "First, for

what he did to you. But tonight, when I saw him forcing his way through your doorway?" He shook his head. "He's lucky he still has a pulse."

I felt warm and loved, plus a measure of pride at my brother's protectiveness. He looked me in the eye while drying his hands, and his expression softened.

"What are you doing here?" I asked. "I thought you had a party to go to."

"I already went," Tyler shrugged. "The party was lame. Besides, I couldn't let my kid sister spend New Year's Eve alone."

I smiled, hugged him, then went into the cabinet where I kept the glasses. "Want some champagne?"

"Champagne?" Tyler laughed. He made a sour face and shook his head. "Fuck no. Got any beer?"

Five minutes later we were sitting on the couch, toasting nothing in particular as the adrenaline drained from our veins. I was pretty sure I'd seen the last of Brian. And that was a good thing.

"You talk to Jace lately?" Tyler asked, out of the clear blue sky.

I panicked. My brain flip-flopped trying to find the correct answer, until my lips spit one out.

"Yes. Sort of."

I took a little too long to answer the question.

"*Sort of?*"

I bit down on my lower lip, which was a tell of sorts. As my big brother, of course Tyler knew every tell I had.

"Just *say* it, Dakota," he reasoned. "We're adults now. You don't have to hide it from me."

For a few seconds I didn't do anything at all. Eventually though, I uncrossed my arms and let the tension go out of my shoulders.

"Fine."

I took a deep breath, wondering what to tell him. Or rather, how *much* to tell him.

"Jace is moving to Colorado," I said, matter of factly.

"I know," said Tyler. "He's headed for civilian life, too."

"Yes," I nodded. "His discharge is already scheduled. He's co-building a house a little about an hour outside Denver. Starting over with a few military friends."

I studied my brother's face, assessing how much he knew or didn't know. I decided to go for broke.

"Anyway, he asked me to come out there and help with the move-in. I'm leaving next week."

Tyler's expression was hard to read. It didn't change, or register anything in the way of surprise or recognition.

"Cool," was all he said.

"So I uhh, I figured I'd check the place out," I went on. "I've never been to Colorado. It looks—"

"As cold as here but twice as amazing?"

I chuckled back at him. "Yeah."

"And you and Jace can catch up," he added.

My brother wasn't stupid. I wasn't going to start treating him that way now.

"Look, you obviously know Jace and I have been... talking."

"Talking," Tyler smirked. "Right."

"Honestly I don't know if there's anything there," I added quickly. "But if it turned out something *was* there, well, I guess I'd want you in the loop."

My brother kicked back a good portion of his beer, enough to make his eyes water. When he stared back at me again, his expression still hadn't changed.

"He's really something, isn't he?"

"Who, Jace?"

"Yeah."

I had to admit that he was. In many more ways than Tyler knew.

"He's a total badass now," Tyler said with a proud grin. "Big. Strong. Super intelligent. Nothing like high school."

My brother went on, staring off into space. I didn't say a word.

"And if you knew even *half* the things he's told me he's done..."

I'd wondered about some of those things myself, honestly. But I never wanted to press. I always figured Jace would tell me in time.

"If you wanted to date him, I really couldn't stop

you."

"No," I chuckled. "You couldn't."

"I wouldn't want to anyway little sis," he said. "Maybe when we were in high school, but not now."

For the first time in my life I looked back at Tyler and saw someone entirely different. He was older now. A little more wrinkled around the eyes, a little bit of grey starting up here and there. But it was his personality that had changed the most. He was a lot more mature now. Much less impulsive, and more thoughtful.

"With all the moving around he's done, I can't imagine how such a thing would've worked between the two of you," Tyler went on. "But now Jace is settling down. Carving out a place for himself." He shrugged and smiled. "I guess when it finally comes down to it, you could definitely do worse."

The ball was dropping now, shimmying its way down the pole at the top of the screen. Tyler and I watched it together. We listened to the roar of the crowd as they counted down the final ten seconds, until the whole thing lit up and the fireworks went off, ushering in the new year.

My brother swept me into a hug, and my eyes welled up with tears. Everything to do with Brian was wholly forgotten.

"This is going to be a hell of a kickass year," Tyler said, toasting with his almost empty bottle.

"For the both of us," I grinned back, as my phone went off in my pocket.

Thirty-Five

MERRICK

She flung herself into my arms and I spun her around, like one of those sappy commercials you're always seeing. In an airport, too. So cliché.

It was even more cliché when I dipped and kissed her.

"Welcome to Colorado," I smiled against her full, beautiful lips.

There was a small crowd around us, and a few of them were clapping. I realized it was less for the romance and more because I'd worn my camos.

"They think you just got back from war, don't they?" Dakota giggled. "And I'm you're sweetheart."

"You *are* my sweetheart," I told her happily. "But yeah. Probably."

"Let's not disappoint them then."

We kissed a little more, some for them and some for us. By the time we finished the little crowd had dispersed. It gave me time to look her up and down again. To drink in all the little details my mind had been missing, whenever I thought about her.

And just like the others, I thought about her *a lot.*

"So Aurelius and Jace are back at the house?" she asked.

"Yup."

"Let's get my bags, then. I can't wait to see it!'

We bounced happily through the luggage area, holding hands and interlacing our fingers like a long-time couple. I couldn't believe it had only been a few weeks. The time apart had felt like forever.

But just seeing her again made it seem like no time had passed at all.

Look at her...

Dakota looked gorgeous all bundled up in her furry parka, her tight jeans accenting every one of those delicious curves I knew so well. I wanted to pull her into the nearest parking lot and give her a proper hello. But it was still very early, and Jace had us on a tight schedule. We had plans for the entire day.

Besides, I didn't want a quickie in a parking lot — as juicy as that quickie might be. After this much time apart, I needed to welcome her here *properly.*

We all did.

The sun was shining brightly by the time we got outside, but it did little to ward off the bitter chill of the spectacularly blue sky. Luckily I'd left the engine running and the heat on full blast. We'd left the Bronco in Hawaii and traded it for an even bigger truck, this one with a double cab and an extended bed.

"This is ridiculous," Dakota breathed, climbing into the passenger seat.

"The cold?"

"No, the scenery!" She laughed. "Cold? I'm from Minnesota, remember?"

"Oh, I remember," I quipped. "Jace wouldn't stop talking about Minnesota, wherever we were. Middle of the Afghan desert? Minnesota. Jungles of Uganda? More Minnesota."

"Yeah," Dakota smiled. "It gets into your blood."

"It gets cold in Boston too," I added. "But it's apparently nothing like where you grew up. Still, it was good to hear him talking about home. It made things better for us. It brought out the same kind of thing for Aurelius and I."

I pulled out of the airport and onto the highway, pointing the nose of our new truck straight into the mountain-laced horizon. While the heat washed over our cold pink faces, Dakota's hand found my thigh. She squeezed it affectionately, if not promisingly as well.

"When did you guys decide to build a house out here?"

"Around the same time we decided to form our own security company. There's lots of opportunity in Denver, especially for ex-military."

"And ex-special forces," she added.

I nodded. "That part certainly doesn't hurt."

I wanted to tell her about the contacts we'd made, the people we were already in the process of bringing on. Jace already had jobs lined up for us. Aurelius was busy working on warehouse space.

As for myself, I somehow had even more connections at NORAD than I'd bragged about, and to be honest I'd talked a big game. The contract work I could get us over at Peterson Air Force Base alone would sustain us for several years, if we needed it to. And that was just for starters.

Still, as exciting as it all was, I didn't want to overwhelm her with too much at once. It was one of the things we'd talked about, as Jace came back from his Christmas visit. We wanted Dakota to feel welcome and relaxed. We wanted to show her a great time while she was here, and let her digest everything else at her own speed.

And of course, we all *wanted* her.

"So what are we doing today?" she asked sweetly, from her side of the truck.

I glanced over and my heart skipped two whole beats. Dakota had a smile that could wash away a thousand doubts, and cerulean eyes that reflected the sky. Her hair bounced gently around her gorgeous face as it cascaded downward, spilling over her shoulders like the beautiful waterfalls we'd seen on Kauai.

"What *aren't* we doing," I grinned back, squeezing her hand as I guided us along the highway.

Thirty-Six

DAKOTA

The house wasn't just big it was totally enormous! And it wasn't just beautiful either, it was outright fucking breathtaking.

"When the *hell* did you start all this?"

I stood with my hands on my hips, staring up at the vaulted, two-story monstrosity the guys were still in the process of finishing. A mortared stone base gave way to a sprawling, log cabin-style home, with at least three or four chimneys and big glass windows that would provide the most incredible views of the sprawling fields and distant, surrounding mountains.

"We're probably going on two years now," said Jace, his voice filled with pride. "Of course, there were delays last year. Material shortages. Work stoppages..."

"Forget all that," Aurelius grinned, pulling me close. "We're in the home stretch and that's all that matters."

After kissing me everywhere he could reach — and

some places he couldn't — the handsome SEAL had slid one arm around my waist and refused to let go. He'd been glued to my side for the past ten minutes.

Not that I minded, of course.

"It looks like you stole Kevin Costner's house right out of the show *Yellowstone*," I chuckled.

"So?"

"Not saying it's a *bad* thing," I relented, adding a chuckle. "I'm just saying."

The inside was every bit as impressive as the rest, even though nothing was painted and only half the rooms were even done. The guys were living with a makeshift kitchen, and in bedrooms that were sparsely furnished. There was enough of their own style to see what was coming, though. And everything that was coming was cool as hell.

Toward the end of the upstairs hallway, Jace pushed a pair of doors open. The two rooms on the other side were mirrors of each other, and totally empty.

"That'll be our office," he said, pointing left. "And that one..."

"Baby nursery?" I chuckled.

I thought the guys would laugh with me. Instead they all stared back at me, their expressions deadly serious.

"Someday, sure," said Merrick. As he folded his big forearms over each other, the muscles flexed. "We built this place with a big family in mind."

"We were going to use both rooms as offices," Aurelius explained. "But with the commercial space we're about to rent in downtown Denver, we really don't need it."

I nodded, peeking into the room. I still didn't understand.

"Which is why," Jace said carefully, "we figured *you* might want it. Not so much as an office, but maybe as a recording studio."

I blinked a few times, then pushed my way inside. The space was perfect, actually. There was enough square footage to set up an acoustically-sealed room and still have plenty of space for editing and retouching equipment. Right now I was outsourcing a lot of the post-production, and it was expensive. But if I had everything I needed, right there at my finger tips...

"The walls are still open," Merrick offered. "We could egg-crate the insides for sound-absorption, then do double-drywall for—"

"You know you guys totally fucking rock, right?" I said, whirling on them.

Jace and Merrick looked at each other. Aurelius laughed. "Well yeah, obviously."

"No, I'm serious. This would literally be the sweetest thing anyone's ever done for me. *Ever.*"

"Well we really haven't done anything," Merrick pointed out. "Yet, anyway."

"No, not yet," I agreed. "But this shows how much the three of you are thinking of me. You're going out of your way to—"

"You're a lot of things, Dakota," Jace cut me off. He

stood in front of me now, his physical presence causing my body to react in all the right ways. "But the one thing you'll *never* be is out of our way."

I hugged him tightly, as the others closed in from behind. It felt so good being between them again. The feelings of safety and security came back instantly, along with the warm contentment that everything was right in my world again.

Beyond the window, a trio of ravens circled lazily in the mid-morning sky. They hovered over a field containing three separate trails, and a distant fence.

"How *big* is this place?" I asked, pressed snugly against Jace's chest.

"Tomorrow we'll take you out in the side-by-sides," said Aurelius. "Show you the extent of the property itself."

"Why not today?"

"Because today," Jace smiled, glancing down at me. "We've got bigger plans."

Thirty-Seven

DAKOTA

"Well shit," I breathed, pulling my goggles onto my forehead for a better view. "This is a far cry from the beaches of Maui!"

I'd only seen Vale in movies and on television, but it was every bit as breathtaking and then some. It had taken less than two hours to drive here. After another hour of suiting up and strapping on ski boots, we were riding the express lift to the Wildwood summit and exiting beneath a dome of crystal blue sky.

"I love that we don't have to teach you to ski," said Merrick.

"Teach me?" I laughed into the brisk, beautiful mountain air. "You might not even be able to *catch* me."

I pointed my skis toward 'Wild Card' the nearest black diamond trail. The name seemed oddly fitting.

"First one down picks where we eat tonight," I suggested, lowering my goggles again. "And I'm pretty damned starving."

"You're on," said Jace. "Although I have to warn you —"

Everyone moved at once, shooting through the packed snow at the top of the trail and into the powder below. Jace was shredding right alongside me. I'd skied with him a few times before as teenagers, but only when my parents could guilt Tyler into dragging me along with them. He had the speed of longer skis and the advantage of being tall, but I could shift my hips better than he could and cut much sharper corners.

On the more narrow, moguled paths I passed him, but on the straightaways he bent his knees and really put his ass to the ground. Faster and faster we raced down the mountain, weaving through the crowds on the lower hills until he edged me out — only barely — right before the lift line.

"Not bad," he said as I skied up, shaking a layer of snow and ice from his hair. "You still got it."

Merrick was nowhere in sight — we'd burned him quickly at the top of the mountain. But just ahead of us, leaning casually on his ski poles, was Aurelius.

"Fuck," Jace grunted. "Really?"

The gorgeous SEAL's face was plastered with a perma-grin. Even his laughter had a sexy accent to it.

"You think you Americans could actually beat someone who learned to ski the Italian Alps when he was just four or five?"

"You're an American yourself, you know," Jace

pointed out.

"And I think you got out ahead of the crowd," I lamented playfully.

"Excuses, excuses."

Merrick showed up next, intentionally snow-plowing us with a fresh wave of fine power.

"Sore loser," Jace grunted.

Merrick stuck his tongue out at him. "So where are we eating?"

"I haven't figured that out yet," said Aurelius, cleaning snow from his ear. "But ask me again after eight or ten runs."

The guys began ribbing each other as we melted into the line again. I admired them silently, watching them interact. Their good-natured banter came so effortlessly and naturally, it was obvious they'd spent incredible amounts of time together.

But it was the *type* of time, too, and I knew that by the very nature of their jobs. These men hadn't just been friends or comrades, they'd had to rely on each other to stay alive. They'd saved each other from death at times. Put each other's lives ahead of their own, creating an unbreakable bond that simply had no comparison.

All three of them had suffered through the gauntlet of combat, and come out the other side. As such, they valued honor. Humility. Sacrifice. They'd adopted these principles as their own personal mantras, which gave them common ground.

I'd seen men who were close before, but even in the case of family or brotherhood ego always got in the way. That wasn't the case here, though. Each of these men were thrilled for the success of the others, and bent on helping maintain that success as a trio. They were more competitive than any men I'd ever seen, yet somehow, they were never jealous of each other.

I swallowed hard, focusing on that last part. It was the one main reason I'd come here. The only reason something this crazy could ever even be *considered*.

"Hey beautiful! You coming?"

Looking up, I realized I was holding up the line. Jace and Merrick were already getting on the lift. Aurelius held one gloved hand out to me. His sexy smile felt like a double-shot of Amaretto, warming my belly from within.

"I'll let you pick the restaurant if you want," he offered, as we slid into the next chair.

"You want pizza again," I chuckled. "Don't you?"

"No, no," Aurelius grinned. "Not tonight. Tonight we're taking you to the village. Someplace special."

Glancing ahead to where the others sat in their own lift chair, he covered his mouth with one hand and leaned into me.

"I just didn't want Jace to pick it," he whispered conspiratorially. "He wouldn't know good food if it slapped him in the face!"

Thirty-Eight

DAKOTA

As incredible as the views from the top of the mountain were, even more amazing was walking through Lionshead village. The three and four-story buildings that made up its quaint, cobbled streets were beautifully painted and immaculately kept, not to mention still decorated in more than a few places with leftover holiday lights.

Aurelius and I decided to choose with our noses, and we ended up at an Italian restaurant that smelled like heaven. We were seated in a booth near the wood-burning stove, which was nice enough. But we also were provided a beautiful, frost-coated window with a full view of the outdoor ice-skating rink, which at the moment swirled with dozens of happy people.

The boys caught me up on everything as we ate, including the construction schedule as well as the transition from their military careers to civilian life. I reminded them they were also going from a nomadic existence to one where they were actually locked down and settled in, all together beneath the same roof, to boot. None of them seemed to mind, though. In fact, they appeared more eager than ever to be granted this new sense of normalcy.

"People tied down to the same place always dream of wandering, right?" Merrick pointed out.

"Sure," I agreed, spearing one of my stuffed mini-shells.

"Well by the same token, when you're on the road and relocated as much as we've been over the years?" He shrugged, as the others nodded. "Sitting in one place starts to sound very, very appealing."

I smiled, feeling lucky and blessed. I couldn't imagine being a part of their lives while they were circling the globe and constantly in danger, wondering if and when they'd ever come back. I'd gotten these men at the perfect time in their lives, really. When they'd already served with honor, and were ready to settle down and start something new and exciting together.

Gotten them, Dakota?

My stomach did a flip-flop. I guess I hadn't really 'gotten' anything. Not yet, anyway.

But I was pretty damned sure I'd captured their hearts.

And what about your *heart?*

I scanned them as they ate, watching each of their rugged jaw-lines moving in turn. They had my heart already, I was sure of that now. I had love for each of them, for all of them. And it was a full gamut of emotions that ran deeper than simple infatuation or attraction, or even pure sexual lust.

So you love them...

That one undeniable realization was both exciting and terrifying. It meant I was opening myself up to all new incredible possibilities, if everything worked out the way I dreamed it could. But in doing so, I was also opening myself up to the possibility of getting seriously hurt.

After dinner we finished nursing our final drinks, while relaxing by the warmth of the fire. The guys had been looking at me all day, but now those stares had become long and lingering. Aurelius ogled me shamelessly, unapologetically. And I could feel Merrick's sexy caramel eyes crawling my body, his expression one of deep satisfaction as if he were already plundering me in his mind.

"We're skipping dessert, right?" I chuckled, playing a slow finger over the rim of my glass. "We're all on the same page with that?"

All three men nodded, silently.

"Good answer," I murmured, throwing back the last dregs of my wine.

Thirty-Nine

DAKOTA

There was no ride back from Vale, and that's because the guys had sprung for a fantastic hotel room. I knew this when they'd made me grab some things from my suitcase for a possible overnight stay, and the things I'd grabbed were exactly the type of things a girl might grab when she hadn't seen her boyfriend — or in my case *three* boyfriends — for several weeks.

My body was tired, almost even exhausted by the sheer number of things I'd packed into the day. My mind however was awake and alive and racing with limitless possibilities. My excitement grew with every step of the walk back, as the guys' hands began finding themselves in more strategic and intimate places on my body. I welcomed every one of them, and by the time we got off the elevator the four of us were practically racing down the carpeted hallway toward the threshold of paradise.

Once inside the room all bets were off, as the guys began kissing me in ways that made me instantly drenched.

I'd imagined this night for weeks. Pictured it in my head as I lay in bed staring at the popcorn ceiling of my little apartment, while letting my fingers take me places only my mind could go.

"This night is going to be legendary," I murmured, moaning into Aurelius's beautiful mouth. I had one hand planted firmly on Jace's incredible ass. The other cupped Merrick's thick bulge, which I couldn't wait to get inside me. "But first... we need to talk."

I stepped back into the center of the hotel suite's living area, so I could address all three of them together. They stood with their backs to the windows, silhouetted against the sprawling nighttime lights of Vale's breathtaking village. A light, lazy snow had just begun to fall. The whole thing was picture-perfect.

"I want you to know I've thought about each of you nonstop, since Hawaii," I started. "But I've also thought about *this*."

I raised my arm and pointed to each one of them slowly, then finished by pointing back to me. The gesture wasn't lost on them.

"I *want* this," I said, and the words put an instant lump in my throat. "I can admit that now. It's entirely unorthodox and it's probably crazy, and I know it'll be way more challenging than any traditional relationship. But it also comes with three times the rewards. Three times the fun, three times the excitement, and... well..."

They were staring at me now, and not just in the way they'd been thirty seconds ago. Things had suddenly gotten way more serious. Their expressions were filled with hope.

"Three times the love," I finished softly.

It occurred to me that I was standing there in my underwear, whereas they were still fully-clothed. Strangely, it didn't bother me. It seemed the perfect metaphor for what I was doing, which was baring my feelings for them. Every last one of my undeniable, emotional attachments.

Maybe even my soul.

"I once told you I wasn't *that* woman," I said. "The one you're looking to share. Only maybe I am. Maybe I could be. We'll never know unless we actually try, and the only thing stopping us from trying this for real has been me."

I took a step toward them, unhooking my bra. I let it fall, noting the three pairs of eyes that follow its movement to the floor.

"Only I'm done resisting," I murmured. "I *want* to be that woman. I know that now." I shrugged my bare shoulders. "Maybe I've even known it all along."

Aurelius and Merrick stood off to the sides, looking at me entirely differently than just minutes ago. Jace, standing between them, was equally motionless.

"You wanted a shared girlfriend?" I asked rhetorically. "Here I am. Only you'd better be ready," I smiled. "Because although there are three of you, I can be pretty demanding."

The sexual tension in the room was palpable. Our bodies were practically vibrating.

"Dakota—"

I killed Jace's sentence with an appreciative look, but also the wag of a finger. This was my show, my time. If we were really going to do this, I needed to get everything out.

"You boys are always worrying about my feelings," I said to him, "and that's sweet. But trust me, my feelings are fine."

I turned around, showing them my thong-covered backside. Hooking my thumbs through the hip straps, I lowered them ever-so-slowly over my naked ass.

"I want you to be selfish with me tonight," I purred over my shoulder. "I want you to take me. Use me..."

My panties dropped, and I bent down with them. But I never broke eye contact.

"It's time to show me exactly how much *you* want this," I whispered huskily. "All three of you."

That's it. That's all it took. The guys scrambled forward together, practically elbowing each other out of the way. But they never reached me. I was too quick.

"But not yet," I teased, leaping in the direction of the bedroom doorway. "Almost, but not quite..."

I slipped into the bedroom, swinging the door closed behind me until it was open only a crack. Then I pointed backwards.

"You boys should probably get on that couch and wait," I winked sultrily. "Three minutes. Four, tops."

My involuntary chuckle came out as wicked, if not evil.

"And when I come out you'd better be wearing a *lot* less clothes."

228

Forty

JACE

She emerged looking like a goddess, wearing a sheer satin cutout with a plunging V-neck and matching garters. All of it was gorgeous. Every inch of it was this shimmering, electric blue.

Holy SHIT.

Only her stockings were black; a pair of sheer, boner-inducing thigh-highs with criss-cross patterns of diamonds and fishnets that ended in lace trim. That trim encircled Dakota's upper thighs, gliding inward and between places I wanted to bury my face in. Down past her shapely calves, a pair of blue stiletto heels matched the top part of her outfit. Right down to the deadly-looking spikes that made her four inches taller.

"Is this what a shared girlfriend might wear?" she asked with mock-innocence.

She teased us by traversing the room slowly, criss-crossing her stockinged legs with every stride. She *dripped* sex. It took my breath away.

"It's what a shared girlfriend might get ripped right off her incredible body," Merrick offered. "Right before we screw her into the next world."

"Speak for yourself," Aurelius countered, his eyes glued to her curves. "An outfit like that? I vote for leaving it on as long as humanly possible."

We were seated on the couch in our boxers, side by side by side. Dakota smiled fiendishly, changing course mid-stride so her journey ended in front of Aurelius. Merrick and I looked on jealously as she bent all the way down to whisper something into his ear.

"What?" Merrick demanded. "What is it?"

Aurelius let out a long breath, his face already two shades more red. "She said the panties are crotchless. There's no need to take anything off."

My friend reached for her but Dakota was already gone, dancing back to stand before all three of us. She'd activated some playlist on her phone when she first came out. Now she stood there smiling, swaying her hips seductively to whatever background music was playing softly behind her.

God, she's incredible.

It was something I'd somehow always known, deep down inside. Ever since the first moment I'd laid eyes on her, sitting cross-legged in the grass in Tyler's backyard.

Even better, she's perfect for what we want.

That part I was still wrapping my head around. Yes, she was everything the three of us had ever wanted. And yes, she seemed to want us just as much.

But she was still Tyler's little sister. A member of the same amazing family that had taken me in. Practically adopted me...

"Jace."

Four slender fingers tilted my chin upward, just in time for Dakota's hot mouth to crash against mine. Her tongue swept forward, gliding past my lips, and the resulting kiss was deep and beautiful. Damn near soul-searching.

Fuuuck.

I wanted to pull her downward, into my lap. To wrap my arms around her and hold her there tightly, kissing her for years and decades to make up for all the lost time.

You can do that, sure, my mind said admonishingly. *But there are three of you now.*

It was a truth I couldn't escape, but also one I didn't want to. I loved Merrick and Aurelius as brothers. Everything we had so far was because of all of us, and together we'd build something ten times greater than any one of us could ever do alone.

And the same went for our woman, as well.

Dakota broke the kiss slowly, her ice-blue eyes lingering on mine. I smiled and nodded, giving her the go-ahead. Silently communicating that no matter how close of a bond we'd always shared, I was thrilled she was making those same types of connections with Merrick and Aurelius, too.

I love you.

I mouthed the words to her, and I saw her heart melt.

With tears in her eyes she mouthed them back and then kissed me again — fiercely and proudly — before dropping to her knees and swallowing Merrick whole.

Wow...

The double-edged sword of jealousy and excitement twisted like a hot knife in my belly. I watched as Dakota's hot mouth moved up and down over my friend, taking him deep. With a delicate hand she flipped her hair to one side so Aurelius and I could watch. We could sense it lending to her own excitement as well, giving us a full, glorious view of everything she was doing.

Our boxers came off quickly, as Merrick's somehow already had. Aurelius and I could only wait our turn, watching the cascade of hot blonde hair glide forward and back over Merrick's rippled stomach. Taking in how incredibly hot she looked in her satin blue lingerie, our eyes slowly devouring every ounce of her beautiful, exposed skin.

Fuck...

Dakota went down on him enthusiastically, gripping him at the base. Eventually she reached out blindly for us, and upon finding us naked and already hard, switched over seamlessly to blowing first Aurelius, and then eventually, me as well.

Tyler's sister...

I had to get over it. I had to get past the idea that what we were doing was somehow forbidden or taboo or anything like that. At one time, maybe. But not anymore. Because now...

Now the beautiful creature kneeling before us was

our *girlfriend.*

The ramifications of the statement still hadn't fully hit home for me, and probably wouldn't for quite some time. That said, she was ours now, and we were hers. And as much as I loved Tyler as a brother, I loved Dakota more.

More, and in wholly different ways.

One by one Merrick and Aurelius slid from the couch, dropping to the floor on either side of our electric blue goddess. I only barely noticed, because right now I was focusing on the pure heaven of Dakota's tongue rolling circles around my shaft. On the incredible heat of being buried all the way in the back of her throat, while her sexy blue eyes sought out and found mine.

There was love in those eyes, but also mischief, wickedness, lust. She wanted to be used. She wanted this night to be legendary.

And fuck the whole world if we weren't going to give her *exactly* that.

Forty-One

DAKOTA

"MMMMMmmmmm..."

I moaned loudly as Merrick's tongue delved into me from behind, his two strong hands spreading my cheeks ever so slightly for better access. I was still on my hands and knees. Jace's rock-hard thickness was still buried deep in my eager throat, as Aurelius slid beneath me, to feed on my breasts.

Talk about being busy!

We'd done these things before, but now it seemed different. The intensity of our connection was stronger, the whole act more meaningful. These men weren't just friends or lovers showing me a good time, ravishing my body to make my vacation unforgettable.

No, these men were my *boyfriends* now. My mates. I was their woman, and the closed-circle exclusivity of our arrangement made me feel all warm and fuzzy inside.

But also, wayyyy more than just warm and fuzzy.

Ohhhh...

At the moment I was blowing my lifetime crush, while being devoured expertly from behind. I was hotter and wetter than I ever dreamed possible. So excited I was ready to do anything and everything; whatever they asked of me, I wanted to please them.

Somehow I pulled myself away from Jace's awesome dick to kiss my way up his chest. After making out with him some more — something I knew I'd *never* get enough of — I slid our cheeks together until my lips were pressed right up against his ear.

"Hope you don't mind if your friends go first," I whispered sinfully. "After all, they didn't get the Christmas present you did."

Jace reached down to clap me hard on the ass, sending a shockwave of pleasure through my body. It didn't stop Merrick's questing tongue though. Not even for a second.

"You can have us in whatever order you want, baby," he murmured back. "But we're going to *use* you. We're going to get selfish with you... just like you wanted."

His hands slid into my hair, guiding me back down and over the saliva-coated head of his manhood again. Jace's two powerful arms guided me up and down, his muscles tensing and flexing as he used my face for his own pleasure.

YES.

It made me feel incredibly submissive, yet somehow powerful at the same time. I didn't have long to think about anything, though, because right about then I felt a pair of hands locking themselves onto my hips.

"Thank fuck," Merrick breathed, as he filled me from behind. I could sense the relief in his voice. The pure euphoria of finally coming home. "This has been *way* too long."

He started pumping me fast and hard, not even waiting to savor the moment. There was a desperation in the way he fucked me. And an equal desperation in the way I fucked him back, screwing my ass tightly against his thick, rock-hard body.

Oh fuck...

The way he filled me was incredible, stretching me almost to the absolute limit. If I weren't so hot for him, it might've hurt. If I weren't so shamelessly dripping wet, we might've had to go slow.

Thank God we didn't though, because his speed and rhythm were incredible. Merrick drilled me like a machine, pistoning in and out of my writhing body as I tried to remember I had Jace to focus on as well.

"It's okay," Jace chuckled, leaning all the way forward to whisper into my ear. His stomach went tight as he pulled himself from my mouth, kissing me wetly. "Fuck him back, baby."

I was breathless. Wordless. Totally without thought for anything but the pleasure being delivered to my delirious body. Jace kissed me yet again, cradling my face in his hands.

"*Enjoy* it."

I fell even deeper in love. Even more in love than ever with the idea of being shared, of being plundered and taken and traded back and forth between these three gorgeous men. I wanted to be consumed by them, until there was nothing left. I wanted to be flipped and tossed and used in ways that no single man could ever accomplish, by three special forces soldiers with bodies made hard by long years of discipline and training.

I wanted to submit to them. Be crushed beneath them! I wanted them to ravage my body and obliterate my mind, as each successive orgasm brought me closer to blissful unconsciousness. I wanted to be stretched to the absolute limit. To walk that razor's edge between pleasure and pain, until their indomitable wills — and bodies tougher than steel — inevitably shoved me over that cliff of my own jubilation, to go spiraling down into a warm, euphoric sea.

Aurelius took over, just as my first mind-erasing climax had me leaving nail-marks in Jace's two well-muscled thighs. My still-open mouth never closed as he glided his way into me, with Jace watching — and stroking himself slowly — the whole time.

"You still okay?"

I bit my lip, my eyes crossing in far-away rapture. Somehow, in my post-orgasmic delirium, I managed to nod.

"Good," Jace murmured, "because after he's done with you I'm taking you into the bedroom and spreading those legs *wide* open."

I let out a breathless sigh, feathering my hands out across Jace's hard chest as I pushed back against Aurelius. He was kissing my forehead, my cheeks, my lips again, by the time I looked up at him.

"And just what are you going to do to me in there?" I

asked, matter-of-factly.

The question wasn't meant to be answered. It was a tease, entirely rhetorical.

Even so, I gushed as Jace leaned forward, put his lips to my ear, and told me anyway.

Forty-Two

DAKOTA

Jace's mouth hovered just millimeters from mine, his hot breath mixing with my every inhale and exhale. Every time our lips brushed he pulled back. No more than a sliver, but just enough to keep me staring deeply into his slate grey eyes.

"Do it."

I moaned softly, squirming as my excitement reached its fever-peak. I was completely under his spell. Totally unable to stop what was coming, even had I wanted to.

"Let it *go*, Dakota."

I exhaled again, straining to kiss him, and Jace evaded me one last time. It was the ultimate tease. I'd never wanted anything more in my entire life than to feel his lips against mine, and right now they were so close. So tantalizingly, heartbreakingly close...

"I–I..."

My eyes crossed, then rolled back into my head. The dam broke. I no longer cared.

"Ohhhhhhhhh!"

I flailed against the softness of the bed, just as the flood of euphoria came crashing over my brain. Aurelius's mouth was locked tightly between my legs. I gushed straight into his mouth, onto his tongue, his lips... flooding him with an eruption of my warm juices that I couldn't possibly control.

And that *exact* moment, Jace leaned in and kissed me.

YESSSSSSSSSSSSSSSSSSSSS!

It was like climaxing at the exact moment the world ended. Screwing myself into the oblivion of endless rapture, as stars collided and planets exploded and nothing else in the universe mattered except my own greedy pleasure.

The kiss was apocalyptic. It connected us tongue to tongue, soul to soul. Four strong hands remained locked on my body, holding me down as I came and climaxed and squirted against one lover's handsome face, all while moaning and screaming into Jace's hot, twisting mouth.

I returned to earth in a haze of warmth and wetness, trembling all over. My legs shook violently. My breath came in ragged gasps.

"Easy," I heard Merrick chuckle. "Take it slow."

I tried to relax, letting my eyes adjust to seeing the dimly-lit room again. I found my third lover off to one side, gently holding my hand.

"That was the hottest fucking thing I've ever seen."

My body was tingling, my mind spinning down from the oblivion of my last amazing climax. The boys had been fucking me for what seemed like *hours*. Over and over they took turns on me, flipping and spinning me into different positions, screwing me from both ends. At times they made love to me slowly, one by one, only to pin me down by the wrists and pound me into all new breathless delirium whenever the mood struck.

I'd come so many times I couldn't count, but the guys hadn't given themselves any release at all. They'd always switched off before they lost control. Tagging each other in like wrestlers, fresh and ready to continue some epic, sweaty bout.

But now...

Now I could sense something was different. The guys were too focused, too aroused. Too wound up from holding out for so long, that their own dams were bound to burst, and soon.

My eyes fluttered all the way open, and Jace was hovering over me with that piercing, yet loving gaze. I was still his helpless prisoner. In more ways than one.

"That was for you," he said, kissing me one more time. "But now..."

Our lips parted, and I saw his expression turn fierce. Almost warrior-like.

"Now the rest is for *us.*"

I held my breath as Aurelius faded back, and Jace nudged his way between my outstretched thighs. He dragged the head of his manhood through my molten furrow, coating it with my own juices. Glancing down over my heaving stomach, it looked oddly beautiful. Like honey.

"You said to use you," he growled. "Be selfish with you."

I nodded, and with that he rolled me over onto my belly. Someone slipped a pillow beneath my face. Merrick, probably.

"That means *nothing's* off limits."

Climbing over my body, Jace straddled my thighs on either side. He lowered his hard body against mine, pushing further, deeper. Forcing me to bite my lip in anticipation of what came next.

But he didn't shove forward. He didn't glide back inside me, or fill me all the way from behind, as I craved he would.

Instead he held his shaft firmly in one hand, before guiding it right up against my asshole.

"Use you?" he growled, low and throatily, into my ear. "Use *this?*"

My breath caught in my throat. I swallowed hard, wracked by butterflies of anticipation. Eventually I nodded.

"That's our girl."

I breathed out as he pushed slowly inside of me, filling my ass, making me feel exquisitely naughty. It was something I'd done once or twice before, but never like this. Never with someone as big as Jace. And never with onlookers.

Relax.

I moaned into the pillow as he bottomed out, pressing his rippled stomach firmly against my soft, round ass. His arms were on either side of me. His beard tickled my cheek, as his face glided alongside mine.

"My God, Dakota. I'm so fucking far *inside* you."

His words made me feel so dirty, so incredibly hot. I responded only with a nod and a whimper.

"After all these years," Jace murmured, his body molding tightly against me. "Now we're one."

He began pumping in and out of me, very slowly at first so I could grow accustomed to having him back there. I screwed my hands into the pillows in front of me. Held on for dear life as Jace increased his speed and tempo, but with every movement he always stayed in complete control.

This... This is...

In the past this was something I could take or leave. Right now though, the whole situation was different.

This is fucking fantastic.

I was liking it. No, I was actually loving it! Maybe it was because I'd come so much and was already so relaxed, but I came to realize there were other reasons too.

I loved Jace. I *trusted* him. All three of these men were warriors with hard, unyielding bodies and fierce, invincible wills. But when it came to me they were lovers. Protectors. They were gentle and sweet and kind, and they'd always put me before everything else.

These men could do *anything* to me... and I would

eagerly let them. That's how deep my feelings ran. That's how much faith I had invested in—

I gasped as Jace's body stiffened again, this time past the point of all possible resolve. A second later he was surging inside me. Dumping his hot, beautiful seed deep in my tender ass, as I cooed and writhed and squirmed hotly beneath him.

He grunted and cursed and let loose a whole string of profanity, but all of it within the scope of his own orgasmic rapture. Then he kissed me on the cheek, sweetly and beautifully, before doing a push up and pulling himself from my warm, naked body.

HOLY—

I didn't have time to reflect, because an instant later I was being plundered again. This time it was Aurelius, guiding himself straight into the warm, wet place Jace had just left.

"You've gotta be kidding..." I heard him murmur. His lungs exhaled a long, pleasure-filled breath, and then he too was pumping away between my supple, rounded cheeks.

I could actually come like this.

The realization was stark and beautiful. I'd heard it was possible. I'd always thought it was bullshit though.

No, my mind admonished me, lost in its own delirium. *Not at all.*

I gripped the pillows even harder as my beautiful Greek lover screwed me tightly from behind. He rode me deep into the bed with long, slow strokes that awakened all new feelings of arousal in the back of my pleasure-addled mind. It was a different type of feeling. An exquisite fullness so radically different than conventional sex, edged with the taboo nature of being fucked in such a forbidden, off-limits place.

Aurelius lasted longer than Jace, but not by much. I was starting to actually buck backwards to meet his thrusts when I felt him go off.

FUCK...

He detonated like a bomb inside me, each throb and pulse of his rock-hard thickness a new jet of warm, wet heat. He continued pumping me full, shooting himself way up deep in my nether-regions. My jaw clenched. My fists tightened. And then he was gone too, being replaced by the massive bulk of Merrick's body, hovering over me.

Oh my GOD.

In the heat of the moment, I'd forgotten his thickness. I hadn't factored in whether or not I could even take him in such a way! But my sexy pilot had other ideas. Instead of taking me in the same place his friends just had, Merrick pushed hungrily past my throbbing entrance and filled my pussy instead.

Ohhhhhhhhhhhhhh...

Taking him inside me was the greatest feeling in the whole fucking world. It triggered another climax almost immediately, as I writhed and thrashed beneath him.

"Next time..."

He growled the words into my ear, while still sawing into me slowly. While he did, I slid one hand down over the flat of my belly to rub at my swollen, aching button.

"Next time I want what *they* had," Merrick breathed hotly. "But for now..."

He gripped my shoulders and drove all the way into me, burying himself deeper than anyone in the world had gone before. I was still spasming around him. Still coming down from my latest mind-numbing climax, while sighing into the linens and twisting the pillows and biting down into the very mattress itself.

How can this possibly—

All of a sudden I was crying out with him as Merrick exploded inside me, splashing my womb with long, beautiful weeks of his pent-up excitement as he filled me to absolute capacity.

Only seconds later my eyes closed, passing me into blissful oblivion.

Forty-Three

DAKOTA

I left Vale on shaky legs, but with rock-hard memories that would last a lifetime. From there we went home, back through Denver and out the opposite side. Back to the beautiful piece of property the guys had pooled their resources in order to obtain.

And 'home' was every bit as welcoming as anywhere I'd ever lived.

I spent the next week or more exploring the breathtakingly large house they were still in the process of finishing, while the four of us explored our budding new relationship. We talked about the past and the present. We talked about the future. We set guidelines and boundaries, eventually outlining the full scope of what it would look like for three men to date one woman.

But no matter which angle we looked at it from, the four of us were always all on the same page.

Our relationship would be exclusive; a closed circle

of love and trust. There would be no other men for me. There would be no other women for Jace, for Merrick, or for Aurelius. That part made me feel warm and secure, but as the sole source of their happiness it also put a lot of weight on my shoulders. It left me with three men to satisfy, emotionally as well as physically. It gave me three times the responsibilities for building those one-on-one connections, and I vowed to give each of them equal time when it came to such things.

In the end though, I shouldn't have worried.

As it turned out, the guys were incredibly understanding of both my feelings and fears. Between them, there *was* no jealousy. There never would be. Each realized that scheduling inequities would invariably exist, and that trying to make everything 'equal' would only drive everyone crazy. In that respect, we decided there would never be any schedule. Anyone and everyone was welcome on every single date, dinner, or place we went to. Wherever the world might take us, there would never be any splitting of my time, my efforts, or my love.

In the week and a half I spent with Jace, Merrick, and Aurelius, there was never anything but positive vibes. I went out with each of them alone, or sometimes with two or three at a time. I slept in their beds, and they slept in mine. Our lives and schedules were interchangeable, constantly moving and always fluid. But the golden rule — the one that would become our mantra, of sorts — was plain and simple:

Whenever we could do something together, we always did.

For me, my life was about to radically change. I

wasn't just moving from one place to another, I was going from being single to having three mates. From being constantly alone to always having someone around. But it would be someone to talk to. Someone to cuddle up with. Someone to love.

And most times, more than one someone.

Throughout my entire time in Colorado there was never a dull or lonely moment, nor did the guys pressure me to make the decision to move in with them. But that decision was a no-brainer. It had been made the very second I'd landed beneath those wide, beautiful skies, only to be crushed against three strong chests and enveloped by six hard, beautiful arms.

I spent my last evening on the couch watching movies and lounging comfortably in three warm laps, mentally going through the checklist of things I needed to do once back in Minnesota again. There was a lot to clear out, a lot of loose ends to tie up. And then there were a lot of goodbyes I had to make too. Some of which I knew would prove to be the most difficult part of all.

"You sure you don't want to go out tonight?" asked Jace. "It's not too late. We could easily—"

"Ice cream."

Merrick laughed. Aurelius bolted upright, like a little kid who thinks he heard Santa come down the chimney.

"I want you to take me out for really good ice cream," I declared. "And then right back here, so I can give you all a proper sendoff."

Jace's eyebrow rose up on one side. It was a little

trick of his that I was always jealous of.

"Aren't we the ones giving *you* the sendoff?" he asked.

"Maybe," I shrugged. "But a good girlfriend knows the value of tiding her man over with something to remember her by, before she goes away."

I stood up, suddenly very excited for ice cream. The guys rose with me.

"A good girlfriend, huh?" smirked Merrick. "And what does a *great* girlfriend do?"

Without missing a beat I set my hands on my hips and winked.

"A great girlfriend does it with *all* her men."

Forty-Four

DAKOTA

Of all my goodbyes, perhaps the most unexpectedly hard one was Naomi. I called to tell her I was leaving on a Thursday, and by that Saturday night I was buying her dinner, explaining to her how I was picking up my entire life and moving it to the mountains of Colorado.

But of all the people I was saying goodbye to, Naomi was the only one who really and truly understood.

"Just like that, huh?" she joked, tracing the salt on the rim of her margarita glass. "Three ridiculously hot guys ask you to move in with them, and you just say yes?"

"No, not yes," I smirked. "I told them 'fuck yes', and then they celebrated by tattooing my ass into the couch cushions."

With anyone else it would've felt like I was rubbing it in. But Naomi wasn't just anyone. When it came to the few friends I had left, she was the only person who knew the actual truth. Plus, Naomi enjoyed... details.

"Well it's not fair," she told me sadly.

"Are you kidding?" I waved my hand dismissively. "You'll find your own guy, the second you start looking. Naomi, you're gorgeous!"

"No, no, I don't mean that," she countered, mugging for an imaginary camera. "I *know* I'm gorgeous."

"Well, obviously," I smiled.

"I mean it's not fair that I have to lose you. After living in the same town all this time we just finally became friends. And now you're going away."

That part sucked, I had to admit. In just the short time we'd known each other, we'd developed some very sisterly bonds.

"Look, it's not like I'm disappearing off the face of the planet," I said. "And the house is huge! You could come down and visit, anytime you wanted. In fact, the guys are really looking forward to meeting you."

My words seemed to cheer her up a bit. We continued chowing down on the free bowl of tri-colored tortilla chips that our waiter kept refilling, as we totally ignored our burritos.

"Well if you're really flying away to your little three-on-one paradise, let me indulge myself one more time."

She reached out and took my phone, then began flipping through my most recent photos. I had nothing to hide, but I rolled my eyes anyway.

"Jesus, Dakota."

Naomi held up a photo of Merrick and Aurelius,

both flexing for the camera. Their arms and shoulders were almost comically enormous.

"Where'd you take this?"

"We've got a home gym on the first floor," I told her. "And they're always hamming it up for the camera."

"With biceps like these, I'll bet."

She kept going, flipping past candid shots of the four of us in various places throughout the house. There were pics of us outside, exploring the wilderness, and shots from downtown when we were picking up groceries. There were even a few pics taken of our weekend in Vale.

"Wow, you really are a lucky bitch," Naomi said wistfully. "But if anyone deserves something like this, it's you."

I gazed down casually, watching the past few weeks of my life flash by. It occurred to me how happy we all looked, and how in every picture we were smiling ear to ear. Until you saw things from the outside in, you never truly realized just how much of a charmed life you led. And I was totally seeing that now.

"Any... good ones?" Naomi asked slyly, still flipping.

"You mean dirty ones?"

Her mouth curled up at one corner. "You know damned well what I mean."

"Then no," I answered smartly, trying to think. "Unless you count a few shirtless pics the guys sent me to whet my appetite, while I was back here getting my stuff."

"Ohhh," Naomi said excitedly. "Let's see those!"

"Sorry, they're embedded in conversations," I smirked, holding my hand out. "And you're not seeing *those.*"

Naomi pretended to keep my phone for a moment, then slid it across the table with a mock frown. "It's because they're dirty, aren't they?"

"Maybe," I chuckled. "Some."

"*Definitely* some."

"Alright, fine."

We'd talked about everything as usual, and for the most part I'd left nothing out. In return Naomi had detailed a lot of her own saga, including roommate problems, a lecherous boss, and a kickass opportunity to switch to a different career. I'd encouraged her to take the leap, but of course it was an easy thing for me to say. Other than her asshole boss, Naomi was comfortable where she was.

Sometimes though, comfort could be a bad thing.

"So if I come down there—"

"*When* you come down there," I countered with a smile. "But please. Go on."

"Fine," she relented. "When I come down there, you're hooking me up with some of your boyfriends' hot military friends, right?"

Lifting my own glass, I put on my best poker face. I hadn't *told* her this yet, but it was a situation I'd already looked into.

"That's a distinct possibility, yeah."

"I mean, if you're keeping all three of those studs to

yourself," she admonished, "the least you can do is hook a girl up with one or two—"

"Two?" I chuckled.

Naomi paused, then shrugged. "We all have fantasies, Dakota. You're just lucky enough to live them out."

It was a point I could never, ever argue. Not that I wanted to.

"I'm going to miss the hell out of you, Naomi. I really am."

"Yeah," she smiled, "well I'm just a phone call or a FaceTime away."

"And trust me, I'll be making those calls," I told her. "In the meantime, save up your vacation days. And... be careful of Brian."

It was the third time I'd told her, just tonight. Naomi smirked as she drained her drink, then clapped the glass loudly to the worn wooden table.

"I think you've got it backwards," she said, with complete and total confidence. "That piece of shit should be careful of *me.*"

Forty-Five

AURELIUS

The snow was falling fast and heavy, blanketing everything in a sleek layer of unblemished white. It stretched in every direction beyond the balcony, past the field where we planned to build a stable. Over the slight rise on the other side, that Merrick had already claimed for his work shed.

No matter how many times I'd seen it, it was still amazing to me. Especially how easily all the whiteness could light up even the darkest night.

"Hey."

A smooth, feminine hand slid over my shoulder, causing me to turn and smile. Dakota stood there in all her semi-naked glory, wearing one of my T-shirts and nothing else.

"Can't sleep?"

I wanted to explain to her that this *was* sleep for me. BUDS training included sleep deprivation tactics designed to reduce the amount of time required for me to rest and recharge. Those lessons had carried over into various missions, followed me back to base, and spilled over into my daily life. Now I slept in small snatches of two to three hours at a clip, with long stretches of being awake in between.

But such sleep patterns also had their advantages. Like now, for instance.

"Sorry if I woke you," I apologized, sliding my arm around her waist. I pulled her close, clapping my hand over one cheek of her warm, naked ass. "But also," I grinned, "not sorry."

I wasn't exactly sure how long she'd slept. It was only a few hours ago that she'd climbed into my bed, all wet and willing and ready for anything. Her thighs felt amazing as I slipped between them, like bundles of warm laundry fresh from the dryer. We'd made love to each other slowly, sleepily, with tons of heavy petting and kissing. We'd even climaxed together too; the culmination of a very deep and beautiful connection.

And now here she was, living with us. Loving us. Sharing our dreams. Dakota was the woman we'd always desired but never thought we'd find, and somehow she'd been under Jace's nose all along.

"So your parents were really that supportive of you moving down here?" I asked.

She nodded, pulling her hair over one shoulder. The way her T-shirt ended at her bare thighs was driving me crazy.

"They think I'm with Jace of course," she answered. "My mother was a little wary of things happening 'too fast', but my father always admired Jace. I think he's secretly thrilled I ended up with him."

But they don't know about us, I wanted to say. Of course I couldn't. Having three lovers instead of one wasn't exactly something you told your family members. Not at first, anyway. If ever.

"If it were up to my father, I'd still be rebuilding engines with him at his shop," Dakota went on. "I pretty much lived there when I was younger. He doesn't understand what I do now of course, or that I could do it from practically anywhere. Then again none of them really understand, and that's okay. It pays the bills, and I was never trying to follow in anyone's footsteps to begin with."

She extended a finger toward the window and traced a heart in the condensation. Chuckling, she added an 'A + D' in the center.

"What about Tyler?" I asked softly.

Dakota paused, then shrugged again. "He's traveling and doesn't know the details yet, but I'm pretty sure he's just being willfully ignorant. Tyler and I talked about Jace over Christmas. He's a lot more understanding now than he would've ever been back in high school."

I turned to stare back out the window. Dakota positioned herself in front of me, pulling my arms around her from behind.

"Aurelius, what's wrong?"

For a few long moments I said nothing. Eventually I sighed, and shook my head.

"Family's important," I murmured. "Isn't it?"

Her hands found mine. Pulling them downward and over her belly, she squeezed.

"It's not just important," she answered. "It's everything."

I bent to kiss her on the top of her head. Her hair smelled absolutely amazing. Probably one of the three-hundred different bottles of shampoo, conditioner, body-wash, foaming scrub, and God knew what else she'd already littered our shower with.

"That's the only thing I worry about," I said softly, "in the dead of night, at moments like these. That eventually, your family will know about us. They'll realize it's not just Jace you're with."

"I know," Dakota admitted. "That's a bridge we'll need to cross someday. But not today."

Snow swirled against the window. Though it was warm and toasty inside, I felt her shiver in my arms.

"What if they don't cross that bridge?" I murmured, wincing as I asked the question. "What if they don't accept it?"

She paused for a moment, then turned into me again. Her expression was placid. Her face, smooth and beautiful.

"Dakota, my family's all but disowning me right now for not wanting to come 'home.' My father thinks my place is in Greece, with everyone else. My mother can't accept that I actually want to stay here."

"But didn't they bring you here in the first place?" she asked.

"Yes. And they raised me here too. But now that my enlistment is over, they expect me to fall in line. To return to my place in the family, as tradition dictates."

She scoffed. "Whose tradition? Theirs?"

I shrugged. "Tradition is tradition. It gets passed on."

"And it gets broken too," she said. "When outdated."

I thought about the last conversation I had with my parents, and how angry they'd been with me. I'd tried telling my father that Jace and Merrick weren't just friends or comrades, they were also brothers. He'd responded by practically spitting into the phone. My mother had tried to convince me with tears, next. She'd told me my only *real* brothers were all waiting for me at home.

The memory created a knot in my throat, just as it had at the time. But I knew how to swallow knots. I'd learned that trick long ago.

"Dakota this isn't about me," I said gently. "I've already made my peace with things. My decision was easy, because my family is *here*. Jace and Merrick are blood to me. True brothers, in ways that few people in this world could possibly understand."

"I understand," she whispered.

"I know you do," I smiled. "But you need to make your own peace, with your own family. Peace with your parents. Peace with Tyler." I pulled her even closer, feeling the comforting softness of her body molding itself against mine. "I can tell you it's not easy, because I've already done it. But it's something you'll have to do on your own. It's the one thing in the world we can't help you with."

I pulled back a little, to gaze into those crystal blue eyes. Right now they reflected the silver moonlight in ways that were unimaginably beautiful. But her expression was still stoic, still unfazed.

"I love you, Dakota," I told her, as my own eyes went glassy. "I love you with all my heart."

Her lip quivered, and her eyes twitched. But she remained strong. Proud. Beautiful.

"As a SEAL I've always been fearless, even in the face of overwhelming odds. Hell, I've even cheated death. More than once, too."

I brushed her cheek with my finger, and it came back wet. The same could be said of my own cheek.

"But the only thing in the whole world I'm afraid of right now," I whispered, "is spending the rest of my life without you."

Forty-Six

DAKOTA

"Check check check!"

I tapped the mic with a stern finger, listening for feedback. For once there was zero. The walls of my recording studio were up, even if they were makeshift and temporary and still a little experimental. But they were *my* walls. *My* recording studio.

For that reason alone, everything was golden.

"We'll nail it all up when you've got everything the way you want it," said Jace. "Until then though, this ought to do it."

"Thank you baby."

I planted a big kiss on his cheek, then laughed as he turned a little red. I guessed he wasn't used to being called 'baby.' He was definitely going to have to get used to it, though.

"The extra soundproofing for the walls should be

here in a day or three," Jace added. "Once they arrive, we'll stuff and spackle them for you."

I looked him over, and I was loving what I saw. The tight T-shirt Jace had stretched over his chest was all covered in sawdust. His arms were pumped from carrying lumber and hammering and all sorts of other good things.

"Stuff and spackle, huh?" I teased. "Sounds dirty."

"Not as dirty as blown insulation," he countered.

"Blown, huh?"

God, I was such a horndog! Then again, I was pretty sure the guys had made me this way. Sure, I'd had a fairly big libido even before our legendary trip to Hawaii, but after a whole month of living alongside the guys I was starting to talk like them. Act like them.

"There should be enough power with the outlets you have in here," Jace offered. "But if we need to run new ones, we can."

"Sounds good," I smiled. "Wouldn't want a *blown* fuse, would we?"

Finally he was catching on. "Hmmm," he smiled. "We might, actually."

I debated dropping to my knees right there. If I weren't already late, I would've.

"Well then," I cooed, gliding my hand over him promisingly. "Later on tonight, we'll have to check into that."

I gave him a squeeze and a kiss, then spun away and bounded down the stairs. Merrick was already in the truck, with the heat running. I jumped in, kissed him as well, and together we took off in a shower of gravel and spinning tires.

"You sure it's ready?"

"Oh, it's ready," Merrick smiled. "I double-checked."

"Because four days ago they said it would be ready 'tomorrow', and then they said two more days, and then—"

"It's ready," my lover assured me again. "Because if it's not, trust me, I'm taking something else."

I squeezed his hand happily, all the way to the dealership. Getting rid of my old car wasn't something I thought would be hard, but it turned out to be quite sentimental. Rather than drive the old girl another thousand miles to an all new altitude she probably wouldn't agree with, I'd sold her and used the money as a down payment for the one thing I'd always wanted.

"There!"

My Jeep was parked right in front of the lease office, looking shiny and new and freshly detailed. Although it was a few years old, the previous owner had garaged it. She'd kept the mileage down, too.

"It's got wheels and everything," Merrick joked, as we rolled to a stop.

"That's nothing," I said. "Just wait until I start customizing it."

I could see it in my mind's eye: a push bar up front, a light bar across the top, complete with a full rack of LED floodlights. Maybe even one of those corny wheel-covers in the back that said 'Jeeps are for Girls'.

"You know what this means, don't you?" he asked.

"Off-roading at night?" I asked, practically skipping toward the sales door. "Parking under the stars in the middle of nowhere?"

"It means you're stuck here now," Merrick pointed out.

"What do you mean *stuck* here?"

"With us," he grinned. "You've got a home, an office, and now a lease agreement, too. You can't go back. You're a full-fledged Coloradoan now."

"Colora*doan?*"

"Yup."

I laughed merrily. "Is that even a word?"

"If it's not it should be," he shrugged. "But yeah. I'm pretty sure it's a word."

I patted my girl on the hood on the way past; an ocean blue Wrangler with charcoal grey trim. Maybe she came with a car payment, but she came with a lot of other things too. Things like pride. Accomplishment. Freedom.

An all new beginning.

Merrick held the door for me, ushering me inside. I kissed him on the cheek as I passed, thinking about all the things we'd accomplish together.

"You're my favorite, baby. You know that, right?"

"I do," he laughed. "I also know you say that to *all* the guys."

"So?" I smiled back. "Doesn't make it any less true."

I loved teasing them. I loved kissing them, touching them, waking up beside them. I loved being a part of their everyday life, from dawn to dusk and beyond. Best of all, I was starting to feel like I was a *part* of them. Like I was somehow on the inside of their tight-knit circle of camaraderie.

And that together, the four of us could rule the world.

Forty-Seven

DAKOTA

"Well it's been fun and all, but we should probably get back," said Aurelius, propping himself up on one elbow. "The house awaits."

I was still flat on my back, staring up at the sky. Enjoying the first real warmth of such a beautiful spring day, surrounded by the men I loved.

"Leave now?" I asked. "Why?"

"Well for one, the beer's all gone," the Navy SEAL replied. "Wine also."

"And two," said Merrick, "we're getting hungry."

Our little picnic had gone on for a few hours now, out in the field of clover beyond where the foundation for the stable was being poured. I'd never imagined I'd be the type of girl to ride horses, much less own one. But that's exactly what the guys' plans were, when it came to developing the property.

"I packed snacks," I countered, still trying to eek out another few minutes on our little blanket in the middle of nowhere. "Why don't you just eat some more of—"

"The snacks are long gone," Jace interjected. "Besides, we're men. We need actual *food*."

I watched as he rose, extending one hand downward in my direction. After a few last seconds of relaxation, I eventually sighed and took it.

"Pizza?" Aurelius offered.

"No, not that again," Merrick grumbled.

Three months — that's how long it'd been since I left Minnesota. To me it felt more like three glorious years, probably because every second of my time here had been so amazing. I'd been busier with work than ever before. Happier, too.

And the guys... well, they'd been even busier.

"We *could* go out," Jace offered. "It is the weekend, after all."

"Out for Italian?" inquired Aurelius.

"What, so you could get pizza?"

"No," he shrugged. "Not necessarily."

In those three months the guys had established a field office, acquired a few new hires, and brought in a good number of clientele. It required long hours, though. One or more of them was usually in Denver at any given time, plus Merrick still ran shuttle flights for the base at Peterson, according to his contract. As a result, getting all of us together for a few hours was a rarity these days. So when it did happen, we took full advantage of it.

"I think we should go out," I declared. "If for no other reason than to take a ride."

Aurelius bumped me playfully with his hip. "We could stay in if you wanted to ride," he countered.

"True," I chuckled. "But you boys would be even more hungry after that."

Jace walked ahead, while I reached out to clasp Merrick and Aurelius by the hand. Our fingers interlaced, as our arms swung happily with me in the middle.

"And by then, the restaurants might be—"

My sentence ended abruptly as I bumped into Jace. For some reason he'd stopped walking.

"Hey," said Merrick. "Watch where you're..."

Everything stopped. All conversation died. The last time something like this happened, it was because a bear had wandered onto the property.

"Jace?"

The voice came from up ahead, at the foot of our stretch of private driveway. I recognized the voice instantly. Under any other circumstance, it would've made me thrilled and excited.

"*Dakota?*"

At the moment, it sent a chill down my spine.

"W—What?" my brother stammered. "I mean, who..."

He stood near the bumper of an obvious rental car, a large duffel bag at his feet. He had his arms crossed now.

His face registered total confusion.

"Umm, T–Tyler?"

Aurelius and Merrick's fingers slipped through mine. They let go at the same time, just as I pulled my arms to my sides.

By then it was far too late, though.

"Tyler!" I ran to him, embracing him in the warmest, least-awkward hug possible. My brother responded by keeping his arms at his sides. Maybe because he was in shock.

"Sis?"

I hugged him again, then stepped back with my most 'pleasantly surprised' look on my face. It was a tough sell, though.

"What in the world are you doing here?" I asked him.

"I... came to see you."

His eyes flitted to Jace, then back to Merrick and Aurelius as well. There was more than a little confusion in them now. But there was accusation, too.

"So you just showed up?" I couldn't help but say.

"Yes," he said mechanically. "We have a tournament tomorrow. The team's back at the hotel, resting up, and you were less than two hours away, so I figured..."

"Well we're glad you're here, bro! " Jace stepped up, all smiles. He jerked his chin toward the house. "Come in, check out the place!"

Unfortunately, my brother wasn't having it. Tyler shrugged him off coldly, refusing to even look his way.

Instead, he returned his gaze to me.

"What the hell's going on here, Dakota?"

The resulting silence was a living, breathing thing. It stretched on for what seemed like an eternity, gathering strength and momentum as no one really knew what to say. It occurred to me that I could lie. That I could simply play it off as three roommates having a picnic, blowing off steam. Holding hands in a silly, funny way.

"Take a walk with me, Tyler."

The words left my mouth sharply, almost defiantly. My brother didn't quite register them right away.

"We need to talk."

Forty-Eight

DAKOTA

There were a thousand things I could've said to appease the situation, or explain it away in a semi-logical sense. Many of them Tyler might've bought. Some of them might even be convincing.

Then I realized... I didn't *want* to lie.

"A lot's happened while you were away," I told my brother, leading him though the side yard and behind the house. "Some of it's downright unbelievable."

"Dakota—"

"Hell," I interrupted him, "some of it hasn't fully registered in my own mind, yet."

The others had gone into the house, which was probably a good thing. I know Jace wanted to talk to him, and it was probably killing him to remain silent. But this was something *I* needed to do. I owed it to Tyler, to the others, and most of all, to myself.

"I know what this looks like..." I began plainly.

"Dakota, it *looks* like you're sleeping with Jace *and* his friends!"

We stopped walking abruptly, as I shot my brother a dark look. "Will you let me finish?"

His eyebrows remained knitted together in anger, but Tyler still bit his tongue. I knew it took every ounce of his willpower to do it.

"I know what this looks like," I said again, "because that's exactly what it is. I fell in love with three men, Tyler. Three men at once."

He just sneered and shook his head. After staring at the ground for a few seconds, he looked back at me.

"I'm gonna kill him."

"No you're not," I shot back sternly. "Not just because you couldn't — and *believe* me, you couldn't — but because I'm your sister and you love me and you owe me at least the chance to explain things."

Tyler's expression was a mixture of shock, indignation, and pure outright disbelief. I started walking again, and this time I took his hand and brought him with me.

Here we go...

We walked for a very long time, all the way to the back of the property and along the cracked picket fence. Step by step I explained everything, from posing as Jace's wife as a favor to our friend, to the trip to Hawaii, and all that happened beyond. I tried conveying how easy it was to fall in love. Not just with Jace, but with the two other incredible men Tyler didn't even know yet.

I talked about honor, respect, brotherhood. That part was harder to sell, because not even I knew the full scope of the inseparable connection between Jace, Merrick, and Aurelius. But I did my best to explain. I pleaded with Tyler to open his heart if not his mind, and try to understand what it was like for me.

In the end I finished with how happy I was, and that was something my brother could plainly see. Historically, Tyler and I kept no secrets. As siblings we had our own connection, and each of us generally knew when the other was bullshitting. If he took anything away from this at all, it was that I was wholly and unbelievably happy. Happy in Colorado, happy with work. And of course, happy with this incredibly loving although admittedly unorthodox relationship.

"I just... I just can't *see* it," he said at last. "I mean Dakota, there's *three* of them!"

"I know," I agreed. "That freaked me out too. At first, anyway."

"But—"

"Remember that summer you were dating two girls? And neither of them knew of the other?"

He nodded guiltily. "Anna and Suzanne."

"Yeah, them."

My brother let out a low whistle. "That was one hell of a summer."

"It was, wasn't it?" I agreed. "But did you set out to date two women? Did you go into that whole thing thinking, 'I want two girlfriends at once?'"

The wind blew a lock of hair into Tyler's eyes. He tucked it back and shook his head.

"No, of course not."

"It just sort of happened, right?"

"Yes."

"And why did it end?" I asked. "What broke it up? It was because you felt guilty, right?"

Tyler pursed his lips. He knew what I was driving at.

"No, my dear brother. It ended because the holidays were coming and you couldn't be in two places at once. You couldn't get away with going over to both girlfriend's houses, meeting both families, and all that. So you dumped one, and you went with the other. Right?"

He looked bitter now, almost angry. But there was admission in his expression too.

"Yeah. That's right."

"Now let me ask you this," I posed. "What would you have done if both these girls knew about each other and agreed to split time with you? Or better yet, just share you together?"

I let him stand there, going over the scenario in his mind. His face remained impassive. For a long time, he didn't say anything.

"Let me answer the question for you," I said. "You would've rolled with it. You would've loved it, enjoyed it,

275

took it for what it was."

He knew I was right. It was in his eyes, his expression, his whole body language.

"I was young," he shrugged eventually.

"Yeah, so what?" I countered. "Tyler, this is *me*. This is my situation. Only these men not only know about each other, and they're closer in ways that even brothers couldn't fathom."

I stepped directly in front of him, until our eyes locked. I could see the struggle. But beyond the struggle, there was also truth.

"I'm not going to pretend anymore, Tyler. This is what I have. This is what I *want.*"

"But our parents..." he pleaded.

"Are going to have to deal with it, eventually," I said, shaking my head. "Everyone lives their own lives, Tyler. Everyone has their own triumphs and failures, everyone makes their own personal mistakes. Maybe this one's mine. If so, I have every right to make it."

I took his hand again, squeezing it gently.

"I don't expect you to understand," I murmured. "And you have every right to feel however you want. You can be disappointed with me, or with Jace, or with both. You can even disown me if you want—"

"I would never do that," he interjected, shaking his head. "Never."

"But I had to come clean with you," I went on. "I couldn't keep lying to my brother. I never wanted to in the first place."

"Yeah, well you also got caught," he pointed out.

"Sort of," I smiled. "Maybe..."

He tilted his head, but at least he was returning my smile.

"Okay fine, I did get caught," I admitted. "But I'm glad I did. I'm so happy we got this out in the open."

The wind picked up again, bringing a late afternoon chill along with it. Tyler turned his back against it, shielding me with his body.

"Dakota... Dakota..." he sighed. He set his hands on his hips and shook his head. "Holy fucking shit, sis."

"I know," was all I could say.

"This is crazy," he breathed. "You know that, right?"

I chuckled. "Yeah."

"And you're aware that our parents will probably—"

"I know, I know," I cut him off. "You don't have to say it."

I stepped even closer, slipping my arms past his ribs for a big, brotherly hug. It felt so good, squeezing him tightly. So much better now that there was nothing between us.

"So you don't think I could kick Jace's ass, huh?"

"You'd give him a run, maybe," I lied. "But—"

"Because when we get back to the house, he's going to expect me to."

I raised an eyebrow. "And will you?"

"There might be a tackle," my brother admitted. "A few headlocks, maybe."

"*Tyler!*" I growled

In the end, my brother let out a long, deep laugh.

"We'll see what happens. No guarantees." His smirk faded a little. "Well, one guarantee anyway."

"And what's that?"

"You're gonna have to blackmail me to keep this from mom and dad."

My brother suddenly looked very pleased with himself — probably because we'd been blackmailing each other back and forth since we were kids. I punched him in the arm.

"Alright," I conceded. "What's it going to cost me *this* time?"

My big brother looked down at me, then scratched his chin and smiled.

"Don't worry. I'll think of something."

Epilogue

DAKOTA

"*Another* one?"

My reaction was one of pleasant surprise, in response to another cork being pulled from yet another bottle. Aurelius swept my glass away. He returned it three-quarters the way full with a delicious, blood-red merlot.

"I thought you guys were going fishing in the morning?"

"We are," said Jace, to the sound of more pouring.

"Not if we keep drinking like this," I laughed.

We were relaxing in a set of Adirondack chairs, at the edge of a wide, long-reaching dock. The house behind us didn't belong to us, but it was ours for the week. A beautiful lodge-like rental on Evergreen Lake.

"You don't worry about us," Merrick told me. "We'll be up, even if you aren't."

"I won't be," I warned.

"Well you're on vacation my pretty, pretty princess," smiled Aurelius. "Feel free to sleep as late as you want."

I let out a happy sigh, just thinking about how amazing it would be. I couldn't remember the last time I woke up naturally, instead of to an alarm clock.

"What about breakfast?" I asked.

"We'll take care of that," said Jace. "You just have hot coffee ready."

My smile widened as I stared out over the darkening surface of the lake. I'd gotten so used to our schedule at home. To waking up at the crack of dawn to feed the chickens and collect their eggs. I'd learned how to ride too, and there was nothing more satisfying than exploring the length and breadth of the beautiful, rolling hills that made up our property.

Two strong arms slid over my shoulders from behind. They settled against my chest, just as a pair of lips found their way to my neck...

Well, *almost* nothing.

"Can I get you something, baby?"

Jace's words were warm and welcoming, his breath hot against my ear. He kissed me some more, right at the nape of my neck, and my whole body erupted in goosebumps.

"Well let's see," I murmured. "Breakfast in bed, lunch on the water." I counted on my fingers as my mind fondly went over the events of the day. "Flowers. Champagne. A spa treatment..."

I slid my hands upward, interlacing my fingers with his. "Haven't you done enough for me today?" I chuckled.

"Shit, she's right," Merrick laughed. "No more for her."

I put on my best mock-wounded face and looked to Aurelius. My beautiful Greek god was always my go-to. The one lover who would always back me, no matter what.

"I hate to say it, but they're right," Aurelius smiled, causing me to open my mouth in shock. He tipped his glass and took a long sip of wine. "Maybe you should be doing stuff for *us,* tonight."

I glanced back to where the lights in the house were glowing warmly. Not even an hour ago, the sun had set spectacularly behind the mountains. The purples and indigos were so deep, making the sky so saturated, it looked like a painting instead of real life.

"It's getting pretty late," I said. "We were supposed to have gone to dinner by now. But if you boys would rather stay in..."

I shifted in my seat, letting my sundress ride even higher up on my thighs. Three pairs of eyes made their way over the newly-exposed skin.

"Well... I'm pretty sure we could find *something* to eat."

I savored their new expressions, laughing inwardly at how quickly and easily I could control the narrative when I wanted to. Yet I couldn't deny it; the boys often did the same to me. They knew how to damn near hypnotize me by walking around the house with their shirts off, or their boxers pulled down just a little too far in front. Those 'V'-shaped muscles just below their rippled stomachs always drew me downward, quite often to my knees. I'd ravaged each of them at the drop of a hat, or a pair of underwear, as the case may be.

And my *God*. I couldn't even begin to count the number of times they'd thrown me over their shoulders and carried me off, despoiling me together and alone in every room of our beautiful home. Stretching me out across every soft bed, and every available surface.

In two whole years of being together, there had never been a dull moment.

"Is that what you want?" asked Merrick. "To stay in tonight?"

He set down his glass, and so did Aurelius. Such movements might've seemed planned ahead or orchestrated, but these were men who'd grown accustomed to moving together. Both on the battlefield and off.

"Sure," I shrugged. "No need to go anywhere, let's order in. Let's just—"

The rest of my words were lost as Jace's mouth closed over mine. He began kissing me slowly, deeply, his tongue rolling delicately around mine as I spent my last breath whimpering into his hot, gorgeous mouth.

Or we could do this... I laughed inside my own head.

My hands went to his upper arms as Jace lifted me to my feet. As always his muscles felt like steel, his biceps and triceps coiling just beneath his warm, unblemished skin as he held me weightless. He made out with me in full view of the others, which was standard procedure in our relationship. It always made me hotter than hell, knowing the others were watching, awaiting their turns with me.

And of course it made them *harder* than hell, too.

Eventually Jace set me down, depositing me in the center of the dock on two shaky feet. I was still reeling from all the kissing. My body was trembling too, but that had nothing to do with being cold.

"You know I've wanted you since we were young, all the way back in Minnesota," he said, his eyes finding mine. "But I didn't realize how much I needed you, until I saw you wearing *this.*"

He tapped my hand, or rather, my finger. When I looked down, I was wearing one of our 'wedding' rings.

The diamond engagement one.

"I love this damned thing," I smiled up at him. "You know that. It made me feel special the whole time I was your wife."

"Oh, I know," he agreed.

"I mean sometimes I even put it on just for nostalgia." I held my hand out. "I mean, look at it. It's beautiful. Symbolic. It reminds me of—"

I never finished my sentence, and that's because Merrick took me next. I swooned as his hands found my hips. His mouth opened mine with a series of slow, smoldering kisses that had me melting into his arms.

My God...

Over and over he kissed me, until I was so woozy I

could barely stand. He was holding my body against his now. The heat inside me rose, as our hearts beat as one.

"We tend to overdo everything," he murmured softly. "Always have. So why not this?"

With that he took my hand, and spread it across his open palm. Before I knew what was happening, he used the other hand to slip a second ring on my finger.

It was another engagement ring, identical to the first one.

"A woman who can handle three men can handle three rings," Merrick murmured softly. "Right?"

Aurelius stepped in, taking my hand from his. He slid another ring on my finger, and in that moment all three diamonds caught the budding moonlight.

"I'm pretty sure he's right," Aurelius smiled, and took over kissing me.

I gasped into his mouth, suddenly realizing what was happening. And then I was crying. Crying and kissing him and looking over his hard shoulder at my bejeweled finger, where three very distinct matching engagement rings clicked against one another.

"They're all real this time," Jace whispered softly. "I had the first one made to look exactly like the one you wore in Hawaii."

"And we had the others made to match," Aurelius told me, placing his forehead against mine. He kissed me again, drinking deeply from my lips. His grin was euphoric. His eyes, glassy.

"You need to marry us for *real*, Dakota," he said. "All three of us. And do you know why?"

I was crying, almost bawling. But they were tears of joy.

"Why? I sniffed.

"Because we can't even begin to imagine what our lives would be like without you."

I was in a state of shock, but also a state of emotional rapture. Everywhere I moved one of them was kissing me, hugging me. Sometimes even spinning me around, before another one took me.

Eventually I stared upward, into what would soon be a star-flecked sky. Right now though, I didn't want anything to do with the stars, or the dock, or the water, or dinner...

Or anything other than our vacation bed.

"Take me inside," I whispered, still in tears. "I need all three of you..."

As if to punctuate the statement I began kissing them fiercely, swirling my tongue through their hot mouths with ten times as much heat. Eventually, I heard one of them chuckle.

"No one's going anywhere until you give us our answer."

I held my hand out as far as I could. It was difficult to see how beautiful my rings looked because of all the tears in my eyes.

"YES!" I practically shouted. "Yes, yes, and YES!"

With that my feet left the floor — or rather, the dock

— and I was carried quickly and efficiently back into the house. With my sundress still bouncing about my legs, I gasped again in yet another level of shock and awe.

"Oh my *God!*"

The house was glowing warmly for a stunningly simple reason: one or more of the guys had snuck back and lit about a hundred candles.

"This is..."

"Too much?" asked Merrick. He pointed to the floor, which was littered in pink and white rose petals. A trail of them led upward, all along the staircase and onto the second floor landing.

"You don't know *anything* about too much," Merrick grinned.

Before I could open my mouth again I was carried upstairs, pinned against Jace's beautiful chest by his two strong arms. Aurelius and Merrick were right behind us, their expressions full of happiness and excitement, but also all new levels of lust.

Within moments we crossed the threshold into the candlelit master bedroom, where I was laid gently down — amidst a sea of red rose petals — into the center of the king-sized bed. The room itself smelled warm and rich and delicious. The scent was so incredibly familiar too, yet I couldn't put my finger on it.

This is unbelievable.

My mind kept repeating the phrase over and over like a mantra, as they took turns undressing me. In just seconds I was down to nothing more than a cute pink G-string.

I can't believe this is really happening...

We'd talked about our future together, of course. About marriage, and children, and being husbands and wife. Until now though, it was all talk, all fantasy. These were nothing more than good intentions we could just keep on putting off, kicking the can down the line.

Until *now.*

I swallowed hard, realizing the ramifications of this moment. They wanted to *marry* me. All of them.

Jace and Aurelius and Merrick wanted to make me their *real,* actual wife.

Yes please.

And I would make all three of them my loving husbands.

Oh, God YES.

The idea didn't just excite me, it thrilled me to near hysteria. It was like a dream, really. An incredible, amazing dream, where I had to remind myself to keep breathing.

"Well?" I said, when I finally managed to speak.

"Well what?" Jace offered.

"Are you just going to stand around the bed like spectators," I teased, "or are you going to strip down and show your new fiancée a good time?"

Aurelius was the first to step out of his shorts. He dropped his boxers too, and his long shaft sprang forth, swinging through the air like a sword blade.

"Now we're talking," I grinned.

I reached out for it, but a hand stopped me. Another hand grabbed my other wrist, and before I knew it I was face down on my stomach.

"So it's going to be like this, is it?" I chuckled.

We'd had nights like these before — nights where the boys tied my wrists or ankles — or even both — to the far corners of the bed. They were sizzling hot nights, too. Fun nights...

"It's not what you're thinking," said Jace. "Although what you're thinking might be fun also."

My pussy throbbed beneath me. My G-string was already soaked through. I strained to look over my shoulder, just in time to see some kind of glass bottle being lifted from a strange-looking device on the corner of the nighttable.

"What the—"

"It's a warming machine," said Merrick. "Trust us, you're gonna love this."

It was my all-time favorite of their many mantras: *trust us, you're gonna love this.* And I always trusted them. And I always loved it.

Still, I couldn't help but glance back over my shoulder as the bottle was tipped downward over my naked ass. A clear, glycerin-like stream poured outward in a razor—thin line, dribbling hotly over first one cheek, then the other.

"Coconut oil?" I purred, squirming into the mattress. I felt almost silly, not recognizing the scent before now. "You're going to pamper me some *more?*"

"We've pampered you all day," said Aurelius. "Haven't you caught on yet?"

The stream continued, dripping onto my lower back, my upper back, my shoulders. They dragged the stream back again, like a soothing waterfall of warm honey. Over my ass, down my thighs. *Between* my thighs...

Mmmmm. Wow.

It was liquid heat, but it was more than that, too. It was pure, unfiltered arousal. Total surrender. I sighed happily, relaxing even further as the boys continued splashing my body with what felt like a whole river of hot massage oil. The more they poured, the deeper I was thrust into absolute heaven.

Then they dripped it down my ass-crack and over my G-string... and I was somewhere else entirely.

"Ohhhhhhh...."

Six hands fell to my body at once, all of them diving through the pools of melted coconut oil. Thirty fingertips traced my skin in places that made me shiver, massaging even more heat into my quivering muscles.

Holy.

FUCK.

Their oil-soaked palms glided up and down my body, all the way from the nape of my neck to the soles of my tired feet. The silky pleasure they conveyed was almost overwhelming, to the point of losing consciousness.

Stay awake!

There was no way I was missing out on any of this.

No way I was losing even a single second to something as ridiculous as sleep, as three of my five senses threatened to be gloriously overwhelmed.

They rubbed and massaged at first, their efforts dedicated solely to loosening me up. I loved the way they kneaded my lower back, my hamstrings, my calves. As good as that was though, it paled in comparison to getting both feet rubbed at once. That seemingly simple little act, which brought tears to my eyes, was truly a religious experience.

After that though, things got wicked.

I twitched in anticipation as one of them stretched my G-string off to one side, then outright jumped as an oil-soaked thumb glided over my tight little asshole. More fingers began kneading the insides of my thighs, working their way upward. They grazed over my tender entrance, rubbing warm coconut oil into places that were already wet, already dripping.

Mmmm.

All three of them knelt beside me now, working the same beautiful area. I felt my cheeks being spread apart, followed by a pair of thick fingers gliding all the way inside me...

MMmmMMmmMMmm...

Nothing felt even close to the sensations overwhelming my brain. I was totally theirs now. Prone and exposed and ready for anything they wanted to do to me. My submission was voluntary and total and indescribably thrilling; made even more so by the fact I wasn't just their lover or girlfriend, I was now their fiancée.

Soon to be their *wife*.

The fingers inside me began thrusting, moving in and out in deep, satisfying ways that rocked me to my very core. And then, even easier than I could imagine, another long finger went straight up my ass. It felt equally wonderful, thrusting and moving on a completely different rhythm. Pushing and pulling through my oil-soaked channel, causing me to gasp into the face of whoever was about to kiss me.

Jace.

His lips covered mine, and together we shared a long, beautiful moment. A kiss so deep and wonderful, so profoundly heartfelt, it was as if we'd always been together, always been in love.

I moaned again as Jace spread out on his knees, feeding me the very head of his long, oil-coated shaft. Of course it tasted like coconut. The oil was everywhere now; the bedspread, the pillows, and on all three men as well. It glistened upon their naked bodies. It glistened brilliantly in the candlelight, as they'd apparently oiled their own skin every bit as much as they'd oiled me.

Whoa. Look at him!

Coated in pools of luscious oil, Jace's muscles stood out in stark, beautiful relief against the rest of his physique. Bracing one hand against his quivering stomach, I rose up on my elbows and took him deep down my throat.

"Mmmppffhh..."

The taste was strange but wonderful. The added slickness made everything slide *that* much deeper.

The boys surrounded me now, penetrating me in all

three holes. Pushing into me from three sides, three places. Making me their own sexy little pincushion. To say I loved it wouldn't do justice to the word. I felt incredible, invincible. Totally and deliciously dominated, yet still oddly powerful in ways I couldn't begin to explain.

I couldn't even imagine being more turned on, but then it happened anyway. It occurred as Merrick somehow slid himself beneath me, our two oil-soaked bodies gliding all over each other until we were stacked like pancakes. It happened again as he grabbed my hips and guided himself inside me, drilling me hard from within while my slick breasts squished noisily against his broad, beautiful chest.

OhmyGod.

I was fucking him. Sucking Jace. Reveling in the feel of their hands reaching and grabbing and exploring every inch of my glistening flesh they could possibly reach, while Aurelius kept sawing one long finger in and out of the place that was even tighter than all the rest.

OhmyGodohmyGodohmy–

And then it wasn't a finger any longer. It was *him.* The ripped SEAL was kneeling behind me, pushing his way past the very last of my resolve. He entered me with a wet 'pop' and rush of movement, filling my backside with the entire length of his granite-like thickness. I should've screamed. I should've cried out...

Instead I let out a moan that was half delirious laughter, half gratification. I was happy to accommodate them and glad to be done. And absolutely, positively thrilled to be *this. Fucking. FULL.*

"Mmmmm, *YES...*"

The guys held me there for a few long seconds, freezing the moment in time. It was the first time we'd all be connected like this. The first time I'd had all three of them inside me, in a way that felt like total, unequivocal completion.

"Yes..." I murmured again around Jace's thickness, while shifting my hips to test the waters. I glided upward on Merrick. Back on Aurelius. I tightened my lips, moving them up and down Jace with every new bob of my eager head.

"I love you," I moaned again. "I love you. I love you..."

Merrick surged inside me, pinning himself deep. At the same time Aurelius pushed forward, and I actually saw stars.

"And I love *this*," I clarified, totally drowning in the moment. My voice was thick with lust. My mind, swimming in rapture. "Oh GOD, I love THIS."

Again and again they surged into me, pumping me full of their warmth and heat and love. I took them gladly, happily, accepting them into my body, my very soul...

Ohhhhhh...

I was their missing link, the last piece of their puzzle. And they were mine. These men had always known a woman like me would complete them. On the flip side of that coin, I never could've imagined how much I actually needed something like this. Not until it came into my life, changing it forever.

My body was on fire now, awash with the flame of total and complete exaltation. The oil made everything slippery, almost to the point of being dangerous! But my lovers held on, holding me tight. Pinning me perfectly between them in a triangle of raw sex and gyrating, carnal heat. Over and over they penetrated my body, their coiled arms flexing tighter as they gripped me with greater force, more intensity...

"FUUUUCK!"

Jace came first, erupting down my throat with a ferocity I never knew he possessed. I took it all, still whimpering and moaning and thrusting backward against the others as I tasted his deliciousness.

God, I LOVE him...

The sheer physicality of the act was humbling; I took each warm surge deep into my belly, eagerly devouring every drop of this man I loved so very fucking much. His hands were on the back of my head now. The cry of ecstasy torn from his chest was primal and powerful, but there was still care and tenderness in the way he gripped me, despite the savagery of his climax.

Jace.

My fiancé.

We'd shared many moments together in the past two years, and more in the decade before that. But this one would always be special. We'd gone from friends to lovers. From lovers to boyfriend and girlfriend, and now, even beyond.

To know that we'd actually be married was something that emotionally blew me away. It was something I told myself I couldn't have hoped or even dreamed about all those many years ago. But then again, was that really true? Was it possible I'd loved this man all along?

VERY possible.

Jace finished, then staggered away as I continued riding the others. His eyes met mine, and we broke into a pair of grins. Along with the normal arousal that came with watching me in action, I saw all new levels of adoration in his expression, too.

I love him so much.

My own climax had been building slowly, and up until now I'd been keeping it down. It was hard to let go completely with Jace still in front of me, and focusing on his pleasure had distracted me somewhat from my own.

But now...

Right now I was free to screw my other two lovers into oblivion. To set my hands down on Merrick's hard chest and ride his thickness to an orgasm of my own, with Aurelius buried gloriously to the hilt, so incredibly deep in my ass.

And so I did.

"Awww, fuck."

Merrick felt it first; the pressure of my insides, bearing down on him. I squeezed him from within, making it even tighter and wetter than it already was. Swallowing him internally, through the magic of kegel muscles and the friction of my own back and forth movement.

"You're going to make me—"

"I know," I growled, leaning low so that my lips were against his ear. I chuckled evilly. "That's the goal, actually."

Aurelius adjusted for my lower position by rising up on one knee. With more control he drove into me even further from that angle, double-penetrating me faster and harder now that Jace was no longer in the picture.

"I'm close," I whispered out loud, to anyone who might be listening. "So close. So fucking close..."

My breath quickened until I was actually panting. My heart felt like it would pound right out of my chest! But I never slowed down, never stopped fucking them. I kept giving it back every bit as good as they were laying into me, and *then* some. And right now, they were laying into me pretty hard.

"Merrick—"

He knew what I wanted before I even asked for it. His hands slid to my breasts, cupping them perfectly. Squeezing them just hard enough to drive me over the edge, but not hard enough to cause any pain.

Then he rolled his thumbs over my oil-slicked nipples... and the lower half of my body went off like a nuclear explosion.

"UNNNGHHHHHH!"

I came like a thunderclap, erupting around Merrick's thick shaft. In response, he began pulsing with a release all his own. He grunted and growled, thrashing beneath me as I rode out his own orgasm and added that pleasure to mine. Our combined excitement made things exponentially more explosive and infinitely more hot, as we could feel one another's throbbing, one another's wetness, and one another's total, wanton release.

"Awwww, *hell*."

Aurelius — no longer able to stand the tightness of my ass — was the last to lose control, but his climax was maybe the most impressive of all. He gripped my hips with vice-like hands as he came and came, filling my ass with his cream. Screwing me so hard and fast that I probably wouldn't be able to sit down later on, much less tomorrow or even the entire weekend.

Jaw clenched, teeth gritted, I took it anyway. I took it because it pleased him, sure, but I also took it because I enjoyed the raw ferocity of being so thoroughly and completely railed from behind, in such a way that I would never, ever forget.

Glancing back into the sweaty face of post-orgasmic bliss, I knew that I was his. That I was *theirs*.

All of them, always.

Forever.

We fell limply into the ruins of the oil-soaked bedding, chests heaving, our legs tangled in a confused, trembling heap. The whole act had been ridiculously hot, incredibly naughty. All that was missing was a mirrored ceiling, so the four of us could gaze up afterward, at our own handiwork.

The thought made me chuckle. I was surprised they hadn't thought of that, too.

"Sooo..." I said when I could breathe again. "When's the wedding?"

Laughter. Smiles. Someone reached out and spanked my ass with a loud, perfect 'SLAP'.

"And the kids?" I continued smartly. "How many did we say again?"

"Four," Merrick answered.

"No, six," Jace stepped in. "At the very least."

"SIX?" I laughed some more.

"Yeah, what's wrong with six?" Aurelius challenged. "Six is a full, round number. Six kids is nice."

"Six kids is a cataclysm," I giggled. "A trip to the asylum! And who's having all of these children? Because it's damn sure not going to be—"

I was grabbed, rolled over, tickled — all in one motion. When I got done laughing, they were all hovering over me.

"Fine, three children," I allowed. "Maybe four, if you boys are lucky."

They tickled me again. I laughed and cried until I could barely breathe, then waved them off with two flailing arms.

"Alright then, FIVE," I coughed. "Final offer!"

I could see the love in their eyes. Sense the warmth of genuine adulation in their swollen hearts. I knew deep inside that I'd give these men a *dozen* children, if that's what they truly wanted. Not just because I'd give them anything, which I would. But because a huge, happy family was what *I* wanted, too.

"Let's see how you all perform during the honeymoon," I teased. "And we'll revisit the topic then." I sat up and my stomach growled, reminding me I still hadn't eaten. Not food, anyway.

"Right now," I said, "I need two things."

"Is one of them pizza?" Aurelius offered hopefully.

My belly tingled. "Actually, yes."

My gorgeous Greek warrior grinned, folding his arms in satisfaction. For a split-second I imagined our children, all shaggy dark hair and bright beautiful smiles. My heart soared.

"And the other thing?" Merrick asked, as I bounced from the bed.

Standing up, I held my still-dripping arms out and chuckled.

"A whole *stack* of towels!"

Wanna read the ULTRA-HEA, sugary-sweet,

super-sexy, flash-forward

BONUS EPILOGUE?

Of course you do!

TAP RIGHT HERE TO SIGN UP!

Or enter this link into your browser:

https://mailchi.mp/kristawolfbooks.com/bonus-epilogue-swsf

to have it INSTANTLY delivered to your inbox.

Need *more* Reverse Harem?

Thanks for checking out *Secret Wife to the Special Forces*. Here's hoping it rocked your socks off!

And for even *more* sweltering reverse harem heat? Check out: <u>The Switching Hour</u>. Below you'll find a preview of the sexy, sizzling cover, plus the first several chapters so you can see for yourself:

The
Switching
HOUR
A Halloween Reverse Harem Romance

Krista Wolf

AMAZON AWARD-WINNING AUTHOR

Chapter One

SILVANA

They say that every second you dwell on the past is a second you're stealing from your future. Slick, right? I don't know how true that is, or even who "they" are. But it was this questionably deep quote — scrawled across the front of a dirty garbage can at the end of a Miami Beach street — that finally broke the camel's back for me.

That stupid little quote sent me home to pack my things. It flung me two full days and sixteen-hundred miles northward, in a tired old car that was already protesting to begin with.

And now here I was, driving to a house I'd never seen, built by a great-grandfather I'd never met. Rolling past midnight through a state so far north I'd never even dreamt of visiting, toward a town so small that zooming into it from Google maps had me laughing my ass off.

I turned the wheel again, growling as the streets grew even darker. Shaking my head with the outrageousness of it all.

I could've stayed. I could've tried to make it work in my shitty little apartment at the ass end of Overtown. On a whim though, I'd made a command decision: that I'd rather try making it in some *other* shitty place, in some *other* shitty town.

Why? Because to hell with the past. My past sucked so much I'd rather drag the future out to the nearest bar and start doing shots with it. Even if in the end, all it wanted to do was fuck me.

Not that I couldn't use a good—

The road — if you could still call it that — suddenly opened left, and there it was: a tiny overgrown trail that could be construed as a driveway. Two strips of dirty gravel overgrown with weeds in the middle.

"No way."

It looked like it hadn't been used in decades. Maybe more.

"No fucking way."

I rolled to a stop. My phone still blinked with the same alert: ARRIVED AT YOUR DESTINATION. The cold rain had finally let up enough to see without windshield wipers, which was good because I only had half a wiper-blade left on the driver's side, and none on the passenger's.

You should just turn around.

I laughed, and my laughter quickly turned hysterical. Imagine that? Coming all this way and just turning around? I could chalk it up to one of the craziest things I'd ever done, and that list wasn't exactly insubstantial.

But for once, I wasn't here for crazy.

"Alright gramps," I grumbled. "Let's see what you got."

I clicked on my turn signal — an action that made me laugh even harder — and rolled slowly up the shadowy driveway. The crunch of gravel beneath my tires was accompanied by the scraping of overhanging branches, from trees that hadn't been pruned since Elvis was alive. The twin path stretched on and on, and for much longer than I expected. When you lived your whole life in a big city as I had, you had no true conception of what owning property was even like.

The letter from the lawyer had arrived half a year ago. It shocked me enough that I even *had* a great-grandfather, but to learn he'd actually known about me in the end was even more of a surprise. Apparently he'd used the last of his money to search for heirs, and in his final days had willed everything he owned to me.

Since the man died penniless in his Oregon rental trailer, that really didn't amount to much. But it turns out he *did* own a big old house in New Hampshire. A house he'd supposedly built with his own two hands, nearly eighty years ago.

I'd signed my name to the deed last spring, sight unseen. The only image I had of the house came from a single black-and-white photo, found at the bottom of the old cigar box the lawyer shipped down to me. In it, my great-grandfather was grinning from ear to ear. He stood proudly in front of the beautiful Victorian, hugging a pretty young woman that could only be my great-grandmother.

My thoughts were mixed at the time. I was thrilled to know I had another relative, yet somewhat angry I'd never known about him until it was too late. Maybe my great-grandfather even felt the same about me. I'd never know.

But the house...

In my spinning, conflicting mind, the house eventually became my savior. My Hail Mary pass. My ticket out of the ruins and rubble of Miami, because after what I'd gone through, there certainly were ruins.

Something large and dark finally faded into view, and I guided the headlights straight onto it. I killed the engine, cracked the door, and swung my cramped legs onto the gravel. By the time I'd pulled myself into a standing position, my jaw was already on its way to the ground.

The house was a complete and total *wreck*. A broken, ruined shell of its former self, it jutted three stories into the air and loomed high over me like some ugly, angry demon.

"Oh, for fuck's sake."

It was well past midnight now, on a moonless, cloudless night. Only the spectral glow of my car's headlamps illuminated the hulking, ghostly form of the old Victorian, just enough that I could see my way up the decrepit steps and to the front door.

Any other person would've run screaming, possibly even in terror. But I didn't have time for screaming. I was a woman down to zero fucks, zero choices, and her last eighth of a tank of gas.

Setting my hands on my hips, I let out an exhausted

sigh.

"Home sweet home."

Two

SILVANA

Six straight hours. That's how long I scrubbed the place. That's how long it took to put even the slightest dent in the stench of mold and mildew, and give the first few rooms a nice, lemony, bleach-tinged scent... over the smell of *more* mold and mildew.

But I didn't care. I'd never owned anything substantial before, and this was my place now. The idea of being a homeowner felt outright bizarre — stranger than anything I'd felt before — but it also came with a certain pride of ownership that I was really enjoying.

I did the important rooms first: the kitchen, the living room, the *other* living room... plus whatever that round, turret room was that contained that amazing, curved wooden staircase. I had no idea about the place, really. Everything was incredibly old, and the doorways unusually narrow. But the house was huge on the inside, even cavernous. The once beautifully-paneled rooms gave way to each other with multiple entrances and exits, like some sort of weird, messed-up maze.

Bit by bit, the dirt and grime was stripped away beneath my furious onslaught. Growing up as a foster kid, the one thing I really learned was how to clean. I'd always been meticulous about whatever little spaces I'd been lent or given, and that was paying off in spades now. And while some things were so old they disintegrated the moment I touched them, the more basic parts of the old Victorian were still proud and strong.

In short, the house had good bones. Maybe the porch was a rotting mess and the railings were failing away, but the front door was as solid as the day my great-grandfather hung it. The plaster and lath walls remained strong and unbent. The planked oaken floors creaked beneath my feet, but there were no holes, and no soft spots.

I'd opened the windows just after getting started, and now the light of dawn was filtering in. I stuck my head out from time to time, reveling in the fresh, sweet pine scent of the forest that surrounded this place on all sides.

Where I was from, the waning days of September were no different than the rest of the summer. They were an extension of light and heat and warmth.

Not up here, though.

In this place it was already cold. There was a snap to the air; a sharp chill that numbed your skin and bit at your lungs whenever you breathed in too quickly. The air had a taste to it, too. The flavor of something crisp and strange and autumn-tasting.

I kinda liked it.

I heard the vehicle before I actually saw it. The low thrum of its engine seemed like an interloper after all my solitude. I continued cleaning through the sound of a car door swinging open and shut, and the heavy sound of boots thumping up the outside steps and across the porch.

My porch.

The front door was open. I didn't even turn around as the footfalls indicated my visitor had stepped inside.

"I figured it wouldn't be long until you showed up."

The man was stout, short, and overweight, with large brown boots and a belt that disappeared beneath the overhang of his belly. His beige-colored uniform seemed stretched tight in several uncomfortable-looking places as he shifted from one leg to the other.

"Did you catch me on the way in?" I asked him. "Because there's no way you saw my car from the street."

The sheriff shook his head and grunted.

"A deputy saw you drive through town last night. He followed you through to the other side, then said you disappeared down this road."

I nodded, dropping my sponge into the latest bucket of my shit-brown bleach mixture. Then I wiped my hands on my 'clean' rag.

"Didn't take long to drive through town," I replied glibly. "I could throw a rock from one side to the other."

The man grunted again. "Maybe see that you don't."

I watched as he reached behind himself and pulled out a large, oldschool clipboard. On top of the clipboard was

312

something else: an IPad, or some other sort of generic electronic tablet.

Ah, crap.

My face contorted bitterly as I leaned back against the counter and crossed my arms. The man's eyes were cold and unfeeling as they shifted to meet mine. Immediately I noticed that one of them was clouded over with a milky white cataract.

"Alright, Ms. Carter," he barked. "Let's see it."

I paused for an extra-long moment, just because I could. Just because it would piss him off, and I enjoyed pissing people off. Especially people like this.

Then, begrudgingly, I put one foot on the opposite counter and reached down to roll up the hem of my jeans.

Three

SILVANA

The electronic ankle monitor was sleek and black, with a green LED that blinked every eight seconds. It was fixed tightly to my ankle by a thin nylon band, just as it had been for the better part of the past eight months.

"Hmm," the Sheriff said, examining it visually. "Alright, now don't move."

He tapped his tablet a few times, punching all different things with his pudgy fingers. The LED on my anklet began blinking furiously, several times per second. After about half a minute, it finally stopped.

"Good. You're all synced up."

The man seemed satisfied as I slowly lowered my leg. He punched a few more buttons, then turned to face me again.

"By the terms of your house arrest, you're not permitted to go beyond fifty yards from this very spot," the sheriff said. "Except under the unique set of circumstances the Miami-Dade probation department has already laid out."

I crossed my arms again, letting my lips go tight. "Fifty yards?" I sneered. "C'mon sheriff, you know that's bullshit."

"Fifty yards is all you need," he said mechanically. "With that radius you can go outside, walk the grounds a little." He sniffed at the moldy, bleach-soaked air, wrinkling his nose. "Get some fresh air..."

"I have a few dozen *acres!*" I protested. "And lots of landscaping that needs to be done."

"So?"

"So fifty yards is nothing," I shot back. "Especially with all the spare time I have."

My guest stared back at me for a moment with his blue-and-white eyes. Eventually his lip curled, and he began punching buttons on the tablet again.

"Fine. I just gave you a little more breathing room."

"Thank you."

"If you reach the edge of the arrest zone," he pointed downward, "that light turns red and your ankle monitor will beep loudly. That's your warning to turn back. If it beeps for more than a minute it shoots me a message, and then you're screwed."

I nodded obediently, though I'd been wearing this thing for almost a year now. It took every ounce of my willpower not to make my best 'no-duh' face.

"If you leave the property," he continued, "or try tampering with that device? I get immediate notification on my smartphone. We'll come straight away. You'll be handcuffed in minutes."

My folded-arm silence didn't seem to be the answer he was looking for. His scowl deepened.

"I *mean* it, Ms. Carter. I won't even ask any questions, you'll just be arrested."

"Yeah, yeah," I waved him off. "Let's get on with the good stuff. Let's talk about exceptions."

Now it was his turn to pause, as he reached up to scratch at the side of his head. The sheriff had very thin, straw-like hair, probably the result of going so totally grey. But he had a lot of it for a man well into his 60's.

"Once a week you're permitted to go into town for groceries, and groceries *only*. You can also bring any trash you have to the landfill. You can also see a doctor, but you'd damned well better have an appointment first. And believe me, I'm going to check."

He reached out and handed me a business card embossed with the sheriff's office logo and a trio of phone numbers on it. I took it reflexively.

"You'll call that first number *before* you leave to go anywhere," said the Sheriff. "And I'll tell you whether or not it's okay to go."

"I have to *call* you first?" I snarled.

"Every single time."

"What if you don't answer?"

"I always answer," he shot back. "That's my personal line. It goes directly to me."

"And what if—"

"What if *nothing*, Ms. Carter!" the man snapped back. Clearly he was already fed up with me.

"But just look at this place!" I protested, waving an arm around. "Give me a free pass to the hardware store, at the very least. If I'm going to fix this place up, I'm practically going to be living there."

"Too bad. *Hire* someone."

I put on my saddest face. "I can't afford to—"

"You're under house arrest, remember?" the sheriff snarled. "This is supposed to be a punishment, not a renovation project."

My expression turned sour again quickly. He wasn't buying it. Smart man.

"I still don't know why you're here, Ms. Carter," he said suspiciously, "or how long you plan to stay in town. Just make sure you abide by my rules. I'll be stopping by to check on you often."

"Awww," I purred, giving him my most saccharine smile. "Sheriff, now that's just sweet as honey!"

"Stuff it, Ms. Carter."

He turned to leave, and I watched him go. Two steps beyond the kitchen's side doorway, his foot cracked one of the porch boards straight through. His ankle gave way and he almost rolled sideways, but caught himself just in time. Before he'd regained his balance though, I think he used every curse-word he ever knew.

"This is bullshit," he finally sneered, flexing his knee

to make sure it was okay. "You shouldn't even *be* here!"

"And why's that?"

"Because it's unsafe! This house ought to be condemned!" He sighed angrily. "Hell, I think it was condemned at one point."

"So?"

"So you don't even have a CO for this place."

"A CO?" I bit. "What's that?"

"Certificate of Occupancy." He glanced upward, probably at the sagging roof that overhung the porch some thirty feet up. "The inspector would have a field day here. You should probably just rent a room in town, while you wait."

I approached the doorway, then leaned out a little ways. I pretended to look at the same thing he was.

"You want me to live in one of those creepy motels I saw on the way in, until I can get this place fixed up?" I laughed heartily. "By then I'll be fifty!"

"Not my problem."

Our eyes locked, in a test of wills. I tried my best not to stare too hard at the white milky one.

"Sheriff, are you saying I can't live in the house that my beloved great-grandfather built with his own two hands?"

He shook his head slowly. "Not until it passes inspection, no."

I laughed again, just before slamming the door in his face.

"*Watch* me."

Four

SILVANA

It probably wasn't the best idea, slamming the door in the Sheriff's face. Especially since his rolled ankle was likely to swell to the size of a softball over the next few days, and that meant I'd be constantly on his mind.

No, that was just one more wrong move in a long series of bad choices I'd been making lately. Only this was the first one I'd actually made here, at the site of my all new beginnings. And that part sucked.

Instead I spent the rest of the day knocking a half-century of dust off the bottom floor of the house, and scrubbing it clean. It was daunting work. Tackling the tiny bathroom off the entry hall had almost made me physically ill, but being the only toilet I'd found so far, it had to be done.

By noon I'd cleared enough space to make the first floor livable, or at least half of it. Even so, I already had much more square footage than my largest apartment. I took an impromptu lunch in the front seat of my car; half a gas-station sandwich I'd picked up somewhere in New Jersey, washed down with warm soda and a stale bag of chips. Then I closed my eyes, just to rest them for a moment...

... and woke up cold and shivering, in pitch darkness.

Fuck.

I had one task left to do today, and it was probably the most important of all. I'd planned on doing it while it was still light outside, but now that option was shot to hell.

Gotta get it done, though.

After stretching some of the stiffness out of my tired body, I popped the hatch and rummaged through the dense pile of everything I owned in the world. My car was so full of miscellaneous crap it looked like I'd been living in it, which really wasn't that far off.

Near the bottom of the pile of clothes, boxes, and laundry baskets full of personal belongings, I found what I was looking for. So much for planning ahead.

Heaving the mother of all sighs, I gathered up everything I needed and headed upstairs.

I went slowly, despite the burden of the big canvas sack slung over my shoulder. I hadn't even been upstairs yet, but I needed to get as high as possible for what I needed to do. The ornate wooden staircase creaked beneath my weight, but it didn't shift or budge an inch. My great-grandfather was apparently one hell of a carpenter. For that I was grateful.

I passed the second floor landing where the staircase continued onward, shining the five-dollar headlamp strapped to my forehead everywhere I looked. The hallway broke off in two directions up here, both of them lined with doorways. Some of them were even open. But the floor itself...

Oh SHIT!

I stopped dead in my tracks. In both directions, the dust on the floor was broken by footprints. *Booted* footprints.

"HELLO?"

My own voice broke the stillness so abruptly it actually startled me. I panned left and right, up and down, half-afraid of what I might see. Dust swirled through the beam of my headlamp.

"Anybody up here?"

It wouldn't surprise me at all to find squatters in the house. Back in Overtown, squatting had become almost a legitimate form of residence. Rents were ridiculous in some places. People simply couldn't keep up.

The weight of my burden was dragging me down. I could explore later on maybe, but right now I had to continue.

"I'll be upstairs if anyone needs me!" I called out loudly. "Make yourself at home, there's beer in the fridge!"

There was no beer and there was no fridge. Hell, I didn't even have a bed or a bedroom picked out yet to set up in. But when you were alone and lonely, it always was fun to play around.

Upward I went, climbing into the vaulted attic on the third floor. The space was massive, spanning the entirety of the house. The dust was so thick it limited visibility to just a few feet in front of me.

"Anyone wanna help me with this?" I grumbled, shifting the weight from one shoulder to another. "It's heavy."

No answer. No footprints up here either, and that was good. I made my way south, in the direction of one of the reverse gables I'd seen from the driveway. This particular one opened out to a tiny, railed balcony with a pair of broken spindles. The door granting access had long ago been twisted backward on its hinges.

There we go.

I stepped through the opening, testing the balcony's rotten boards with one foot first, then the other. Satisfied, I climbed over the railing and onto the precariously sloped roof just outside. Being careful the whole time not to look down.

It was pitch black and moonless again, but now the wind had picked up. I could hear the sound of leaves rustling as the trees swayed. The canopy was a mass of shifting shadows, just above me.

"This is nuts."

Saying it out loud didn't make it any less crazier, but I continued unpacking the bag anyway. The metal bars of the tripod went together easily enough. In no time I had them positioned against the roof's moss-covered tiles, as best I could considering the angle I was working with.

Bracing my feet for maximum leverage, I grabbed the .22 caliber Ramset tool and loaded it with a half-dozen drive pins. Then I started blasting.

"OOOHH!"

The first pin I fired into the anchor hole on the tripod blew me backward a couple of inches, but a couple of inches was all it took. I was slipping. *Sliding.* Pain flared on my hands and forearms as I scratched for a handhold on something, anything, but it was just too late. Gravity already had me. It pulled me downward, faster and faster, moving me inexorably closer to the edge of the roof.

Tiles slid free. Rotten pieces of ancient plywood disintegrated beneath my scrabbling fingers, as I flipped backward and hurtled helplessly over the edge.

"HANG ON!"

And then I was falling... falling through the crisp, night air. The beam of my headlamp swept wildly across the trees as I winced hard, waiting for the excruciating pain of my inevitable impact.

Five

CYRUS

"HANG ON!"

By the time I got the words out, it was already way too late. Thank God she flipped backward before going over though, because it gave me that one extra second. Just enough time for that one last step, which positioned my body more or less perfectly beneath hers.

"*UNNNFFF!*"

The air was forced from her lungs all at once, in such a violent way I knew it would hurt like hell. My elbows bowed painfully, my locked arms giving way beneath the weight of her acceleration. I caught her across the back and just behind the knees, as the force of her momentum eventually knocked us both to the ground.

But I caught her. And that was all that mattered.

"Gotcha!"

I held her for an extra few moments, while her face

went tight with alarm and panic. My God, she was beautiful! Even as she clutched me, gasping for air.

"It's okay, it's okay!" I said quickly. "You're gonna be alright. Your wind might take a minute to come back though, so just try to relax."

Her hands were still death-locked on my arms, her fingernails digging in like claws as she clutched onto me for dear life. Eventually her blue-grey eyes shifted to mine. I saw the fear slowly draining.

"Don't say anything. Just *breathe*."

We were on the ground now, at the foot of the vast, wraparound porch. She'd missed the railing by inches. She'd missed even worse than that, only by the grace of good timing.

"I saw you climbing around up there," I said slowly, "so I made my way over. At first I thought you were trying to break in, but—"

"Why... why would I break in..."

She was talking, even though I told her not to. The pretty ones were always the most stubborn.

"... to my own *house*."

I glanced down at her strangely, then smirked. "This isn't your house," I said. "This isn't *anyone's* house."

The woman I'd just saved from certain death pushed off me, then scrambled to her feet. Her chest was still heaving, as she worked to force air into her deflated lungs.

"W—Who are you?" she demanded.

"Me? I'm Cyrus."

326

Her head cocked curiously. "And why are you here?"

"I'm here for the house."

For the first time I noticed that the lights in the lower level were on. There weren't many of them, but they were definitely running.

"You got the *lights* on?" I gasped incredulously.

The woman swallowed hard, regarding me coldly. Eventually she nodded.

"How?"

"I called the electric company," she said. "I had the power turned back on a few days before I got here."

"But—"

"I told you already, this is my house."

Though her words were registering in my ears, I still shook my head. I'd been here a hundred times, inside and out.

"No one would buy this house," I disagreed with a laugh. "It's too—"

"I inherited it," she cut me off coldly. "From my great-grandfather."

Inherited! Now I was interested! I couldn't help my eyes from going wide.

"You're a relative of old man Carter?"

The woman glanced up at the spot she fell from, a good two-and-half stories directly above us. I saw her shiver involuntarily.

"I guess so, yeah," she replied. "That's my last name."

"Got a first name?"

She looked at my arms, fixating on the torn right sleeve of my leather jacket. A good portion of my bicep and tricep was exposed. The skin there was bleeding from three distinct puncture wounds.

"Silvana," she said, her eyes softening. "My name's Silvana."

"Silvana?" I whistled. "Damn that's beautiful."

She went to roll her eyes, then somehow stopped herself before she did. She pointed to my arm.

"Did I do that?"

I looked at it and shrugged. "Better than you hitting the ground, no?"

"I guess so, yeah."

"What the hell were you doing up there?" I pointed. "That roof's like a hundred years old!"

"Eighty," she corrected me.

"Still—"

"And I was installing something," she went on. "Trying to, anyway."

"Installing *what?*"

Her eyes shifted away from me for a second, as if trying to determine how much she should tell me. Eventually I guess she relented.

"A satellite dish."

I couldn't help it. I laughed. "A satellite dish! On *that* roof?" I let out another chuckle. "You must take your television routine very seriously."

Silvana Carter folded her slender forearms across her chest. "No, I take my *work* very seriously."

I noticed that she was bleeding also. And shivering. Hell, she ought to be shivering, she was only wearing a T-shirt.

"What did you mean when you said you came for the *house?*" she asked me skeptically.

"You're bleeding too," I pointed out.

"Answer the question."

I bit my lip. She was a tough one. I had the urge to pull off my jacket and drape it around her, but I knew for certain she'd refuse.

"I... sort of work here," I said awkwardly. "Have been for the past five years."

Her face remained impassive, unchanged. Cold and beautiful.

"So that's your footprints I've been seeing around?" she asked.

I flicked a finger in the direction of the newly-lighted windows, and therefore the front door.

"Let's get out of the wind and I'll tell you."

Six

SILVANA

"And you bring people here? To my *house?*"

It probably came out a lot snottier than I actually meant it. Accepting the clean wad of paper towels I'd just given him, Cyrus nodded.

"Small teams of people, yes."

"For... what did you call it? Ghost hunting?"

"We prefer the term paranormal investigation," he smirked. "But yeah, that's the gist of it. We set up cameras, recorders, EMF meters—"

"In *this* house," I said again, pointing to the floor.

"Sure. What's so hard to believe about that?"

Cyrus peeled off his leather jacket and draped it over the counter. Almost immediately, all thoughts of everything else went straight out the window.

Holy shit.

My guest's body was utterly *ridiculous*. Two broad, dream-like shoulders flowed into a pair of long, powerful arms that dabbed at the scratches I'd given him. I was all but hypnotized watching them flex into tight, striated muscles.

But his chest...

Cyrus's enormous pectorals stretched his T-shirt tightly over his V-shaped body. I could see the curve of his muscles straight through it. All the way down to the taut, rippled expanse of what *had* to be the best rack of abdominals I'd ever seen on a man's body.

"You still haven't thanked me, by the way."

"For what?"

"For saving your life."

My eyes crawled back to those incredible arms. If they hadn't been so big... so strong...

"You're right," I admitted. "I definitely owe you one."

Cyrus chuckled and turned on the faucet. "Big time."

A disgusting stream of air and water sputtered from the faucet, vibrating the very walls the pipes were housed in. As it spit out into the sink basin, I sighed and shook my head.

"If you give it a minute it'll go from sludge-black to shit-brown," I said. "And then if you're really lucky, you'll get yellow."

"Yeah, you've definitely got well problems," Cyrus agreed. "Water down there's stagnant from sitting so long."

I felt a flash of panic. "So I need a new well?"

He shook his head. "Nah, probably not. You just need to run it hard, for maybe a day straight. Get all new water in there."

"Run my water for a day straight?" I scoffed. "I could only imagine the water bill."

"You don't have a water bill," Cyrus pointed out with a smile. "It's a well, remember?"

God, even his smile was beautiful! Cyrus had thick, flowing dark hair, offset by a pair of intense, ice-blue eyes. His face was clean of stubble, his angular jaw covered in stubble so perfect it would make George Michael jealous.

"I still can't believe the work you've done in this place," my guest said, glancing around the kitchen. "And you're saying you just got here?"

"Yesterday."

"Man," he whistled low. "Have you started on upstairs yet?"

I paused for a moment, then shook my head.

"That's gonna be an uphill climb," he lamented, finally wetting his paper towel. He switched the sink off. "You should probably get help."

"I'm not in a rush," I countered. "I've got plenty of time."

As I watched, Cyrus began dabbing at his wounds. He had thick wrists. Big hands. The kind of hands you could imagine all over you.

Stop it.

"Is that a *Datsun 280z?*" he asked incredulously, peering out the window.

"So what if it is?"

"It's pure awesome."

Something occurred to me as I shrugged off the compliment. "Hey, where's *your* ride? I don't see one, and I didn't hear you come in."

"I left it parked out by the road," he said. "There's a path that runs along the other side of the house and comes up from behind. I usually take it, to check the trail cams."

I blinked in astonishment. "There are *trail cams?*"

"Yeah. Motion sensor deer cams, actually."

"I want them gone."

I'd spat the words quickly, defensively. Without giving it much thought.

"They're not aimed at the house or anything," Cyrus explained. "Not directly, anyway. They're more focused on the yard, and the old—"

"Still," I cut in, trying to remain diplomatic with the man who saved my life. "I'd feel better if they weren't there."

He finished cleaning the scratches on his arm, which were starting to look sort of deep. Eventually he nodded.

"Alright, they're history," he agreed. "I'll come by in the daylight to make sure I get them all."

Guilt crept in. It was mixed with a few other emotions I couldn't quite put my finger on.

"Okay. Umm.. thanks."

"You're welcome," said Cyrus. He unrolled a new wad of clean paper towel and wet it all over again before taking a step in my direction. "Now you."

"What about me?"

"Look at your forearms, Silvana. Your hands..."

The stinging was something I'd filed away almost immediately after regaining my breath. Now I looked down, and for the first time I saw the abrasions on my arms and hands. There were trails of dried blood running down to my elbows, where they stopped abruptly. Sliding down the roof had done a number on me, my palms especially.

"You got any peroxide?" he asked. "If not, there's a twenty-four hour place in town that we could—"

"No, no, I'm fine."

He took another step toward me. "At least let me help wash off the—"

"I said I'm *fine.*"

Cyrus stopped, shrugged, and dropped the paper towel in the sink. By the time he'd slung his jacket back on, I felt like an asshole.

"Look... I'm sorry," I fumbled awkwardly. "I really don't mean to be an asshole."

"So it just comes naturally?" he joked.

"Something like that," I finally smiled. "I'm just really tired and strung out."

"Not to mention cold," he said, pointing to my shaking hands.

"Yeah. When the sun goes down, it's freezing in here."

Cyrus nodded. "There was a pot-bellied stove in the common hall — a real beast of one, too. It used to heat most of the house, but someone broke in and scrapped it a few years back."

"Great," I grumbled.

"The fireplaces in the library and some of the bedrooms still work though. And there's a wood-pile out back. It's old but there's a lot of it. Should burn hot and fast."

My shoulders slumped, and very slowly I felt my body start to relax. This guy wasn't a problem, he was a bunch of solutions. Plus he'd just saved me from a serious trip to the hospital... or worse.

On top of all that, he was straight up yummy as fuck.

"Think you could help me mount that satellite dish?" I asked, picking up the paper towels again. "I'll let you keep the trail cams."

Lifting one arm, I began washing the dried blood away. I intentionally avoided his gaze while awaiting an answer.

"On another part of the roof, sure. Maybe a part that's not rotten."

I shook my head. "Can't be on another part of the roof. I need south-facing exposure for the satellites."

Cyrus paused, scratching at his stubbled chin. For

the first time I noticed a long scar trailing across one of his cheeks.

"I could pull it all up and put down new plywood. We'd need tar paper. A couple squares of asphalt shingles..."

"Would that cost a lot?"

"Wouldn't cost anything if you don't mind hunter green shingles," he shot back. "I've still got some left over from the last roofing job I did."

I raised an eyebrow. "You do construction?"

"I do a lot of things," he winked. "But off and on, yes. I do carpentry."

My mind raced with conflicting thoughts, weighing merits and drawbacks. I hated relying on people. I hated not doing things myself. But considering the circumstances...

"O–Okay, sure," I relented. "That would be great."

I punched up my contact list and handed him my phone. Cyrus put his number in, and headed for the door.

"Where are you staying, anyway?" he asked.

"Hmm?"

"In town. Obviously you're not staying *here*, at least not until you get all set up."

"I... don't know the name of it," I lied. "One of those little strip motels."

He regarded me curiously for a moment, then nodded.

"Call me early enough, and I'll show you the best place to get breakfast."

THE SWITCHING HOUR
IS NOW ON AMAZON!

Grab it now — It's free to read
on Kindle Unlimited

About the Author

Krista Wolf is a lover of action, fantasy and all good horror movies... as well as a hopeless romantic with an insatiably steamy side.

She writes suspenseful, mystery-infused stories filled with blistering hot twists and turns. Tales in which headstrong, impetuous heroines are the irresistible force thrown against the immovable object of ripped, powerful heroes.

If you like intelligent and witty romance served up with a sizzling edge? You've just found your new favorite author.

Click here to see all titles on

Krista's Author Page

Sign up to Krista's VIP Email list to get instant notification of all new releases:
http://eepurl.com/dkWHab

Printed in Great Britain
by Amazon